HEARTBEATS

SUN VALLEY SERIES BOOK 2

KELLIE COATES GILBERT

Dedicated to my dear friend, Cindy Taylor.
Our hearts have beat side-by-side for a lot of years. Love ya.

PRAISE FOR KELLIE COATES GILBERT

"If you're looking for a new author to read, you can't go wrong with Kellie Coates Gilbert."

— LISA WINGATE, NY TIMES BESTSELLING AUTHOR OF
WHEN WE WERE YOURS

"Well-drawn, sympathetic characters and graceful language"

— LIBRARY JOURNAL

"Gilbert's heartfelt fiction is always a pleasure to read."

— Buzzing for Books

ALSO BY KELLIE COATES GILBERT

Mother of Pearl

Sisters (Sun Valley Series Book 1)

Heartbeats (Sun Valley Series Book 2)

Changes (Sun Valley Series Book 3)

Promises (Sun Valley Series Book 4)

Otherwise Engaged – a Love on Vacation Story

All Fore Love – a Love on Vacation Story

A Woman of Fortune - Texas Gold Book 1

Where Rivers Part - Texas Gold Book 2

A Reason to Stay - Texas Gold Book 3

What Matters Most - Texas Gold Book 4

More information and purchase links can be found at:

www.kelliecoatesgilbert.com

HEARTBEATS

SUN VALLEY SERIES – BOOK 2

Kellie Coates Gilbert

"Blast it! Look out!" Joie Abbott swerved to miss a cat that darted in front of her jeep as she pulled into the parking lot of the office where she'd be spending the next months, and hopefully years, of her life.

She screeched to a halt and yanked on the parking lever. Early morning sun peeked through bare trees as she reached across the worn seat and grabbed her briefcase. Unable to help herself, she stood mesmerized, gazing up above the door at the freshly mounted sign.

Crane and Abbott, Attorneys at Law.

Joie blinked twice, stared. A strange giddy feeling welled up in her chest. She'd never been the sentimental type, but she had to admit no small amount of pride at seeing her name there in those gold letters.

Only months ago, she'd been at her lowest point. That was saying a lot, given all the dips in her life's journey, the times where she'd taken one too many risks or one too many drinks, thrown caution to the wind and plunged into what would only later reveal itself as a pit.

She'd spent a lot of time trying to climb back from those

choices. No one knew how hard it was to lift her chin and talk herself into trying again. It was so much easier to simply strap on a parachute and dive from an airplane, or buckle on a pair of skis and race the mountain, taking no heed of personal safety— always determined to be a Tigger, never an Eeyore. Even when she'd made the biggest mistake of her life.

She'd graduated at the top tier in her law school. Recruiters had come knocking and she had her choice of law firms, had quickly climbed to junior partner at a prestigious litigation firm in Boise. She'd been brilliant and downright bold—yet in a blink she'd morphed into the woman everyone scorned. And, she'd never even seen it coming.

It had a name. Andrew Merrill.

If she never saw that lying married scum again, she'd be happy.

Joie squared her shoulders and gazed at the sign again, determined not to let that man steal even one more second of her happiness. Even if the effort killed her.

Instead, she'd focus on the future, and all that was ahead.

The new office was located in Giacobbi Square, a tiny retail area in the dead center of Ketchum, a bedroom community to Sun Valley. Kind of like Minneapolis and St. Paul, only on a much smaller scale.

The one downside to the location was the front door's proximity to the Painted Lady Art Studio owned by Trudy Dilworth. Miss Trudy and her sister, Ruby, were known for monitoring the comings and goings of everyone in the area. Anyone wanting local news could pass on the newspaper and go directly to the Dilworth sisters. Not exactly ideal for a person who cherished her privacy, but hey—the central location would be perfect for future clients.

Besides, nothing could tarnish the thrill Joie felt standing in front of this door. *Her* door. To *her* law firm.

Suddenly, that door swung open.

"There you are, darlin'! Come on inside and take a peek. The furniture arrived." Madeline Crane threaded arms and pulled Joie through the door. "I hope you like it."

The waiting area looked like something out of a Georgian mansion, with its sweeping draperies and claw-footed furnishings. Not exactly Joie's taste and certainly a departure from what you'd see in most law firms. That, and the fact her new partner wore a flowing black skirt topped with a ruffled light pink blouse and stiletto heels decorated with tiny bows. Frankly, this fifty-something gal looked like she'd just stepped off the set of a *Designing Women* rerun.

Never mind all that. Joie would agree to paint the walls neon green and wear a bunny costume herself in order to work with the petite blonde standing at her side.

Most people called her Maddy, with the exception of a few attorneys who had the misfortune of facing her in the courtroom. They called her Mad Dog. "Behind my back, of course," her new law partner liked to remind her friends.

Joie couldn't help but be impressed as she approached the wall opposite the windows where ornate frames in various sizes encased press releases and newspaper clippings. "Wow, look at all these!" she exclaimed.

Her new partner and mentor patted her back. "You'll have a wall of fame soon too. Just wait and see."

Joie examined a news article with the headline: "Wrongful Death Lawsuit Nets Record Damage Award." She remembered then, seeing a news segment featuring a bereaved couple who'd told how no amount of money could recompense them for the loss of their baby. Prescription error, if she recalled correctly.

Maddy's biggest win, and perhaps her most notorious, involved a case that took down a high school football coach who had been inappropriate with students. The win had garnered her a lot of time in front of the television cameras. She'd even appeared on a segment of *60 Minutes*—an exposé of sorts that explored the issue of teachers crossing the line.

Joie could barely believe an accomplished attorney of her stature had made the decision to move her practice to Sun Valley and had invited her to join as a full partner.

"Everything looks great!" Joie told her.

Maddy beamed. "Just wait until you see your office, sweet thing." She clasped Joie's hand and led her to a closed door. "Ready?" she asked.

Joie nodded.

With great fanfare, Maddy swung the door open wide. "Ta-da!"

Joie 's hand immediately went to her mouth. "It's . . . it's amazing."

Maddy's face broke into a wide grin. She clapped her hands in delight. "Oh good! I was so hoping you'd like it, darlin'.

Joie let out a breath and looked around. "It's so . . . me."

Maddy gave her shoulders a hug. "It is, isn't it?"

She wasn't sure exactly what she'd been expecting, perhaps a replicate of Maddy's massive glass-topped desk and white sofas. Instead, her office was decorated in natural woods and earth-toned colors. Massive windows framed a view of Baldy Mountain. But what really struck her was the wall of framed photographs—one of her skydiving, another of her at the horse stables leading Fresca through her circle training. There was a shot of her in a suit at her swearing in ceremony after passing the bar, and yet another of her standing on the steps of the Supreme Court building in Boise, one she didn't remember having seen before.

She slowly shook her head. "These are—where did you get all these?"

Maddy moved behind the desk, pulled out the leather chair and motioned for Joie to take a seat. "A woman has her ways."

Joie sunk into the offered chair. "My sisters."

Maddy fingered her gold earring. "Let a guilty plea be entered into record." She laughed and took several steps back, spread her arms wide. "So, how does it feel?"

Joie closed her eyes briefly, savored the moment. "It feels great."

Looking extremely pleased, Maddy moved for the door. "Well, enjoy. Tomorrow the work begins. We have clients coming in at ten. There are the files." She pointed to a small stack on the credenza.

Admittedly, despite the prestige of working with Maddy Crane, the decision to make this massive move in her career had not come easily. It was a no brainer in many respects. What long-term future did she have at the stables? Besides, she hadn't invested multiple years and more than a few dimes in law school to train horses and take guided tours up Dollar Mountain for the rest of her life. Never mind the humiliation of moving back into the guest house on her father's ranch—especially at her age.

Still, it'd been hard to break the news to Clint Ladner, the stable manager. Despite a rocky start, Clint had been there for her at one of her lowest moments. He was thrilled for what the move could mean for her future, of course, but as she broke the news she also saw something in his eyes that told her he might be as disappointed as she was that that they would no longer be spending their days together.

She wasn't ready for another romantic relationship. It was just too soon. But he'd been a friend when she most needed one.

Joie swung her chair around and gazed out the window.

Being her friend—that counted for a lot.

LEIGH ANN BLACKBURN picked her way across the snow-packed parking lot of Atkinson's Market to her car, her arms loaded with grocery bags. Despite being in a rush to get home, she paused long enough to watch three young girls all bundled up in parkas and snow boots. They were holding hands as they would start to scamper across the street, then stop; start again, stop. Finally, the oldest quickly looked in all directions, then clasped the others' hands firmly and propelled them forward. Following her lead, the younger girls bolted across to the other side of the street and began to laugh and push each other in celebration, exhilarated by their successful survival.

Standing at the car door, Leigh Ann's eyes met with those of the tallest girl, and they shared a silent understanding, one that comes from being the oldest sister. She smiled and loaded the car with the groceries, thinking about the past months, all that she and her sisters had been through.

Only months before, she'd nearly pushed her marriage over a cliff by letting a hurt propel her into a dangerous situation. Believing her husband was having an affair, she'd foolishly tried to climb into the arms of another man out of spite. Of course, she'd soon learned Mark was indeed faithful. He'd only been distracted with a new business venture. The woman who had left texts on his phone was his new business partner.

Her middle sister, Karyn, had finally taken positive steps to move past her deep-seated grief. It couldn't have been easy for a young widow who had lost her husband to a ski accident to embrace the possibility of loving again, but she had. And Leigh Ann was proud of her. Her sister had even established some much needed boundaries with her former in-laws.

Of all of them, Joie had perhaps made the biggest strides. For years, Leigh Ann wondered if her baby sister would ever get her act together and quit making foolish, and often risky, life decisions. Her heart broke to learn Joie had been struggling with a secret she'd been too ashamed to share with her family. Of course, like all secrets, the truth usually came out. Often, a result of circumstances beyond our control. Joie certainly learned that reality the hard way.

Thank goodness Joie had the good sense to tell that two-timing married man she'd been dating to hit the road. What a jerk! And her former boss, no less. Her sister was right to kick that liar to the curb—write the whole thing off as a bad mistake and move on.

Besides, Joie had a lot to look forward to. After tabling her law degree, living at home with Dad and working at the stables for over a year, she'd taken a leap and made the decision to go into private practice with that cracker jack attorney from Boise—Madeline Crane. Which is exactly why Leigh Ann needed to get a move on. She had a party to get ready for.

Leigh Ann moved for the driver's door and climbed in. She'd just started the ignition when her phone rang. Her sister's name flashed up on the instrument panel of her dashboard. Grinning, she pressed the answer button on her steering wheel. "Hey, Karyn. What's up?"

"Oh, glad I caught you," her sister replied. "I know I could have waited to talk to you tonight, but I didn't want to detract from Joie's celebration."

Leigh Ann frowned and turned down the radio volume. "That sounds ominous. What's the matter?"

"No, nothing that bad. Just something I'm worried about." Karyn hesitated. "I learned Jon scheduled a companywide meeting in the morning. Rumors are flying that big changes are on the horizon."

"Ah, rumors. Well, I've learned a lot about listening to rumors and—"

"I heard the news from a reliable source—the Dilworth sisters." Karyn didn't bother to mask her concern. "If true, I can only imagine what those potential changes could mean to the Sun Valley Lodge."

"Okay, but often change can be good." Did she have to remind her sister how positive the recent changes in her life had ended up being? Take, for example, her new relationship with Grayson Chandler.

"And scary."

"Yes, change can be scary. Even so, you won't have much choice but to embrace the new situation and make the best of it. Besides, why borrow trouble?"

There was a brief pause on the other end of the line. "Okay, yeah. You're absolutely right. I remember that first meeting with Jon. I was so nervous, but look how that turned out."

Leigh Ann grinned as she pulled out of the parking lot and headed home. "Exactly! Everything will be fine. You'll see."

"So changing the subject, do you think Joie suspects anything? About tonight, I mean."

Leigh Ann's insides tightened with excitement. "I doubt it. How could she? We've been careful to keep everything a secret. I know Joie claims to hate surprises, but remember the time we blindfolded her and led her out to the barn? She squealed when she saw the horse Daddy bought her."

"A new horse is a lot different from a room full of people gathered with the spotlight on her. Besides, Joie was eight years old back then."

Leigh Ann huffed. "You worry entirely too much! Trust me—this will be a wonderful evening she'll never forget."

"Okay, so long as this party is for her—" Karyn paused. "—and not for you."

This was posed as a question but Leigh Ann realized she wasn't expected to answer. Nor would she. Yes, she had the reputation amongst her sisters of being the *bossy one*. A title she didn't necessarily deserve.

She preferred to think of her role as the family cruise director. When her sisters' boats were sinking, she became their oarsman. Now that they both had their sea legs under them, especially Joie, it was time to celebrate.

An hour later, Leigh Ann stood at her kitchen sink looking out over her back yard while deftly wielding a paring knife across the outer skin of a butternut squash. She would make a decadent soup for the first course, one with real cream and served in the tureen she rarely got an opportunity to use.

Karyn pushed for an evening with simple hor d'oeuvres. "Make it easy on yourself," her sister had argued.

"Absolutely not!" she'd argued right back. "Joie has turned the corner, is finally making something of herself. That deserves at least five courses."

Outside the window, a tiny chipmunk scampered up the trunk of an aspen tree, its limbs now bare. For several months now, snow blanketed the bedding areas that once displayed her gorgeous red geraniums and blue lobelia, her pink petunias and proud daisies. How she missed summer and all its flowers!

Winter had its own glories. Not only did the season bring the ski tourists en masse, which was good for the local economy, but no one could argue that the beauty of the snow-covered mountain peaks surrounding this area could take your breath away.

Each season had its own delight. Especially here in Sun Valley.

Finished with the peeling job, she wiped her hands on a kitchen towel and retrieved the cream from the refrigerator. She set the bottle on the counter next to the burners of her Thermadore stove.

She picked up a tiny remote from the counter and pointed it at the Bose music component. Immediately, one of her favorite songs started playing—*Landslide* by Fleetwood Mac. While working, she sang the words to the familiar song out loud, her butt swaying to the rhythm of the music—back and forth in a little sinkside dance.

A noise pulled her attention. Her breath caught in surprise as she found Mark leaning against the door jam, arms crossed, watching her. "Mark! What are you doing?"

Her husband's face broke into a wide grin. "I'm watching a beautiful woman." He quickly closed the space between them and nestled his fingers in her hair, pulling her face to his. He kissed her, long and hard—a kiss filled with wanting and needing and all the feels.

Despite the fact she had guests arriving in a few hours, she gave in to the moment. There'd been a time not so long ago when she'd wondered if the spark that had ignited their love had been forever extinguished. She'd dreamed of this—wanted her husband's attention so badly it hurt.

Mark's fingers traced the line of her chin, drifted slowly across her neck before boldly trailing lower. As he pushed her toward the floor, she could barely speak. "Mark, here?" She fought for breath.

Despite her husband's sudden ardor, she snuck a glance at the clock on the wall and mentally calculated she'd have no time to finish the soup if she gave in to this sweep of passion. Regardless, she smiled and did what any woman who had been married since she was eighteen would do. She brushed aside her long to-do list, closed her eyes and enjoyed the unexpected respite with her husband—right there on her new and very expensive hard-wood kitchen floor.

2

Joie stood on her oldest sister's front steps with her finger poised on the doorbell, dreading the evening ahead. She loved her family, but she was drop-dead tired and would have preferred to wait and have this little family get-together over the weekend, but there was no altering her sister's mind.

Leigh Ann had an unreasonable need to celebrate everything —from getting her bathroom remodeled to what she called *life's milestones*. Every holiday had to be at a level ten. She moved a six-foot elf around the neighborhood in the days leading up to Christmas. She delivered personalized boxes of Ethel M chocolates to all her family and friends for Valentine's Day. No pre-made plastic Easter baskets for Leigh Ann. She stuffed Chihuly glass bowls with Pinterest-worthy ombre-colored eggs and jelly beans she made from scratch using a recipe she found on the internet. She even tried to hold half-birthday parties until the family yelled uncle and put an end to it.

One thing Joie had learned. There was no changing her, so the best she could do was play along and make the best of the

situation. Besides, as their sister, Karyn, so often reminded—
Leigh Ann's heart was in the right place.

Taking a deep breath, Joie pushed the button and waited.

Almost immediately, the door swung open and Leigh Ann
appeared dressed in cream-colored slim jeans, a teal-colored top
with matching peep-toed booties.

Joie looked her up and down. "Wow, Leigh Ann. It's good to
know you've seen the softer side of Sears."

Leigh Ann grinned and quickly quipped back. "Yes, and how
many times have I told you not to buy something just because it's
on sale?"

Joie laughed, shrugged off her jacket and handed it over. "I
was afraid I'd be late, but looks like I beat Dad and Karyn."

That's when she saw it—that glint in Leigh Ann's eyes. The
look she'd seen so often when her sister had cooked up some
plan. She groaned. "Oh no, you didn't—"

"SURPRISE!"

Out popped people stepping from the kitchen, the hallway
and even the coat closet. Joie felt a knot form in her stomach.
"Oh, Leigh Ann. You shouldn't have—"

Her sister clasped her hands and smiled widely. "Oh, but I
did!"

Joie's eyes ticked around the room at everyone in attendance.
Her dad was among the guests, of course. Her sister, Karyn. And
Karyn's boyfriend, Grayson Chandler. Joie gave them all an oblig-
atory hug before turning to the Dilworth sisters.

Miss Trudy swept forward and wrapped her ample arms
around Joie. "Congratulations, my dear. This new business
venture of yours is so very exciting. The furniture trucks were out
front all day yesterday."

Ruby joined her sister's chorus. "My, those moving men have
muscles. Don't they, Sister?"

Miss Trudy's heavily-ringed fingers twisted at her bright red
curls. "They most certainly do."

The proprietor of Joie's favorite bar stepped forward and placed his hand on Joie's shoulder, his face earnest. "We're all so very proud of you."

She gave him a tight hug. "Thanks, Crusty."

Terrance Cameron, a fellow bar patron, tipped his smoking pipe her way. "Yes, well done."

Madeline Crane stepped from the kitchen, a glass of champagne in her hand. "Just remember, darlin'—what I'm about to tell you is very important. No matter how ladylike you are, there will be boys trying to look up your dress as you climb up that ladder of success." She winked and everyone in the room laughed.

Over near the sofa stood all her buddies from the drop zone. In unison, they all raised their cans of beer. "To Chill!" One night Dick Cloudt, a fellow skydiver, teased she was an ice queen after she refused to date him, hence the nickname.

She brushed Cloudt's scrubby cheek with a kiss. "Glad you guys could come."

Despite the fact she was exhausted and starving—her stomach was feeling a bit queasy from skipping lunch—Joie grabbed a flute of champagne from a nearby tray and mingled, determined to make the best of the well-intentioned surprise. While she was now a respectable, practicing attorney—let it not be said she passed up a good chance to party, even if Leigh Ann's style of getting down was not exactly her own.

Unlike the guest house out at the ranch where Joie lived, Leigh Ann's home was a showplace. And she loved to show it off.

Overhead, soft notes from a Chopin prelude drifted through the great room from tiny Bose speakers poised inconspicuously behind a large fern. A framed child's drawing decorated one wall —one her nephew, who was now away at college in Seattle, had drawn as a child. The scene was of an army tank and soldiers, a fascination he entertained until he entered junior high, discovered girls and outgrew the notion.

"Cute," Crusty remarked, leaning in over her shoulder.

"It is, isn't it? The artist is grown now and in engineering school in Seattle."

Crusty slowly shook his head. "Well, they do that. Grow up, I mean."

Leigh Ann clinked a fork against a glass. "Hey everyone. Let's all make our way to the dining room for our first course, a roasted beet and carrot lentil salad with feta." She motioned to her husband Mark, who led the crowd to a table set with beautiful burgundy and crème-colored dishes and personalized place card holders hand-written in calligraphy.

Karyn angled toward Leigh Ann as they made their way to the table. "I thought you were going to serve soup as the first course."

Leigh Ann looked over at Mark with an impish smile. "Something came up and I ran out of time."

Joie slid into her designated place seated next to Clint. Despite repeated assertions that they were just friends, Leigh Ann was like a whale in a koi pond when it came to meddling.

He tilted his head, considered the line-up of forks at the side of his plate. "So, this is all pretty great, isn't it? I mean, your sister's house—this party—well, it's all amazing."

She leaned close, whispered. "Yup, ritzy like a cracker."

He laughed. "Well, you're handling all this attention pretty well."

That's what she loved about Clint. He got her—well that, and his bear tattoo. And the way he smelled. But that was all beside the point. Like she said, they were just friends. As much as she'd like to let loose with him, it was neither the time or the best idea. If she allowed herself to travel down that path, it would surely ruin what they had—and she didn't have many good friends who fully understood and accepted her. Even if his blunt style sometimes got under her skin.

When they'd finished their salads, her sister announced the main course—hazelnut-crusted pork tenderloin with roasted winter vegetables glazed with Madagascar vanilla, bourbon and maple. Joie made a mental note to speak to Karyn in private about doing an intervention—their sister had crossed the crazy bridge into over-the-top pretention. The table decorations alone looked like something straight out of a Martha Stewart blog.

While being served, her dad cleared his throat. "So, Ms. Crane—tell us a bit about yourself."

Joie's new law partner dabbed at the corner of her mouth with her napkin. "Oh, darlin'—call me Maddy."

Her father nodded, granted her a warm smile. "Maddy it is."

Karyn picked up her fork. "What's it like, Maddy? Being in the middle of all those high-profile cases, I mean."

Maddy's expression drew into an assured smile. "Well, I'll tell you this. There's rarely a dull moment. One time I was representing a client in the middle of a heated divorce." She leaned toward Joie's father. "The wife drank until she was more cabbaged than cole slaw—and spent my client's money like it was the special sauce. Left her husband no choice but to protect himself financially."

She reached for the salt shaker. "She once broke down along the road and a benevolent trucker stopped and gave her a lift." She smiled at Crusty from across the table. "By the time the day was over, she'd bought not only his truck for three times what it was worth, but the entire load of pigs he was carrying to market. Opened her Christian Dior purse and wrote the guy a check for a mighty big amount of money, right there alongside the road."

They all laughed as she buttered her roll. "Oh, that's not all," she said. "Months into all this, we're trying to value the marital assets so we can get everything wrapped up. And she's having none of it. The old gal fought us every step of the way. For example, no matter how many times her counsel urged her to comply, she refused to open the door when the appraisers showed up to value the art and furnishings. We had no alternative but to seek relief from the court, and a few days later, armed with a court order, we show up again."

Karyn moved a slice of pork from the serving platter onto her plate. "Goodness! What happened?"

Maddy grinned. "Well, sweet thing—she opened the door and complied with the order all right. But she did so without wearing a stitch of clothes. Bless her little heart, she followed us all around that house in full wrinkled glory."

Clint nearly choked on his food. "You're kidding! What did you do?"

Miss Trudy's hands went to her cheeks. "Oh my, yes! What did you do then?"

Maddy swirled the wine in her glass. "We simply hurried and got our business done. When we left, I thanked her—but not before kindly reminding her it was below twenty degrees outside, that she might want to don a coat if she went shopping."

Crusty swiped at the corners of his mouth with one of Leigh Ann's linen napkins. "That's quite the story. I suppose she hoped you all would back off and not come inside."

"Perhaps," Maddy agreed, her eyes twinkling. "Mad Dog learned the signs of a lion fight long ago. This woman knew she wouldn't win, but she needed to roar."

Leigh Ann motioned for the server she'd hired for the evening to take the now empty meat platter. "Well, our girl is very fortunate to be working for you."

Joie flinched. Wearing a plastered well-worn smile, she stared at her sister across the table, unsure which part of her sister's statement ticked her off her more—that Leigh Ann could so easily make her feel like she was ten years old again, or that she had single-handedly demoted her to an employee in front of all her friends and family. Sure, Madeline Crane was bankrolling everything, but she was a full-named and equal partner in their new practice.

Across the table, Karyn seemed to pick up on the slight as

well. No doubt, she was rummaging for how to correct the situation when Maddy spoke up. "Oh, I'm the fortunate one. I've practiced over twenty-five years—always solo. If you want to know the full truth of the matter, I never could find anyone I wanted to work with. Oh, I was made offers—lots of offers. Turned them all down."

That had Joie's attention. And her father's. His face broke into a half smile as he placed his fork by the side of his plate. "So . . . why Joie?"

Maddy reached for her glass of wine. "Your daughter—well, she reminds me of who I used to be. Someone I like to think I still am. Smart, shrewd and delightfully fearless." She looked across the table. In her eyes, Joie saw an understanding, a shared level of vulnerability that came from taking uncommon risks. What was a sprained ankle or a bloody knee next to adventure?

Joie straightened in her chair, lifted her chin. "Thank you, Maddy. I appreciate you saying that." She'd chalk being bold and brave up as victory any day.

Oblivious to the exchanged glances passing at the table, Leigh Ann pushed her chair back. "Yes, we have ample reason to celebrate. So, let's eat up everyone. But save room for dessert—I dropped by the Konditorei Bakery and picked up a fabulous three-layer German chocolate cake."

Karyn pushed back her seat. "Let me help you." She followed her older sister into the kitchen.

"And when we get back," Leigh Ann called out over her shoulder. "I think Joie needs to tell us all what she's most looking forward to."

Joie groaned inside. She put her fork down, straightened the napkin on her lap.

That's when it hit her—a wave of nausea like none she'd ever experienced. For a few brief seconds, the room fogged over and she felt lightheaded, like she might pass out. She couldn't tell whether the sudden queasiness was caused by all the people drilling their attention on her or what. Or, maybe this was what people often described as a panic attack?

Just as quickly, the dizzy feeling was over.

Clint leaned close. "Are you all right? You look a little pale."

Her hand involuntarily went to her mouth. "I—I'm not sure. I think so," she whispered, while waiting for a couple of sneaky hurdles in her stomach to settle down. "No—I—I think I'm good."

Concern pleated his forehead. He clearly saw right through her attempt to make light of the moment.

"I'm fine," she quietly assured him, taking care to not invite concern from those sitting around the table. She needn't have worried. Her family and friends were busy eating and talking.

Whatever made her feel so woozy left as quickly as it had come. Like she thought, it must have been all that spotlight on her, and those couple of sips of fancy champagne. She never could drink champagne.

Regardless, she felt better now. Even so, she thought better of eating any of the rich chocolate cake and begged off. Maybe she was coming down with a stomach bug. That would be just her luck, with the firm opening tomorrow.

Whatever it was, the feeling did not return. For that, she was grateful.

Suddenly, she had to pee. She excused herself and made her way to the bathroom where she splashed some cold water on Leigh Ann's embroidered hand towel and held it to her forehead. Joie could count on one hand the number of times she'd been sick over the last couple of years. Hopefully, she would not have reason to amend that statement.

After relieving herself, she stood in front of the mirror, taking in the dark circles that had formed under her eyes. Despite everything, maybe her nerves had gotten the better of her—that, coupled with her irritation with Leigh Ann for planning this silly party given in her honor.

She should be home reading those files. As it was, she wouldn't get home for at least another hour or so, meaning she wouldn't get to sleep until the wee hours of the morning. She'd wanted to be at her very best on the first official day. Instead, she'd be exhausted.

Armed with that surly attitude, she made her way back out to the table. "You okay, Sis?" her dad asked, pushing his empty dessert plate aside.

She quickly nodded. "Yeah, I'm fine," she said, a little sharply. "I guess I'm just a little tired and have a big day ahead of me."

On that cue, the party started breaking up. Crusty and her skydive buddies all bowed out from staying later, claiming they too had work obligations that would come far too early. Dick worked for the county, and they were scheduled to lay some pavement at the break of dawn. Likewise, the others had early morning jobs.

"We should go too," Ruby said.

Miss Trudy's shoulders seemed to droop like a flower that had been left in a vase too long. She nodded, not bothering to hide her disappointment. "Yes, Sister. I suppose we should. We'd like to stay, but the Women of Sun Valley committee is meeting for breakfast in the morning to plan the Valentine's Day bash." She turned to Leigh Ann. "You'll be there, won't you?"

Leigh Ann looped her arm through Mark's and followed her guests as they made their way to the door. "Of course."

Miss Trudy placed her dimpled hand on Grayson's arm. She looked between him and Karyn. "I hope you two lovebirds will join us. There will be a kissing booth," she reported with a hopeful expression.

There was no doubt she had more she wanted to say, but the color that immediately bloomed on both Karyn's and Grayson's faces kept her from needling them further. Instead, Miss Trudy waved off the situation. "You two are so adorable. You remind me of that cute couple—Lindsay Griffin and Jess Barnett." She looked Karyn's way. "You remember her? The little gal from Atlanta who wanted to learn to make jewelry?"

Karyn nodded. "Yes, our sous chef's new wife. I really like her." Mark retrieved a leopard-printed wrap from the closet. Miss Trudy swept it over her ample frame. "I've been working with her. She has real talent."

Maddy turned to Leigh Ann. "Darlin', everything was wonderful. Thank you for a lovely evening."

Her oldest sister drew her new law partner into a tight hug. "Thank you for coming—and for everything," she added.

Goodbyes seemed to take forever, especially with all the final congratulations each felt the need to bestow. Finally, she reached a point where she could politely head home.

Unfortunately, Leigh Ann had other plans. She closed the door and invited the few remaining guests to retreat to the den for an after-dinner drink.

"I really need to head out," Joie protested.

Her sister waved off her objection. "Nonsense. It's still early."

Mark placed his hand on Grayson's shoulder. "I have a great pear brandy we picked up on our last trip to Napa Valley. It's made entirely of Seckel pears and is aged to perfection, with incredible oak and bourbon notes."

"That's an offer I won't pass up." Grayson took a seat on the edge of the sofa, motioned for Karyn to join him.

When she did, she patted the seat next to her and quietly mouthed to Joie, "Just a little while?"

Not wanting to seem ungrateful, Joie put up her hands in surrender. "Okay, but just for a little while. And I'll pass on the alcohol. I have a big day tomorrow." She didn't tell them she worried her stomach might go all carnival on her again.

Later, after everyone but Joie had all sampled the bourbon served up in warmed snifters, Mark put an arm around Leigh Ann and drew her into the La-Z-Boy with him. She laughed and they bent so that their foreheads came together, smiled at each other like there was no one else in the room.

Karyn dropped to the sofa between Joie and her dad. "Love seeing that," she said, not bothering to hide the fact she found her sister and brother-in-law's antics endearing.

Joie clasped her middle sister's hand and gave it a squeeze. "Last summer, I wasn't sure those two would make it."

The doorbell rang. Leigh Ann playfully slapped her husband's arms away and scrambled from his lap. "Now, who could that be?" She straightened her sweater and moved into the foyer and for the door. She opened it. "Colby?" Her voice filled with alarm. "Son, what are you doing here?"

Mark jumped up and joined her. "Son, you're supposed to be at school. Why are you home?"

Everyone in the room exchanged confused glances. With a straight-line view to the door, Joie saw her nephew hold up open palms. "Look, I can explain."

"Are you—" Leigh Ann's voice went up several octaves. "Did you get kicked out?"

Mark's hand immediately went around his wife's shoulder. "Hold on, Leigh Ann. You always jump to the worst case scenario." He turned to Colby. "Son, come in. We're letting the cold in."

Colby noticed then that they were not alone. The fact seemed to both complicate and ease the situation in his mind. "Hey, everybody." He shrugged off his down coat and handed it off to his dad to hang in the closet.

Colby moved into the room, gave his grandfather a hug, then turned to his Aunt Karyn who drew him into a tight squeeze. "Hey, kiddo."

Joie was struck by the conflicted expression her nephew's face carried as he shook hands with the men. When he reached her, she simply patted his back. "Hey, what's up, Buddy?"

Leigh Ann planted her fists on her hips. "Colby! What are you doing home?" she demanded.

Her son slowly turned to face her. "I have news," he reported with the widest smile he could muster. "I—I made a decision."

"A decision?" his mother asked.

Colby took a deep breath. "Yes. I quit school."

Mark's face drained of color. "You did what?"

"I quit school," he repeated. He looked past his parents to his grandfather, hoping for support. "I decided I didn't want to be an engineer. So, I quit—and I enlisted in the army."

Leigh Ann's hand clutched her chest. "You're kidding, right? I mean, you didn't just throw away your future, let alone the thousands of dollars your dad and I have invested in an out-of-state university, to—to go into the U.S. Army?" Her eyes pooled with tears. "That's horribly dangerous—especially with all that is going on in the world right now." She looked at Mark with a silent plea to help her end this nightmare.

Unfortunately, her husband was of little help. "Son, is this a bad joke? You're barely twenty years old. Did it occur to you to talk with us before you did something so—" He paused just short of saying stupid. "Why did you do something so rash?"

Colby's grandfather set his brandy snifter on the coffee table. He stood and moved in their direction. "Colby, why don't you come and sit—help us all understand why you made this very big decision. Especially without consulting your parents. You must have had a reason for doing something so extreme—" He seemed to be searching for the words to say next, something what would support Colby. Joie wanted to do the same—but, what was the kid thinking?

Colby straightened, scratched at his ear. "I have something else to tell you—" Before he could utter another word, the doorbell rang again.

Leigh Ann and Mark exchanged confused glances. Colby darted around them and went for the door. "Let me—"

He swung the door wide. On the step stood a girl who looked to be about eighteen or nineteen—maybe twenty.

The young girl had naturally curly copper-colored hair, long and untethered and no make-up to speak of—not that she needed any. Joie would kill to have those big brown eyes rimmed with thick black lashes.

Instead of a parka, she wore what looked like a thick hand-knitted wool poncho over jeans with a cool seventies-style leather belt with fringe that swung wildly as she crossed into the room. "Sorry, Colby. It was getting cold out in the car."

By now, everyone had gathered in the foyer, anxious to assess the mystery guest.

Leigh Ann nervously fingered the pearls at her shirt collar before remembering her manners. She extended her hand. "Hello," she said, taking inventory of this girl. "I'm Leigh Ann—Colby's mother." She turned to her husband. "And Mark, his father."

Colby shifted his weight, dug his hands into his pockets. "Uh, sorry. Yeah, these are my parents." He pointed at the semicircle. "And that's my grandpa and my Aunt Karyn and Aunt Joie, and their friends."

Leigh Ann scowled at her son's unexpected friend, no doubt still reeling from his news. "And you are?"

The girl beamed. "I'm Nicole. Colby's wife."

3

K aryn was in bed nearly an hour when the phone rang. Barely awake, her hand reached for her cellphone which was plugged in on her bedside table. "H-Hello?" she mumbled.

"Thank goodness you're still up!" Leigh Ann blurted from the other end.

"I wasn't really." She lifted and flicked on the lamp, rubbed at her face.

"Well, I finally got them all down. They're asleep. Do you know what it was like to close that door on Colby's room knowing she was in there with him? In his bed?" Leigh Ann barely paused for a breath. "I don't know where to start. I mean, he thinks he's going to go off to play soldier? And my baby boy has a wife? Which, by the way, he thinks he's leaving here with us until he returns from basic training. After that—well, who knows?"

"Leigh Ann, I think—"

"Oh no, you don't think she's pregnant, do you?" There was a rattle on the other end. "I need to go ask—"

"Leigh Ann—wait. There's time for that in the morning.

Besides, Nicole seemed pretty open. I'm not sure they were hiding anything more we don't know."

"Oh, Karyn. Did you see her? For goodness sakes, she's a hippy!"

Karyn pulled the duvet up around her waist. "I think now they're called granola girls—or crunchies. I saw something on the internet once about the rebirth of that movement and how young girls are reverting back to all that Mother Earth stuff."

"Karyn, *we're* young. Why have I not heard about all this?"

She couldn't help but smile. "We live in Sun Valley. We have earth girls. They just don't stroll the Brass Ranch and Sturtevants. They shop the Eddie Bauer store online."

"Really?"

"Yeah, don't you remember that girl Joie told us about? The one Clint hired on to help with the stables tours?" She waited to see if Leigh Ann remembered. When there was no response, she continued. "Surely you haven't forgotten how he had to let her go for refusing to wear a bra?"

"Oh, that's right. I remember now. Some resort guests complained the jiggling of her rather well-endowed assets was distracting some of their teenaged boys."

Leigh Ann sighed. "That answers a lot. I found Nicole's account on Instagram. She posts photos of these succulent plants in clay pots, and she's named them all—the plants, not the pots."

Karyn rubbed at her sleepy eyes. "Look, I know all this is shocking. But it'll all turn out fine. You'll see."

"How can you say that?" Leigh Ann argued. "My baby got married without even telling me. I didn't even get to be there. Now, he's enlisted and goodness knows what the future holds. He's ruined his life!"

She could almost hear the lump build in her older sister's throat. "C'mon, Leigh Ann. We don't know that."

"Are you kidding me? Even you have to admit his choices are

pretty bleak. I have a girl sleeping down the hall and she's my daughter-in-law—a girl I only met less than a few hours ago."

Karyn flung the covers back, knowing she wasn't going to get back to sleep anytime soon. She padded to the kitchen in her bare feet. "He must love her."

"They're too young to know what love is." Leigh Ann argued.

"You were barely out of high school when you married Mark," Karyn reminded her sister. It went unspoken that her sister had been pregnant with Colby when she walked the aisle.

"That was different—Mark and I were different."

"Maybe, but I think you might find that this situation turns out just fine," Karyn encouraged, trying to help her sister see the bright side. "Look, tomorrow morning you'll get up and cook a great breakfast. You'll start getting to know Nicole. You might find you really like the girl."

Her sister huffed on the other end of the phone. "I don't like any of this, Karyn."

"I know, but Colby is over eighteen. He can legally do what he chooses." She rummaged in the refrigerator for the milk, poured some in a pan and put it on the stove to heat. "You don't have any option here but to accept his decisions and make the best of them."

Even as she said this she knew her sister's fretting had only begun. In a platoon of helicopter moms, her sister was definitely a five-star lieutenant. She'd be hovering over all this for weeks, maybe even months.

"This was certainly not the grand finale I'd wanted for Joie's celebration dinner. By the way, I don't think she was feeling all that great tonight. I thought she looked a little pale."

Karyn turned on the stove burner. "I don't think you have to worry about Joie. My guess is that she was reacting to the surprise. We both know she hates to be the center of our attention, and we placed a pretty big spotlight on her last night."

"I don't know about that." Irritation rose in Leigh Ann's voice.

"Someone who doesn't like to draw attention to herself wouldn't show up late to her brother-in-law's memorial auction because she was too busy jumping out of an airplane at an altitude of 15,000 feet . . . after staying out all night."

"Yes, but she could care less if anyone is watching. Besides, I think that last episode with Andrew changed her. I don't think she's as willing to jump without thinking things through. Metaphorically speaking, of course."

"True," Leigh Ann admitted. "Anyway, I tried to call her but she didn't answer. Likely, she turned her phone off."

Karyn dipped the tip of her finger into the surface of the milk in the pan. She was going to need to drink something warm to calm down and get back to sleep. "Remember, her big day is tomorrow. The first time practicing law in almost two years. I'm sure she's a bit unnerved."

Leigh Ann huffed at that statement. "Our Joie unnerved? Never."

4

Joie maneuvered her jeep into the Giacobbi Square parking lot at a quarter of nine, feeling utterly and completely exhausted.

She'd had a rough night. Not only had her mind been racing about her new law practice, but she couldn't seem to shake off the emotional residue of that little scene last night with Colby and his new wife.

She was the last one to point fingers or criticize anyone's decisions. But what was that little dude thinking? While she admired his independence, she had to agree with Mark and Leigh Ann. Chucking his education and getting married at such a young age could easily be a huge mistake. Some mistakes were not easily survived.

She'd learned that the hard way.

Besides all that, her stomach was giving her fits again this morning.

She tossed a couple of antacids in her mouth then pulled her Salvatore Ferragamo briefcase from the seat and headed for the front door. The nice leather case, a law school graduation gift from her family, felt good back in her hand as she greeted the receptionist slash secretary they'd hired. "Morning, Heather."

"Morning, Miss Abbott."

Joie held up her hand. "Please, enough with the Miss Abbott. Call me Joie."

The girl beamed. "Sure thing. Can I get you anything? Coffee?"

"That's not necessary. I can get my own coffee. But, thank you."

Heather nodded her appreciation. "Well, sure. That'll work."

The door opened and in walked Maddy Crane in a knee-length fur coat and boots with two-inch heels. She unwrapped a scarf from around her blonde hair and shook it out over the pale-yellow carpet. "Morning, sweet things."

They returned the greeting.

"Today almost feels like the first day of school," Joie noted, blushing. "I mean, everything is new and all the office supplies, and such." She pointed to a container of pens and freshly-sharpened pencils on the counter.

"That it does." Maddy motioned for Joie to follow her down the hallway. When they reached Joie's office door, Maddy paused and turned. "See you in the conference room in a half hour? We have a client coming in for her intake interview. A nasty custody issue."

Joie nodded, wishing she'd gotten a little more sleep. It was a sin to be this stinking tired so early in the morning. "I'll be there."

When it was time for the meeting, Joie gathered up her files and headed for the conference room. Maddy stood when she entered. "Joie, this is Mary Peterson. Mary, Joie is my law partner. We'll be working closely together on your legal matter."

Joie extended her hand. "It's nice to meet you, Ms. Peterson."

Maddy slipped back into her chair at the head of the conference table. "Mary has an unfortunate situation she's facing. Her ex-husband lives in Florida. After having very little contact with her young children over the past two years, he has filed for shared custody, which means Mary would have to send her babies to live with him and his new wife for six months out of the year. Of course, we fully intend to interrupt that little plan of his. Help the court see that what he's really after is to weasel his way into his children's finances." She turned to face Joie. "Mary's mother recently passed. They were left with quite a tidy sum. We believe this is merely her ex-husband's attempt to get his hands on that money." She opened an animal-printed portfolio and pulled out a pen, smiled at their client. "Okay, darlin'—let's start out with you telling us the entire story."

Joie took furious notes as the woman sitting across the table further explained the situation. She recounted how she'd met her ex-husband, told them about the arduous years of marriage and her former husband's inability to keep a job—the tension that created and how at times he'd gotten down right mean with both her and the children. She paused, looked down, clearly ashamed. "I—I should have left him years earlier, but I kept holding onto hope." Her eyes filled with tears and she angrily brushed them away. "For years I wanted Elliott to take interest in the children. He just didn't—not even in the beginning. Early on in my pregnancy, I was often sick. I mean, I'd have these unexpected waves of nausea overtake me, almost from day one. And dizzy spells." She shook her head. "Couldn't keep a thing down."

Joie frowned and jotted "*severe morning-sickness*" in her notes.

"Elliott didn't want children right away. I knew that—took all the proper precautions. But accidents still happen, even when you're careful. Of course, we never expected twins." She shook her head. "It didn't matter how much I pleaded, he wouldn't take any interest. None at all. He refused to take me to any doctor visits, even when I could barely drive myself. Some women only experience those queasy episodes early in their pregnancies. I was one of the lucky ones who was sick as a dog the entire nine months. At times, I was so fatigued I thought I'd die."

Joie's pen went still. She couldn't seem to move the ink across the tablet.

Queasy.

Feeling faint.

Fatigue.

Her insides started to roil as she considered her own situation. In her head, she quickly calculated the number of weeks since . . . Oh, my goodness! Had she even had her period since she broke things off with Andrew—sent him packing back to his wife in Boise?

She was often irregular, but it'd been over two months—ten weeks to be exact.

As if on cue, the room began to get hot and she had to fight to breathe. Something akin to a wrestling match in her stomach pulled her attention away from the discussion at the table.

"Isn't that so, Joie?"

Her head jerked up. "I'm sorry. What?"

Maddy looked at her over jeweled reading glasses and smiled. "I told Mary that you and I would be in her corner every step of the way. Our hope is to stave this off at the pass."

Joie nodded with fervor. "Oh, yes. We're absolutely going to provide the best legal counsel available. You are in good hands."

"I feel better already," the distraught woman told them. "And thank you for seeing me on such short notice. But I have to warn you, Elliott rarely backs down when he's set his mind to something."

"No problem, sweet thing. Let's just see how this plays out." Maddy pressed a button on the phone set on the table. "Heather dear, please get me Jay Teeler on the line. First, be a darlin' and bring in some tea. And maybe some of those little crème puffs from the Konditori. You'll find the box on the counter in the kitchen."

Heather complied and showed up minutes later carrying a large floral tray filled with dainty cups on saucers and a basket draped with the linen napkin. Maddy reached for one of the pastries and offered the basket to the client. "These are messy, but so worth it."

Minutes after the tea was poured, the phone buzzed and Heather reported she had Mr. Teeler on hold.

Maddy wiped her fingertips on the linen napkin and reached for the phone. Grinning, she pressed the speaker button. "Good morning, Mr. Teeler. May I call you Jay?" She didn't let the man answer. "Madeline Crane here. I was wondering if you had a few minutes to discuss a very urgent matter?" She pronounced her words without the R—like any good southern woman would.

A booming voice came on the line. "The famous Mad Dog Crane. I'm honored. How are you? And welcome to Sun Valley!"

Maddy's face broke into a broad smile. "Why, sugar. I'm just fine, and thank you." She winked at Joie and Mary.

"Look, I don't have a lot of time to chat, but I wanted to extend a professional courtesy and tell you that by the end of the week we'll be filing for a temporary restraining order putting a stop to that little charade you're launching on behalf of your client, Elliott Peterson. You see, after his former wife contacted my office and explained the situation, I had a little investigation done." Maddy paused, adding drama to the moment. "I surely hope I'm not the first to tell you. Unfortunately, word has it Mr. Peterson's former employer is missing a bit of money—to the tune of four and a half million dollars. Nothing has been proven yet, of course. But if these allegations are authentic, then your client could easily be facing a felony charge for embezzlement and be spending time in a federal penitentiary. Now of course, we both know white-collar crime perps are sentenced to places that are often nicer than a lot of high-end hotels. It's rumored Bernie Madoff sleeps on four-hundred count sheets. Still, I doubt very much the prison wards are equipped to handle children as young as my client's." Maddy's jaw set, and her blue eyes turned steel gray. "Wouldn't you agree, Jay?"

The man on the other end of the line stuttered. "Where did you learn this?"

Joie's cunning law partner slid a paperclip around on the marble table with her manicured nail. "Now, Mr. Teeler. A mannered woman never reveals her sources."

"I—I'll have to get back with you," their opposing counsel muttered.

"Of course, sugar," Maddy replied. "You take your time."

She hung up, looked across the table at Mary and smiled. "I don't think you'll have much to worry about, darlin'. The best wins are often made outside the courtroom, and I think that one just landed in our column." She winked at Joie. "Wouldn't you agree?"

Joie swallowed, struggled to focus. She nodded her agreement, but all she could think about was the outrageous possibility taking form in her mind.

5

K aryn strolled through the lobby of the Sun Valley Lodge wishing she'd gotten more sleep. Hours after she'd hung up from talking with Leigh Ann, and despite the warm milk, she'd lain awake thinking about Colby and his new wife. Even more, Leanne's reaction to it all.

The news left her oldest sister nearly apoplectic. Not that Karyn blamed her. Finding out your son had dropped out of school to enlist in the army and had gotten married without telling you would leave anyone a bit undone—most specially someone like Leigh Ann, the ultimate pageant mom who believed if she primped her son just right, he'd march down the aisle, accept his engineering degree and make her proud.

Unfortunately, life had a way of throwing some curves. She'd certainly learned that. Few women her age were forced to wear the label *widow*.

Who could have imagined she'd lose Dean to a ski accident while he was preparing for the Olympic trials? Certainly, not her. She'd always believed in fairytale romance. But sometimes, life made you adjust your idea of happily ever after.

Luckily, after barely surviving two years of despair, she'd met

Grayson Chandler, a backcountry pilot from Alaska who also knew heartbreak.

She supposed they were meant for each other, Grayson and her. Two hearts shattered and learning to love again. His wife had tossed him aside for another man, leaving him to wonder if his own heart would ever mend.

Karyn smiled to herself. Often she'd doubted her ability to ever feel this again, the way her heart raced a little whenever he came to mind. Change was never easy, but that didn't mean a shift in the expected could not still end well. Following some of the loneliest months of her life, she enjoyed being with someone who made her feel wanted and secure.

Even in hard circumstances—you could end up blessed.

Armed with that attitude, and despite her earlier nerves about what a suddenly-called meeting might mean, Karyn slipped her bag into her desk, grabbed a notebook and a pen and headed for the conference room, determined to face whatever changes might be coming.

"Hey, girl." Melissa, from the front desk, stood at the back of the crowded room filling her mug from the coffee urn. "Liz is manning check-in. We flipped a coin to see which one of us got to be the lucky one to attend the meeting. Not sure who won—her or me." She grinned. "What do you think all this is about?"

Jess Barnett, their new sous chef, tapped the table with the end of his pen. "Yeah, why the big meeting?"

Karyn took her seat at the granite table. "I don't know anything more than you guys." She heard Jon Sebring's voice outside the door. "Guess we'll know soon enough."

Their resort director entered the room, accompanied by an older woman with white hair, clipped in a stylish short cut. She wore an alpine ski sweater and black slacks, and a friendly smile. Karyn recognized her as the same woman in the portrait in the lobby.

"Good morning, everyone." Jon's hand went to the woman's

back. "For those who might not recognize our distinguished guest, let me introduce you to the owner of the Sun Valley Resort, Nola Gearhart."

Polite applause went up from around the room. Karyn held her breath. This was an honor, and certainly not what she'd been expecting.

Ms. Gearhart held up an open palm. "Thank you, everyone. And good morning."

Karyn was broadsided by the gray-green intensity of Ms. Gearhart's eyes as she smiled sweetly out at the employees gathered in the room.

"I'm sure my showing up without much warning is catching everyone a bit off guard," she said. "But I felt it was important to announce some news to all of you personally before we go public. A press release will be issued later today." She cleared her throat. "First, I'd like to personally thank each of you for your part in making Sun Valley Lodge one of the most enduring icons of quality and hospitality in the world. I am absolutely committed to maintaining all that makes the resort, and especially this lodge, so very special."

Jon nodded. "No one needs to tell any of you that we face a lot of competition for vacation dollars."

"Yes," Ms. Gearhart quickly agreed. "If we are to remain America's number one vacation destination, we'll have to work hard. We can't afford to rest on our past laurels. Today, I have some good news that will help in that effort."

The nervous part of Karyn relaxed, at least a little. Nola Gearhart's direct and honest approach was refreshing. And disarming.

"In light of that, I'm excited to announce a development that will bolster our reputation, and our revenues." Ms. Gearhart paused, glanced over at Jon, her eyes glistening with excitement. "While the details must remain confidential at this point, soon we will have the extreme honor of hosting the film crew for the new remake of *Bus Stop*, right here at the lodge. As many of you know, the original movie, starring Marilyn Monroe, was filmed in Sun Valley in 1956." She grinned. "We'll want to be at our very best, and while I know this milestone will add to everyone's load over the next month or so, the publicity will be well worth it. I know I can count on all of you to make Robert Nygard and the folks from Tanasbourne Media feel welcome."

Karyn's mind raced. A movie crew? Here at the lodge?

Celebrity sightings were common here in Sun Valley, but only twice had actual movies been filmed here—*Bus Stop* and *Sun Valley Serenade*. Nothing recent.

Melissa timidly raised her hand. "Uh, can you tell us who's starring?"

Jon offered a big smile. "Mia Larimore and Rick Hudson. My understanding is that the studio will be casting secondary roles from right here in Sun Valley. The public is urged to participate."

The room immediately buzzed with excited chatter.

The girl sitting next to her, Melissa from housekeeping, grew giddy. She leaned close. "Are you kidding me? How cool is that?" She nibbled her knuckle. "I wonder—I mean, maybe I'll try out."

Karyn groaned, and made some swift notes in her tablet. The big announcement had just taken on a different edge, for she could see Melissa's reaction repeated in the eyes of almost every employee in the room.

LEIGH ANN CREPT down her hallway, tray in hand loaded with homemade scones and French-pressed coffee. She paused at her son's door, hesitating momentarily before convincing herself to move forward with her plan.

She hoisted the tray on one hip and knocked on the door. Leaning close, she nearly pressed her ear against the wood. After all, it was almost eleven and—wait—it sounded like they were up.

Armed with renewed confidence, she knocked again and turned the knob.

Her entrance was met with immediate protest.

"Mom!" Colby shouted. "What gives? I mean, geez Mom!"

Her son's new wife pulled the covers up tight around her chest and smiled. "Morning, Mom."

The term of endearment jolted Leigh Ann before she remembered. "Uh, good morning you two. I—uh—well, I figured you wouldn't want to sleep the morning entirely away. And I thought you might be hungry."

Colby scowled.

At the same time, his new bride's expression brightened. "That was really nice. Thank you." The girl maneuvered herself into a sitting position while maintaining her modesty.

Only then did Leigh Ann realize the couple was naked and she may have interrupted a private moment. The thought left her rattled. "Well, here. I hope you enjoy."

Her new daughter-in-law reached for a scone. "Are these gluten-free?"

"Are they what?"

"Are the scones gluten-free? We don't touch wheat products."

Leigh Ann scowled, quickly glanced between the two of them. "We?"

Colby nodded, his face filled with admiration for the woman leaning her head against his bare shoulder. "Yeah, Mom. The proteins in wheat are like splinters digging into the lining of your gut, causing an inflammatory response. It's really bad for you."

"But the coffee looks great, Mom." Nicole reached for the mugs. "Thanks!"

Leigh Ann didn't know what to say, or even think. Who was this girl her son had married on such a whim? She certainly had odd ideas on eating—and an uncanny influence over her son she wasn't exactly thrilled about. Okay, yes—she was his wife—well, barely. That didn't entitle her to overwhelm her son with a bunch of silly ideas.

Despite what she'd like to say, Leigh Ann judiciously held her tongue. There'd be time for her to approach Colby and ask what in the world was going on with all this nonsense—when they were alone. Right now, all she had to do was play host to this girl —her uh, new daughter-in-law.

She said as much to Mark when he came home for an early lunch. "Honey, I have an uneasy feeling about his girl."

"Her name is Nicole," he reminded, grabbing the sandwich from his plate.

Leigh Ann rolled her eyes. "Oh, don't start. I know her name. That's not the point. You're not hearing what I'm trying to tell you."

Mark looked at her with patience. "Well, I'm with you on one thing—showing up on our doorstep with a surprise wife and an announcement he's just imploded his future is the last thing I'd hoped for, or expected, from our son. I assure you, Leigh Ann. I feel just like you on this situation. The reality is there's very little we can do about it."

"Don't you think I know that?" Leigh Ann argued, taking care to keep her voice lowered. "Still, he can change his mind."

"I beg to differ." Mark lifted his sandwich. "The army doesn't let you change your mind. And what would you have our son do? Divorce the girl? What if he loves her?" He took a bite.

She shook her head vehemently. "How could he love her? He doesn't even know her!"

"We don't know that." He poised the sandwich in front of his face, ready to take another bite. "He married her, didn't he?"

Angry tears pooled in Leigh Ann's eyes. "So, that's it? We have no choice but to accept this mess? This is our son, Mark."

He laughed, literally out loud. "Babe, we're his parents—not his caretakers. At least, not anymore."

Of course, that wasn't true. Did their jobs as Colby's parents end just because he had turned eighteen? Of course not! She still needed to protect him—even from his poor choices. Now more than ever.

She hadn't even known how many things there were to be afraid of before she had a child. Yes, love opened her up to joy, but simultaneously to fear that was unending.

From the time Colby was an infant, she lay awake at night surrounded by monsters of possibilities she'd never considered— a drunk on the street, candy he might choke on, mean kids on the playground who would nick his self-esteem. There was a never-ending list.

What if he missed the bus? What if there was a demented man lurking around the school, or in the store bathroom? What if he flunked his math test and eliminated the possibility of being accepted into the best schools, the best playgroups?

As a mother, was she supposed to just shut all of that off? Technically, Colby was an adult. That didn't mean he didn't need guidance. This last move only proved he wasn't ready to make life decisions without their input.

A silent shudder slid down Leigh Ann's back. The fact her only son had scrapped his life means she'd failed—and she had to find a way to fix it.

She rubbed at her forehead. "Honey, we have to do something. We can't just let him throw his life away. Especially with some girl who doesn't even eat flour!"

Mark suddenly cleared his throat. He frowned and nodded his head in the direction of the door directly behind her.

Leigh Ann held her breath, slowly turned.

There stood Nicole wearing Colby's robe.

6

"You want me to order something in for lunch?" Heather asked as Joie darted through the reception area. She wrapped her woolen scarf around her collar and headed for the door. "No, I'm good."

Perhaps the smarter thing would be to order from Amazon, have a discrete package delivered the following day. But, what if she wasn't home and Leigh Ann decided to drop out to Dad's for an unexpected visit? Her sister had no boundaries, wouldn't think twice about opening the cardboard box. How would Joie explain the contents?

No, she'd have to risk the grocery store aisle and execute her carefully constructed plan.

Atkinson's Market was just across the street, also in Giacobbi Square. Unfortunately, Joie could tell from the number of cars out front that the grocery store was packed. Her mission would be more difficult than she anticipated.

She stepped through the automatic doors and took quick inventory. Ariana, her fitness instructor from Zenergy, stood in the check-out line. Dee Dee Hamilton was inspecting a head of lettuce over in produce. There were others mingling the aisles, but she didn't recognize any of them. Likely tourists.

One, a scruffy-haired guy who looked barely out of high school, had his arm draped around a girl of about the same age. Joie smiled and moved toward the couple with determination. Perhaps they would agree to help her out.

Steps away, she came to an abrupt stop. They wore ski gear. What if they were someone's nephew or niece here on a ski vacation? What if they told that someone that some crazy lady asked them to buy a pregnancy test for her? She shook her head, knowing she couldn't take that chance.

In the soup aisle, an older woman pushed a full cart. Their eyes met and Joie smiled.

Nope. While she couldn't quite place her, she probably lived around here and knew one of her sisters. Or, her dad. She might even be one of the women who had their eyes on her father—the ones she and her sisters had dubbed the *Bo-Peeps*.

Goodness—this was harder than she'd expected.

Joie glanced at her watch, realizing this was a mission she'd have to tackle all on her own. It was the only safe alternative— and safe was a relative term in this instance.

When the coast appeared clear, she darted to the pharmacy area and grabbed the first test box she came to on the shelf. She glanced around to make sure no one was watching, then tucked the little box under her arm and out of sight.

As she made her way down the aisle, she nabbed a bottle of aspirin, a tube of toothpaste, an enormous bottle of multi-vitamins supplemented with iron and piled all her purchases on the counter at the pharmacy check-out.

The clerk, a girl with spiky hair and a penchant for chewing gum, gave her a weak smile. "Did you find everything you were looking for?"

Joie's heart pounded. She looked around to make sure no one was watching. "Yes. Thanks."

The girl picked up the vitamins. "Oh, these are good ones. My mom buys these. But I think we have a sale going on." She reached across the cash register for an advertisement insert from their local paper. "Oh, yes—see right here. Buy two, get one free." She shook her head. "No thanks."

"Are you sure? Because that's a bargain."

Joie drilled her with a look. "Not today, thanks."

The gal chomped on her gum, shrugged her shoulders. "Okay, suit yourself. Just trying to be helpful and provide great customer service. Save you some money." She reached for the toothpaste. Rang it up.

"Uh, could you put this in a paper sack?" Joie swallowed and lifted the little box from its hiding place under her arm and held it out.

The girl stopped chewing, looked Joie in the eyes and slowly nodded. "Well, yeah. Sure." She took the product, swiped it across the pricing scanner and into a little brown bag.

Joie sighed with relief.

"Joie? Is that you?"

Filled with dread, Joie turned to find Miss Trudy approaching, dressed in an ankle-length fur coat with matching hat. Joie pasted a smile. "Hi, Miss Trudy."

The woman waved her jeweled hand. "I saw you heading over here and hoped I'd be able to catch up with you. Your party last night was just lovely, and I wanted to thank you. Leigh Ann is the consummate hostess. Ruby and I had a glorious time." She leaned forward, her brows drawn together. "I heard after we left, a bit of a surprise showed up at the door. Your sister must be simply beside herself with the news. Not only has Colby gone and left school but he has a wife?"

She fanned herself as if the news was just too hot to handle. "Poor, poor Leigh Ann."

Joie wondered how Miss Trudy had learned everything so quickly. More, she wondered what she might have just seen. If

Miss Trudy knew she was buying a pregnancy test, the news would be all over town by nightfall.

Thankfully, there was no indication her secret had been breached.

"Boy, Miss Trudy—I'd love to stand and chat, but it's my first day at the law firm, and as you can imagine, I'm already swamped. I really need to get back." Joie turned and handed her credit card to the clerk, but not before giving her a grateful smile.

"Oh, certainly dear! I understand." She waggled her dimpled fingers. "You do what you have to. We're all so proud of you, dear. Well, of all you girls." She smiled. "Give your sisters all my love. And your father. I think Ruby was planning on dropping off some of her bread pudding."

Joie snatched the bag of her purchases from the clerk and returned her credit card to her purse. "Gotta go!" She waved and hurried for the front door, even while Miss Trudy was still talking.

~

JOIE SAT on the edge of the tub holding a tiny plastic wand in her hand.

Outside, temperatures dropped another twenty degrees as the sky dumped more snow. That didn't keep sweat from beading on her brow as she tried to convince herself to dip the end in the little cup waiting on the counter. As promised in the instructions, in less than five seconds she'd know what her future held.

But she simply couldn't take that giant step. Not yet.

People lied when they glibly championed the notion that a person does not have to be defined by their mistakes. She, for one, failed to subscribe to that line of thinking. For reasons that were obvious.

Joie stared at the little white plastic wand in her hand as if it were a snake poised to bite.

All the times she'd felt almost too tired to move came rushing into her head. The nausea. Even the fact that her favorite tight-fitting jeans were a little too snug the last time she'd zipped them. No longer could she wave it all off as simply nerves caused by upheaval. No—it hadn't been that—or hadn't been entirely that. Sure, her life had taken a few severe twists in the past couple of months. But, all that time—had it been a baby, trying to make itself known?

Suddenly, she stood, placed the test stick on the counter by the sink and marched into the kitchen. Outside the windows, the sky was blanketed with darkness. With determination, she flung open the freezer door and withdrew a lone package of frozen waffles.

Joie slammed the door shut and flung the crumpled box onto the counter, stomped to the cupboard and pulled out the toaster. She scowled, pondering when the appliance had last been used.

She shrugged and plugged it in. Didn't matter really. What mattered is that she was starving and she wanted a dang waffle.

The toaster—an old chrome-plated Toastmaster—had been her mother's. And one of the few things connected to her mom that she actually remembered. At five years old, after her older sisters climbed on the school bus in the mornings, her mama would allow her to stand on a kitchen stool and wait for the toasted bread to pop up.

Funny, it's not the big things that stick in your mind, but the little. Joie remembered the toaster, and the little glass of juice her mom always had nearby in case her diabetes sent her blood sugar levels plunging.

With her teeth, Joie ripped open the cellophane package, dumped the contents onto the counter. The frozen breakfast pastries had seen better days. She brushed off the large frost crystals that had accumulated in the tiny square indentations and plopped the waffles in the toaster.

Minutes later, she was at the table scraping her fork across a plate sticky with maple syrup and melted butter.

Joie envied her sisters their memories—how their mother doled out chores, decorated their room with lavender bedding ordered from the J.C. Penney catalog. The times she played paper dolls with them on the floor. The special way she braided their hair for school.

She'd heard it all over the years, had secretly wondered what it was like to know her like that.

Suddenly, her hands were in fists, thumbs clenched around fingers. How could she ever *be* a mother when she'd never had one? I mean, she didn't even know how all this worked.

Joie marched to the sink, grabbed the sponge and scrubbed her dish, struggling to keep her emotions in check, not able to stop rare tears that overflowed onto her cheeks.

Her breath caught, and she stood at the counter, pressing the palms of her hands against the tiled counter. With her eyes filling with tears, she slammed off the faucet and sunk to the floor, buried her face in her hands.

No little blue line was going to tell her something she didn't already know deep inside. She'd messed up again—big, this time.

7

J oie rammed the spikes of the pitchfork into the pile of dirty straw scooping as much as she could, then heaved the smelly mess into the wheelbarrow at her side. Without hesitation, she repeated the effort—again and again—stabbing at the straw with all her strength until the wheelbarrow was full.

Satisfied it would hold no more, she straightened, rubbed at her lower back for several seconds before she donned her down jacket. With grand determination, she pushed the unwieldy and heavy load outside into the bare light of morning, lumbering as she made her way to a pile by the side of the barn. There, she dumped the mucky contents.

If only dumping her own messes were so easy.

Weather this early in the year could be cold, but this morning was particularly frosty. She could see her breath as she crunched across the crystalline blanket of snow, unbroken except for the indents made by her boots as she made her way back inside.

Without taking any break, she tossed her jacket to the barn floor and returned to her task, jamming the pitchfork with increasing force each time she tore into the pile inside the empty stall.

"Hey, somebody forget they don't work here anymore?"

She turned to the familiar voice, huffed. "This barn could use a little more ventilation, especially in these winter temps. Ammonia isn't good for the horses' respiratory tracts."

Clint leaned against the wooden plank wall, folded his arms across his flannelled chest. "Noted."

"If you place a layer of diatomaceous earth underneath, you'll lower the potential for build-up." She rammed the pitchfork into the straw with extraordinary force.

"Got it." His head tilted slightly. "You okay?"

"Yeah. Why?" She brushed her sleeve across her brow.

He drilled her with a look, challenging her forgery of truth. "You sure?"

She diverted her gaze to the stalls. "The horses are all looking good."

"Yeah? Well—" The corners of his mouth quirked up. "We do our best."

Joie tucked a strand of hair behind her ear. "You know what I meant."

There was a long pause. "Anything you want to talk about?" He stared at her yet again, looked deeply into her eyes.

Uncomfortable under his scrutiny, she turned away, shook her head slowly. "I don't know what you're talking about. I'm fine." And then, "I mean, you got a taste of my wacky family the other night. But hey—everybody's got some crazy going on. Right?"

She longed for a shot of something strong right now. Never mind it wasn't yet seven in the morning, or that—well, yeah that.

She sighed—drinking wasn't the only thing she'd have to give up. That is, if she decided to go forward with all this—she could always decide not to keep it.

You'll keep it.

Sometimes she hated that small voice inside—the one that seemed unable to varnish over the truth.

Her grip tightened on the pitchfork. She drew a breath of air that had grown heavy with unsaid words, things she wasn't ready to reveal. Suddenly, she felt an overwhelming urge to cry. Instead, she swallowed, checked her watch. "Crud, turn around."

"Turn around?" Clint raised his eyebrows.

"You heard me. I said turn around." Without waiting for him to comply, she ripped the buttons open on her sweat-drenched shirt.

He half-chuckled and did as she demanded. "Okay, I give. What's all this about?" he asked, his back to her.

Without bothering to answer, she dipped her hands into a bucket of water located near her feet and splashed the icy water on her face. She pulled off her shirt, dried her face and tossed it on the ground before lifting a freshly pressed one from a peg on the wall. And a pair of black dress pants.

Joie quickly switched pants and drew her arms into the sleeves of the shirt. "You know, it's possible you need to add an additional fan. Dad just had some installed in the lambing sheds. He says they're working great. I could get you the name of the supplier if you want."

"I'll let you know," he told her, amused.

She shook off her annoyance and buttoned her shirt. Finished, she stood and faced him, a well-practiced pleasant smile pasted in place. "Okay, you can turn around now." She tucked in her shirt and fastened the buckle on her belt. A pair of pumps waited in the car.

Ignoring the half-smile on Clint's face, she grabbed the pitchfork and tossed the handle his way. "You'll have to finish this up. I have a client meeting."

∼

LEIGH ANN STARED at Nicole standing in the doorway, nearly choked. "Nicole—good, uh—good morning."

Mark gave his wife a stern look before scooping up his plate from the table. He stood and granted his new daughter-in-law a wide smile. "Are you hungry? Leigh Ann makes wonderful strawberry blintzes. Not too sweet."

Leigh Ann pretended she hadn't just blurted what they all knew was a put-down and jumped up from the table, scooped up her dirty dish. "The scones earlier—I mean, I can make you something else, something without wheat products." She headed into the sink, realizing she was talking way too fast. "Something with protein."

Mark grabbed the dish out of his wife's hand and rushed for the counter. "Well, I'd love to stay," he said, placing the plate in the soapy water. "Unfortunately, I have a big conference call with Andrea DuPont and the others from Equity Capital Group. So, I've got to get on my way. I'll see you both tonight." He charged from the kitchen like he was escaping the Chicago fire, not even bothering to kiss her goodbye.

God love him, it was just like Mark to leave her to deal with this mess.

"So, a salad?" Leigh Ann looked at the girl hopefully.

Nicole tightened the ties on Colby's robe and slid into a chair at the table. "Sure, but I'll wait for Colby."

Leigh Ann nodded. "Oh, yes—of course. Is he getting dressed?" She gathered the remaining dishes from the table.

"He's in the shower." Nicole swept some crumbs onto the floor. "On second thought, I would take a cup of hot water. And a slice of lemon if you have it."

"Oh, sure." Leigh Ann made a mental note to vacuum up those crumbs and headed for the pantry. "I have a huge assortment of tea bags, including a package of oolong from the Wuyi Mountains in the south of China. A gift from one of Mark's business associates."

Nicole ran her hand through her long light-red hair. "No thanks, just the water and lemon. And maybe a bay leaf," she added. "If you have one."

"Oh, okay. I think I do." Leigh Ann frowned. *A bay leaf?* She filled the teapot and placed it on the burner, turned the stove on. "So, tell me about yourself. Do your parents live in Seattle as well?" She wondered if they'd been given the courtesy of some foreknowledge before these two leapt into matrimony.

"No. My dad is an environmental attorney in Portland. My mom's currently in San Francisco."

"Divorced?"

"No, they love each other. They just don't believe in marital unions." A grin sprouted on Nicole's face. "I kind of freaked them out when I married Colby."

Leigh Ann's breath caught slightly. They had a lot in common —her parents and she. At least in the *freaked out* department. "Oh, well—but they don't live together?" she asked, still fishing for information.

Her new daughter-in-law knotted her hair at the nape of her neck. "Sometimes."

Now she was entirely confused. She went for the refrigerator, retrieved a lemon. "Do you want—"

"Just cut in wedges is fine."

Leigh Ann slowly nodded. The girl certainly didn't lack any confidence. "So, what does your mom do? For a living, I mean?" she asked, trying to keep a casual tone to her voice.

"She doesn't really work—to earn money, I mean. My dad's pretty successful. She mainly organizes his protests."

She pulled out the knife drawer, stopped midway. "His protests?"

Nicole nodded. "Yeah, and she carves kettle gourds on the side. Sells them to fund various causes she advocates for."

"Hey, Mom." Colby entered the kitchen, his arms stretched

high as he let out a yawn. "You're not interrogating my bride are you?" He grinned.

Leigh Ann jabbed the knife into the lemon. "No, sweetheart." She huffed, sliced off a wedge. "I'm simply trying to learn a little about our—uh, new family member."

Her son lacked a brain if he thought he was going to blow in like a tornado, whisk the entire household into a foreign land and then paint her as the wicked witch in the story.

She watched him kiss the top of Nicole's head. He straightened, rubbed his chest. "What you got to eat, Mom? I'm hungry."

Leigh Ann cemented a vision of him in her arms as that endearing baby she'd adored in an attempt not to walk over and smack him for this nonsense.

She drew a deep breath. "Sit down. I'll fix you some bacon and eggs."

The newlyweds exchanged glances.

"Sorry, Mom. We don't eat that stuff either." Colby explained.

Her brows knit into a tight line. She drilled her son with a look. "Since when?"

A glint formed in Nicole's eyes. She smiled up at her sweetly. "We don't consume animal products."

Leigh Ann swung back to the counter, finished slicing the lemon and grumbled under her breath, "Of course you don't."

8

J oie cut through the lobby of her office, her briefcase hanging limp at her side.

Heather, still on the phone, put her hand over the receiver. "Morning, Joie. I have Candy Newberry Tubbs on the line. She's running a little late and would like to move your meeting back a half hour."

Joie nodded. "Tell her that's fine."

Heather's voice went all syrupy sweet. "It'll be no problem to move your appointment to a little later, Mrs. Tubbs."

Glad for the respite, Joie made her way to the kitchen hoping to eat something before her empty stomach did another Jersey yodel. On her way down the hall, she passed framed photos and media articles chronicling Maddy Crane's enviable career—one she desperately wanted to emulate.

Joie's own initiation into the practice of law came when she was hired at a prestigious litigation firm in Boise only days after graduating at the top tier level of her law school. Even though her duties as a summer intern had been limited to primarily administrative tasks while she studied to take the bar exam, she'd stepped off the elevator that first day and walked into the lobby eager to show off her capabilities, impress the partners and make her mark.

She never counted on Andrew Merrill entering the picture— a highly respected trial attorney who became her mentor and coached her on the nuanced skills needed to sway a judge and jury, how to zealously represent a client with a goal to win.

Unfortunately, he also taught her when it came to the laws of attraction, some rules were never meant to be broken.

Pregnant.

She couldn't believe it. She barely had her junk together. Now she was supposed to be someone's mother?

And, the timing couldn't be worse. Maddy Crane had given her this lucky break, and she was grateful. Nothing would induce her to let her mentor down, not even her current predicament. This was a once-in-a-lifetime opportunity and she would not mess it up.

"Well, there you are, sweet thing." Maddy greeted her with a wide smile as she entered the kitchen. Her partner was dressed in silk black pants and a tiger-print tunic. Her blonde hair was coiled on top of her head fastened with a clip formed into the shape of a tiger head, the eyes amber jewel stones. "You must be busy. I haven't seen you all day."

Before Joie could form an answer, her stomach curled. She swallowed hard.

Maddy's face grew concerned. "You okay, darlin'?"

"Yeah, sure." Joie took a deep breath. "I'm fine." Thankfully, her tummy settled as quickly as the nausea appeared. She swallowed, forced a smile. "By the way, I really appreciate you coming to the party. I mean, my sister always goes over the top with the celebration thing."

"The entire evening was lovely," Maddy assured. "I was glad to be included." She reached for a tea bag and tore the package open, dangled the bag in a dainty cup filled with hot water. "My mama was a lot like your sister. She'd celebrate a bad toenail."

She pointed to a bakery box on the counter. "Well, I've got a stack of calls to make. But, help yourself, darlin'." With that, Maddy retreated from the room, tea and pastry in hand.

Joie lifted the box lid and surveyed the contents. Not exactly a nutritious meal, but hey—it was food. After settling on an apricot-filled strudel, she made her way down the hall, taking care not to get any powdered sugar on her black pants.

In her office, she pulled her laptop out of her briefcase and turned it on, ready to focus on her upcoming client meeting.

She clicked on an electronic file labelled Candy Newberry Tubbs and quickly scanned the contents again to see if there was anything she'd missed in the limited information recorded. Candy was very well off and had moved from Denver to Sun Valley only last year. When she'd called to make the appointment, their potential client had only indicated she had a business matter she needed to discuss with legal counsel. A quick internet search revealed little more except that Candy was widowed and served on multiple boards—primarily charities.

Joie glanced at her watch.

Despite her best effort to focus on the upcoming meeting, her thoughts again wandered back to that little blue line on the wand and what was growing inside her.

A baby.

Her hand drifted to her stomach.

Suddenly, fear like she'd never known crept up her back and lodged in her head. It was one thing to consider her reckless life and screw ups. It was entirely another to realize another life—that of a tiny child—might be affected by her poor choices.

She slowly turned in her chair and faced the window overlooking Baldy, gazed out at the familiar ski runs winding down the mountain.

It dawned on her she'd have to tell Andrew—I mean, wouldn't she? How could she not? No doubt he'd be as shocked as she. He may even try to trap her into resurrecting their relationship, perhaps promise to raise the baby together.

That wasn't going to happen!

Especially given his lies—and of course, the wedding ring.

Besides, someone like Andrew wouldn't want to be burdened with raising a child. Admittedly, she didn't want that jerk in this baby's life. He simply wasn't father material.

She supposed she could take solace in the fact she already felt protective of the tiny human growing inside of her. Guarding the baby from his influence would be her mission. She might even consider adoption. Some lovely couple out there could be the perfect solution.

There would be a lot of talk, of course. Joie Abbott had messed up again. People would judge any decision she made. None of that mattered. *She* didn't matter.

What mattered was her choosing the very best for this baby.

Unlike many women her age, she'd never much considered parenthood. Only that being a mother might be important to her —someday. Just not right now.

A deep sadness sprouted. She gnawed at her bottom lip considering a multitude of questions. If she relinquished this baby in an adoption process, might her child eventually come to hate her for it? Would she hate herself?

The phone intercom buzzed, jerking her from her thoughts. "Joie? Your client is here."

Joie swung her chair back to her desk. "Thanks, Heather. Show her in."

Seconds later, her potential client entered her office. Candy Newberry Tubbs was dressed elegantly in knee-high boots and thin black pants, her long, perfectly highlighted brown hair appropriately straightened. She had a distinctly exotic look— eyes a bit squinted, full lips slightly pursed, with high cheek bones that looked like they were carved from marble. Even the way she walked signaled this was a woman of influence.

Joie swallowed, slipped from behind her desk and extended her hand. "Ms. Tubbs, it's nice to meet you."

"Please, call me Candy."

Heather entered the room carrying a tray filled with coffee service and some tiny cucumber sandwiches, set it on the guest table. "Can I get you anything else?" she asked.

"Thank you, Heather. No, we're fine." Joie eyed the sandwiches, her stomach rumbling again. She motioned for her client to take a seat.

With a quick nod, Heather retreated, shutting the door behind her.

Joie made small talk as she poured the coffee, then settled into the arm chair across the table. "Let's talk about why you're here," she said, her pen poised ready to take notes on a waiting notepad.

The elegant woman took a sip from her coffee, brushed a stray crumb from her pants. "I guess the best place to start is the beginning."

Joie smiled back at her. "Yes, that's always a good place to start."

Candy nodded and looked across the table. "When my husband was still alive, he fell in love with this area. He loved to ski. We spent a lot of time here in his last years, before he got sick."

Joie nodded sympathetically.

"Headquarters for our business enterprise is Denver, where we made our home for years. While here on vacation several years back, William encountered some enterprising young men who were involved in a start-up that William believed had incredible potential. We invested—heavily. More than I was entirely comfortable with, frankly."

Joie recorded that fact in her notes.

"Over the years, my early reservations were put to rest. The investment did very well, just as William projected it might. We made a substantial sum." She disclosed a figure that caused Joie's pen to skip over the paper a little.

"Unfortunately," she continued. "We've suffered an odd reversal over the past twelve months or so. Despite economic factors that would seem to dictate otherwise, our material costs have risen substantially. We're losing our best talent, with top managers getting lured away with unheard of offers. We've been hit with an abnormal number of lawsuits, many making frivolous claims, including some product liability assertions that are simply unfounded. I could go on, but you get the picture." She drew a deep breath. "The important factor is that all this is driving our stock prices down."

"Meaning?"

Her eyes grew thin and guarded. "Meaning it has become apparent that the company is being targeted."

Joie raised her eyebrows. "Targeted? In what manner?"

Candy leaned forward, her arms resolutely folded on the table in front of her. "This often happens when a company finds themselves in the crosshairs of aggressive corporate raiders willing to pull a few unethical strings to accomplish a take-over."

Joie clicked her pen and laid it down on the notebook. "Crane and Abbott is happy to help, but I'm not convinced what you've suggested is actionable in a court of law. People, and companies, act unethically far too often. That's not breaking the law. To make a case, we'd have to prove a statute has been broken."

"Exactly." Candy caught Joie's eyes, held them. "I need your firm to investigate—to identify any acts that would allow us to legally protect ourselves and hopefully sue for damages."

"We would certainly be happy to do that. I do have a question —you must have in-house counsel. Is there a reason your corporate legal department isn't handling this? Or, someone local to your headquarters. I mean, there are some really successful firms in Denver."

Candy leaned back in her chair. She steepled her beautifully manicured fingers. "For now, I think it's extremely important we keep everything I've shared confidential. If what I suspect is true, we can't risk going public. No doubt, this will be a game of cat and mouse. If we're going to catch the culprits, we're going to have to quietly lure them into a trap."

Joie's mind raced. "Well, I appreciate your trust. I'll review what you've told me with my partner, Maddy Crane. Together, we'll determine exactly how our firm should proceed." She quickly glanced over her notes. "Oh, I don't think you mentioned the name of the company."

Candy took a last sip of her coffee, her expression now more relaxed. "The company is no doubt one you'll recognize. It's Preston, USA."

9

The day Karyn met Grayson Chandler, she'd been sitting on a stone bench at the Hemingway Memorial, unable to do the one thing she and Dean had agreed upon before he died—spread his ashes in the little creek that ran in front of the statuary.

Of course, Grayson hadn't known that until much later. He'd only known he'd stumbled on a woman in tears. Mesmerized, he'd crouched and stared. That is, until she caught him in the act.

Despite his attractive rugged appearance, she'd thought him rude—accused him of spying on her. Not in so many words, but she'd gotten her message across.

A tiny smile nipped at the corners of Karyn's mouth as she remembered the look on his face. Apparently, Grayson couldn't stand to leave her with that initial impression, because he'd shown up at Dean's memorial auction with an apology. Shortly after, she ran into him again at the lodge, right after her interview with Jon Sebring. The interview that landed her the job as hospitality director.

Perhaps it was the upbeat mood she was in as a result of that interview, but she agreed to go house hunting with him. That was the first day she knew that their acquaintance might grow to be more than that. The first time she'd allowed herself to consider even a tiny bit that there might be someone else after losing Dean.

Grayson Chandler flashed those pewter-colored eyes at her, and she wanted more than anything to let her head junk all go— to embrace a bit of hope for a brighter future and believe that everything was going to turn out okay.

Even so, she and Grayson faced some challenges in the early months—she'd nearly lost him due to her need to please, her insane fear of confrontation. After foolishly allowing her former in-laws to wedge themselves into this new relationship and cause strain, she'd finally come to her senses and put their relationship first.

Now she had an entire evening ahead to look forward to, an evening spent with the man who made her happy to wake up each morning.

Karyn wedged the bottle of chardonnay in the bucket of ice, checked the clock on the wall and dried her hands on the towel. Despite a frantic day at work, she'd hurried home and made a pan of homemade lasagna—Grayson's favorite. And a salad, complete with Kalamata olives and feta. Bread would go under the broiler at the last minute.

The smells—that of garlic, rosemary and red wine—all transported her to Italy. She'd gone to Livigno with Dean in the early months of her former marriage. The final trip they'd taken together.

Perhaps she and Grayson could also go there someday. The entire area was like a postcard, and the food—well, Ristorante La Pioda was glorious. She'd try to get them a table at the back, near the wall made of rock.

The doorbell rang. She untied her apron and hurried to answer it. "Hey, there you are!"

Grayson gave her a quick peck on the cheek, then pulled his

down jacket off and hung it in her coat closet. "Mmnn . . . smells good in here."

"Hope you're hungry." She motioned for him to follow her into the kitchen.

Grayson was a backcountry pilot. Despite loving Alaska winters, he'd grown tired of the endless seasons without sun. He'd flown with a friend to central Idaho and spent a few weeks in the Sawtooth primitive area, losing his heart to the jagged mountain area known as the Frank Church River of No Return Wilderness. Outside of Alaska, few places in America could provide such pristine wilderness—a land of clear rivers, deep canyons, and rugged mountains.

The move also allowed him to escape rugged emotions from learning his wife had fallen in love with someone else.

Grayson leaned against the counter, patted his stomach. "You and your sister are going to have to quit feeding me so well. If I'm not careful, I won't be able to get my plane off the ground for the added weight."

Karyn winked back at him playfully. "Oh, somehow I don't think that will be a big problem."

Suddenly, he caught her hand and pulled her to him, cupped her chin and lifted her face to his. He pressed his lips to her own.

This is what she'd missed most after losing Dean—kissing while standing in her kitchen barefooted.

When she finally pulled away to check on dinner, she didn't even try to hide her shy smile. A similar sphinx-like grin played about his own lips. "Anything I can help with?"

She slapped at him with the kitchen towel. "Yeah, you can set the table."

He grinned and moved to her cupboard. She loved that—the familiarity, that he knew where she stored her dishes and that they no longer needed to measure every word and action.

"I learned some news today," she told him as she filled a pitcher with ice water.

"Yeah, what's that?" She could hear the smile in his voice.

"Remember that meeting I was worried about?"

He nodded. "Uh-huh."

She shut the water off, turned. "Well, I'd over thought everything, like I do. Turns out, there was little to be concerned about. The owner of the resort showed up in person, Nola Gearhart."

Grayson pulled down two plates. "Really? What's she like?"

"Quite warm and lovely, actually. If you met her on the street, I'm not sure you'd think of her as such a wealthy woman." She turned off the oven timer. "She wanted to let us all know that the lodge will be hosting a film company which is coming to town to produce a remake of *Bus Stop*."

"The old Marilyn Monroe flick?"

"Uh-huh. The production company has cast Mia Larimore and Rick Hudson in the starring roles."

Grayson let out a whistle as he centered the plates on waiting placemats, then turned for the silverware drawer. "That *is* news."

"I know, right?" She grinned as she filled the water tumblers. "Everyone will be staying at the lodge while the movie is being filmed. That's not all. The plan is to cast locals in secondary roles."

"No kidding?"

"No kidding. And, you know what that means. Everybody suddenly has stars in their eyes and wants an audition."

He moaned and shook his head. "I never did understand that mentality. I mean, none of the Hollywood thing appeals to me—except perhaps sitting in a dark theater with a bucket of popcorn."

"To me either," she told him. "But I had a steady stream of employees stopping by my office today, asking if I'd put in a good word for them." She rolled her eyes. "As if I have anything to say about the matter."

"Need some help getting the lasagna out of the oven?"

"Sure." She tossed him a couple of pot holders. "Word spread and by mid-afternoon the lobby was filled with people all wanting to be in this movie. Miss Trudy and Ruby. Dee Dee Hamilton. Even Nash Billingsley left Bistro on Fourth in the hands of Lucy, that air-headed waitress of his, and came over to see what all the talk was about."

Grayson chuckled. "I guess it's not every day Hollywood comes knocking. Even in Sun Valley."

What he said was true. Sun Valley was no stranger to the rich and powerful. Founded on notions of exclusivity and luxury, the resort had always drawn the wealthy and famous to its powdery slopes.

"People you would least expect can get a little starry-eyed about these things," she told him. "I only hope the lodge doesn't suddenly morph into a studio backlot. That could prove to be a handful. I've been personally charged with hosting the film crew and making certain the resort gets positive publicity."

Grayson set the hot pan on top of the stove, then tossed the pot holders onto the counter. He turned, grabbed Karyn and pulled her close. "I can't think of anyone more qualified. Jon's trust is well placed." He kissed the top of her head.

Karyn smiled. "Well, don't polish my halo just yet."

As if on cue, her phone buzzed, signaling an incoming text. She pulled her cell from her back pocket to find a message from her former mother-in-law.

"Karyn, dear. It's Aggie—Bert and I are just back in town from Bali. Learned of the plan to remake Bus Stop and that the production company is looking for extras. As you know, I took acting lessons a few years back. Could we have lunch tomorrow to discuss?"

She started to laugh. She couldn't help it.

"What's so funny?'

"Nothing important," she said, still chuckling under her breath. "Only that the Hollywood stars still shine brightly."

10

Less than two weeks after Colby had shown up at the front door with his little surprises, the time came for him to report for basic training. He'd spend ten weeks at Fort Benning in Georgia, exactly two thousand two hundred thirty-three miles away, then return home for a brief time before his deployment. Leigh Ann didn't even want to contemplate where her son would be sent after that.

She carefully folded the final pair of pants and slid them neatly into his duffel bag. "There, I think that's everything." She looked over at her son, willing herself not to tear up.

"Don't forget this." Nicole waved a tiny wooden box in the air.

"Forget what?" Leigh Ann asked, knowing every item on her list was checked off and packed.

"His box of essential oils," her daughter-in-law replied. Then looking at Colby, "Baby, I packed three bottles of your pepper-mint oil in case you get one of your headaches."

Leigh Ann scowled. Had they both lost their hoody-oody-loving minds? "Didn't you read the instruction pamphlets they gave you? No pharmaceuticals or medicines of any kind without a prescription. I'm sure that applies to—uh, oils as well."

Nicole gave her a look, no doubt perplexed as to why her new mother-in-law continued to sound so ticked off. So be it. Her patience was running thin with that girl's silly ideas.

In the short time since Nicole had walked through her front door, Leigh Ann had learned more than she ever wanted to know about the *crunchy* lifestyle. Yes, that's what you called it. She'd looked it up on the internet.

Nicole didn't wear antiperspirant, insisting the ingredients were unhealthy, especially aluminum. Instead, she made her own all natural deodorant of bentonite clay. "This product doesn't block the pores," she'd explained. "Which allows for the body to eliminate toxins."

One morning she walked into the kitchen and asked for some baking soda, which she used to clean her hair. "I've been *no poo* since junior high school," she proudly reported. "I also make my own reusable sanitary products."

At that point, Leigh Ann lost it. Over the past several days, she'd immersed herself in articles written by highly regarded psychologists, learned that new daughters-in-law often felt criticized when their husbands' mothers offered too much advice. The recommended advice was to refrain from commenting, unless offering up support. None of those doctors' sons had married *this* girl. "Do you really think women get cancer because they use and discard tampons? Really, Nicole. I think you've drank the Kool-aide on all this hippy stuff."

The bomb had shot out of her mouth before stopping to think of the impact.

Colby's expression grew immediately stern. "Mom, can I talk with you? In the other room?"

She and Nicole exchanged looks. "Sure, Son." With a thudding heart, Leigh Ann following Colby into the den.

When they were safely out of earshot, he turned. "Mom, you've got to stop," he pleaded.

"Stop what?"

A vein popped in her son's neck. "Stop criticizing Nicole."

"I wasn't criticizing," she argued. "I was simply trying to help her rethink some of this nonsense." She shook her head. "I mean, really? She makes her own—"

Colby looked like he was going to explode. "That's what I'm talking about! You always think your way is the only way. I mean, can't you just back off once in a while?"

They both got quiet.

There was simply no way to hide that his words had lacerated her heart. She fought for the next breath—and the next.

"I—I didn't know you felt that way." Her quivering chin shot up. "I'm not sure you completely understand the sacrifices I've made on your behalf. And I won't be talked to in that manner."

She sensed he was fighting not to roll his eyes.

She was battling tears.

It was at that point Nicole intruded by appearing at the doorway. "Everything okay in here?" she asked, as if she had the right to insert herself into her relationship with her son. There were boundaries to be respected. At least in *this* house.

Leigh Ann laughed lightly, but of course her attempt to conceal the situation didn't ring true. Instead, her response came out sharp and defensive. "Everything is fine."

Her daughter-in-law looked skeptical, but nodded just the same. "Good." She walked over, draped her sweater-covered arm across Colby's shoulder. "Because I sense a great deal of negative energy. I think it's important we create a happy aura in our living space, don't you?"

With that, she led Colby back to the kitchen, leaving Leigh Ann to stew.

She could just pop her head off. I mean, really. Who did that granola nut think she was coming into *her* home, poaching her relationship with her son?

He'd never before treated her with disrespect. She didn't

mean to sound over dramatic, but now it was as if they were an army of two and she was the target on the battlefield.

From the other room, she could hear Nicole blather on about making some kind of herb omelette using egg whites and goat cheese.

Her hands fisted as she strode in to join them. "Here, let me help. You need to use the proper omelette pan or the eggs will stick."

That night, she nestled her head against her pillow and cried until she couldn't, like she used to when she was a little girl and felt the weight of the world on her young shoulders. Finally, she wore herself out. She was nearly asleep when Mark came home.

"Hey, babe." He flicked on his bedside lamp, sat on the edge of the bed.

She couldn't hide her sniffles.

He stopped in the middle of removing his tie, turned. "Leigh Ann? You okay?" He rested his hand on her blanketed shoulder. "What's the matter?"

She wiped her eyes on the corner of her expensive pillow case. "He hates me," she moaned in a choked voice.

He turned her face toward him. "Honey, who hates you?"

"Colby." She sat up, recounted the terse interaction from that morning, lamenting she'd lost her one and only son to some girl she didn't even know—a girl with strange ideas and the power to alter everything she'd so carefully trained Colby to believe.

"He doesn't hate you, Leigh Ann." Her husband looked at her patiently. "And neither does his new wife. The fact is, they're married now. Sure, maybe they were impulsive and far too young to make this commitment. Maybe they didn't even think it through carefully. But what's done is done. They are husband and wife. Like it or not, our son has to pull away from us so he can bond with her."

Reluctantly, miserably, Leigh Ann wiped her eyes again, this time on a tissue he offered. She blew her nose. "But—"

He drew her against his shoulder. "No buts, sweetheart. It's the way it's supposed to be."

She had wanted to argue with Mark, but deep down knew he was right. Even if she hated the idea.

Now, all these days later, nothing had changed. She still resented the interruption in her carefully plotted life.

Leigh Ann slowly closed the suitcase, the click sounding like a coffin closing.

As mad as she was at Colby for everything he'd done, he was her son—the little boy she'd bathed and powdered. The tiny guy she'd rocked to sleep each night because he was afraid of the dark. The boy who had fallen into inconsolable tears because the neighbor's dog chewed up his favorite stuffed Care Bear. Did he even remember she'd driven clear to Boise the next day to replace it?

She loved him. Would do anything for him.

Even so, when Colby indicated he wanted to leave his new wife here to live with them while he was away, she'd immediately balked at the idea. "Oh, Son. Don't you think Nicole would be more comfortable in Portland with her father. Or with her mom? Surely, she'd rather be with family."

Colby's expression had immediately challenged that sentiment. "She *is* with family," he corrected. "And I want her here with you and Dad while I'm away. How else are you going to get to know one another?"

Leigh Ann didn't exactly buy into the notion that a clubby relationship was necessary. Lots of in-laws simply spent time together at the holidays, politely smiling across the table at one another. Why couldn't they do the same? Especially given the volatile situation.

Unfortunately, her son had put his hand on her chin and made her face him. "Please, Mom. For me?"

Less than two years ago, she and Mark drove Colby to school for the first time. Leaving him alone in Seattle felt a lot like leaving her credit card on a subway bench. It took everything in her not to snatch him back, tuck him safely where he belonged—at home.

Now, because of one impulsive move, he was in the army and heading off to basic training. This time he wouldn't be sleeping in a dorm with his buddies and attending class to prepare for a bright future in engineering. He'd be sleeping in barracks. Her baby would face grueling and rigorous exercises meant to prepare him for the unthinkable—for possibly going off to some of the most dangerous places on the globe to fight with weapons.

It was almost too much to bear.

She put her face in her hands and pulled away when Mark tried to hold her on the sidewalk. "Come on, honey," he whispered. "He's going to be just fine."

"I thought hippy-types didn't believe in war. The least she could have done is talk him out of this nonsense."

Mark stroked her back, whispered, "She loves him—the fact she's supporting his decision is proof."

Leigh Ann watched as Colby approached. Despite his earlier bright smile, she noted a slight quiver in her son's chin as he leaned and kissed her cheek. "I love you, Mom." He pulled away far too quickly. "I'll email and we can Facetime. Maybe not every day, but we'll talk often. I promise."

Her voice wobbled. "I love you. Stay safe." She patted his back as he turned from her.

She forced a brave nod, folded her arms across her chest and watched him slide his arm around his new wife's waist. Leigh Ann hung back as they walked down the snow-lined sidewalk.

At the car, Colby took Nicole's face in his hands, said something she couldn't make out. He caressed her cheek, then kissed her before he ducked into the car, leaving his new wife huddled at the curb like some lost pup.

The engine started. He gunned the motor, waved big and pulled away, the snow crunching under the weight of the tires.

Mark wrapped his arm around Leigh Ann. Chilled, she tucked her head against her husband's shoulder wishing she could magically fast-forward through these next ten weeks. Nicole turned then, her face completely wrecked. Leigh Ann saw and immediately tossed off Mark's arm and made her way down the frozen sidewalk to her new daughter-in-law.

"He'll be back soon," Nicole muttered through stifled tears, more for her own benefit, while fingering the end of her long red braid.

Leigh Ann immediately drew the girl into a protective hug, squeezing her shoulders tightly against her own. "Yes, he'll be back in no time."

Overhead, the gray murky clouds let go and it began to snow —light airy flakes that drifted to the ground without strain. With a deep breath, she looped arms with her new daughter-in-law and led her back inside.

11

With Valentine's Day right around the corner, time seemed to be marching on at breakneck speed. At nearly four months, Joie's pregnancy would begin showing soon. The fact that motherhood was in her future was about to get very real. Especially when she had to start telling others—especially her family.

And she needed to tell Andrew.

Soon, she promised herself.

More than once she'd considered her options. Wondered if she'd made the right decision in deciding to go forward with the pregnancy and keep the baby. Could she pull off starting a law practice, working full-time and raising a child?

Yes, other women juggled life and motherhood well—Leigh Ann for example. But Joie wasn't like her sister. Homemaking was not exactly her strong suit. Neither was putting her carefree life-style aside in order to make someone else a priority—a little scrunch-faced infant she wasn't sure she could even love properly. Was she even mother material?

There were lots of reasons to say no to that question.

Being a mom was a big deal. It took a lot of self-talk to

convince herself she was up for that kind of responsibility. Even then, she wavered and often doubted the fact.

For one thing, her life was not especially set up for all the changes ahead. She couldn't very well raise a baby in her father's two-room guest house out at the ranch. Given that, she supposed it was time to go house hunting.

Without telling a soul, she set out on Wednesday to look for a place. "I'll be out for a bit," she told Heather. "If anyone needs me, I'll have my phone with me."

She couldn't remember the last time she'd left the office during a work day. Normally, she used every spare minute between client meetings to research the situation for Candy Newberry Tubbs.

So far, she'd had little luck and had only run into walls when it came to finding out who was behind the schemes to keep Preston USA from prospering. "Keep looking," Maddy Crane urged. "Eventually, we'll get our break and when we do, we'll trim the tail feathers of whoever is behind all this."

Joie's email pinged on the way out to her car.

Hey, Joie – Don't forget the Women of Sun Valley Foundation is holding the torchlight parade this weekend. Community dinner at the lodge after. You're coming, right? ~Leigh Ann

Crud, she'd forgotten all about the big fundraiser. Normally, she'd jump on participating. She loved the event where skiers made their way down Dollar Mountain at night holding red flares. The entire town turned out to watch the beautiful parade down the slope.

Guess it wasn't the smartest move to risk a fall. Besides that, her ski pants were growing too tight. Still, she hated missing the annual tradition.

Never mind all that now—she had a small window of time to find a place to rent. She needed to focus.

Joie wasn't terribly picky when it came to where she lived. She'd even slept on her share of sofas. Now, she had a lot of considerations. Would she need a backyard? And, at what age? She didn't want to have to move again very soon.

The internet had a list of available rentals in her price range, which ended up being a very short selection, even on her new salary. Sun Valley property was not exactly known to be economical.

She circled three she was particularly interested in and set out to find a place to live. The first one she looked at fit the bill perfectly—a condo on River Ridge Lane. The front window overlooked the base of Baldy and provided a clear view of the tram. The Wood River ran several yards in the distance which would provide nice ambient noise while sitting on the tiny deck in the backyard.

The kitchen was small, but then she didn't cook all that much.

It was the little bedroom just steps from the door to the master that cemented the decision. She stood in the middle of that room, daring to imagine a nursery, when she felt a movement inside her stomach—like that of butterfly wings flapping against the inside of her skin. The flittering was nearly undetectable at first, then grew immediately stronger. There was no mistaking the origin of the movement.

Without thinking, her hand went to her stomach. She couldn't help herself. It was as if her unborn baby had just signaled from inside the womb, telling her this was their new home. She teared up, hating how her emotions seem to drive her into doing things that were totally out of character. Like crying over some silly bedroom.

Joie wiped the moisture from her eyes and pulled out her phone, dialed the number and made the necessary arrangements to move in.

With that task complete, it immediately dawned on her she didn't even own a stick of furniture. When she'd lived in Boise, she'd leased a fully-furnished apartment and had eaten out of cardboard take-out boxes, that is, when she wasn't dining out with Andrew.

Last she remembered, there were some pieces stored up in her father's attic—items that were considered surplus after her dad updated the ranch house and bought new furniture. Her limited budget would stretch further if she could simply add items to his cast asides.

As soon as she left work that evening, Joie drove out to the ranch. After changing clothes at her place, she made her way out to the lambing sheds to find her dad.

She's always loved lambing season. Seeing new lambs being born was the closest thing she'd ever seen to magic and watching one take its first shaky steps on impossibly long legs was nothing short of a miracle. It made all the sleepless nights of every-two-hour barn checks, all the waiting and worrying seem like minor inconveniences.

According to her father, this year's lambing season had gotten off to a great start. The first four ewes to lamb each had a set of twins—five girls and three boys—all healthy and perfect and absolutely adorable. Now, the lambing sheds were nearly filled each night with newborns.

In her last year of junior high, Joie had successfully talked her dad into letting her skip classes to help out. It was the year Sebastian had to fly home to the Basque country to tend to his ailing mother.

It was her job to stay awake through the night and scout the drop pen, looking for ewes about to give birth. It was critical to move the newborn lambs inside as soon as possible to keep them from freezing.

Four days into this came Itty-Bitty, a premature lamb so small and weak that at first Joie refused to give him a name. Itty-Bitty was the smallest lamb she'd ever seen, a third the size of their cat.

Her father didn't give much for his chance of surviving the

hour, let alone the night, but Joie was determined to do her best to save him.

The little lamb was so weak that there was no way he could nurse on his own, so she started tubing him—dropping a thin tube down his throat into his stomach and pouring milk in, every two hours, 'round the clock. At first her efforts seemed futile, but the next morning he seemed to be improving. On day two, the lamb stood and even took a few steps. Later he surprised everyone by nursing from his mama all on his own.

Needless to say, Joie was elated. She cut back his feedings to every four hours, then every eight. Every time she went out to the barn she marveled at Itty-Bitty's will to live.

But then, Itty-Bitty took a turn for the worse. His breathing was labored and he seemed weaker than ever. She got some milk into him along with a vitamin treatment, but he never responded.

That was the dark side of lambing season. She'd done everything she knew how to do to save that lamb, but in the end, it was not enough.

Ranchers like to say that if you're going to have livestock, you're going to have dead stock. But it never got easier to lose an animal.

What about . . . a baby?

Babies became sick all the time. They came down with something called the croup, their skin got jaundiced, they fell into any number of illnesses. What would she do if faced with any of that?

She could jump out of a plane and pull into a perfect barrel roll before racing five thousand feet to the ground. She could do a Nac Nac from the back of a Triumph Bonneville T100 while racing seventy miles per hour down the highway. She could outdrink most of the boys down at Crusty's and had memorized every word on the old Fleetwood Mac Rumors album. But she'd never been a mother before.

Joie pushed open the door on the lambing shed, a long structure filled with tiny pens lined with straw. Inside, a pot belly stove kept the interior toasty warm.

"Dad?" Joie peered down the empty aisles. "You in here?"

"Coming," her father called from the adjacent shed. He slid the pallet door open and appeared, his face looking tired, but happy. He made his way to her, gave her a hug. "How are you, sweetheart?"

"I'm good," she told him, lying.

He pulled the red cap from his head, swiped his arm across his brow. "Been a busy night already and it's not even six o'clock."

She leaned and kissed his leathery cheek. "Yeah? You eaten?"

He nodded. "Had some beans with Sebastian earlier." He lifted a dented stainless steel pot from the stove. "You want some coffee?"

"Sure," she replied, then just as quickly shook her head. "Nah, I'd better not." This pregnancy stuff was going to be the end of her.

"It's not like you to pass on a hot cup of java. What, has the caffeine been keeping you up at night?"

She gave him a weak smile. "That, and a lot of other stuff."

He nodded. "Life can get like that sometimes. How's work?"

She let herself smile. "What is it you always say? It's not work if you love doing it."

Her dad rubbed at his scrubby cheek. "That's right. Can't ask for any better myself." He grabbed a can of red paint from a nail on the wall.

She followed him down the aisle, watching as he marked the lambs. If the lamb and mother later got separated outside, the marking would allow the herders to pair them back up. Later, they'd be ear-tagged.

"Hey, Dad?"

"Yeah?" He spread a large swath of the temporary color across the backs of several pairs of mothers and lambs.

"I was thinking, now that I'm back on my feet with a good job and all, well, I think it's time I found my own place. So, I rented something this afternoon. In town."

Her dad stopped, looked at her. "Oh?"

Joie couldn't tell from his expression what he was thinking. "Yeah, I mean—I really loved living back out here again. But you know, I'm an adult and—"

He surprised her with a reassuring smile. "Sweetheart, you don't have to explain. I understand."

She breathed a sigh of relief. "And I was wondering—do you think I could pick through the furniture you have stored in the attic and maybe use some of it?"

"Help yourself to whatever you want. It's not doing anybody any good up there."

Sebastian burst through the door. "Edwin, we have a problem."

Her father looked up from his chore. "What's the matter?"

Their old ranch hand ran his fingers through thinning hair. "The main faucet froze up. Water line burst. We're going to have a skating rink soon."

"I'll head and get my tools, get that water turned off. In the meantime, summon Pedro and let's move those sheep to another pen before that mess ices up." He turned and gave Joie an apologetic look. "Sorry, sweetheart. I've got to go."

She watched him pull his hat down over his ears and follow Sebastian out.

Alone, she picked up the paint can and finished marking the animals, stopping on occasion to marvel at the newness of life— how the ewes licked their newborns clean and then stood patiently as the lambs suckled for the first time.

This motherhood thing seemed to come naturally to them. Could she dare to hope the same be true of her?

Twenty minutes later, the task was completed. She wrapped her scarf tightly and headed back out into the frosty night.

An immense scattering of polar-white stars pierced the black night sky—like something so much bigger loomed behind the curtain of darkness just out of sight. She'd always been taught to believe there was a God. Sadly, she was likely a disappointment to him, her mess-ups stacked stone on stone, a monument to the lines she'd crossed.

Her dad often warned not to look back unless you were going that way, but despite recent attempts, she was finding it more and more difficult to pull the crown of shame from her head and hold her head high.

Especially now.

Shrugging off the thought, she gathered what confidence she could muster and headed for the main house, convinced it didn't matter all that much. Her dad was right. There was no undoing the past. She could only move forward.

Inside, Joie made her way into the familiar kitchen. A plate of oatmeal raisin cookies rested on the counter with a note from Elda Vaughn, a woman she and her sisters long suspected delivered these regular treats with romantic intent. Elda was one of the ladies they'd dubbed the Bo-Peeps.

She grabbed one from the plate and slid it into her mouth before moving through the spacious living room with its vaulted ceiling and log beams, past a river rock fireplace sporting a log mantle lined with framed photographs.

One caught her eye—a photo of Leigh Ann and Karyn on either side of her when she was little, holding her hands and leading her across the lawn. As she recalled, the shot was taken the same summer their mother died. Leigh Ann had been fourteen, Karyn ten. She was only five.

After losing their mom, her sisters had filled the roles of caretaker and nurturer. She often thought them bossy, especially Leigh Ann who was determined to rein her in when she all she wanted was to fly.

Joie bent at the base of the stairs to pet her father's border collie, Riley. "How you doing, girl?" she said as she rubbed behind the dog's ears.

Following a final pat on the head, she took the stairs two at a time just to prove she could, taking care to skip the one that always creaked—the one that had served to signal every time she'd come home past curfew. Slightly winded, she moved on down the hallway lined with doors to bedrooms that remained just as they had when they slept there each night.

While her sisters' walls were covered with Jason Priestley and Justin Timberlake posters, their dressers lined with hair products and cosmetics, she'd adorned her room with horses and ribbons won in barrel-racing competitions.

At the end of the hallway, tucked just past the bathroom they'd all shared, was the door leading to the attic. Joie turned the knob and pulled. The door creaked as it opened.

Immediately, stale air and the smell of dust hit her nostrils. She coughed and waved the door back and forth, hoping to let the bad air out, then flicked on the light and climbed the narrow set of steps leading into the large storage area with bare wood floors and open rafters.

The furniture she was looking for was at the far side, under a tiny window. The pieces had been covered with blankets. She lifted one of the coverings and inspected the sofa beneath, thinking it had seen better days. She recognized a familiar ketchup stain on one of the cushions. She'd need to buy a cover.

In the end, Joie made a mental list of items to move to her new place—a list much shorter than she'd anticipated. That was okay. She'd just have to be patient and add to the furnishings as she could from her future salary draws. The baby wouldn't be here until the middle of summer. That gave her plenty of time.

She tucked the blankets back in place and retreated for the door, when a black trunk she'd never seen caught her eye. There were two lamps stored on top of the lid, and several small unmarked boxes.

Curious, she unloaded the items off the top and attempted to open the lid. It didn't appear to be locked, but it sure wasn't yielding easily. The latch caught and it would take some sort of tool to get it to release.

She looked around and found a toy baton, no doubt one of her sisters' Christmas presents from years gone by. Turns out, her dad was a bit of a pack rat.

Joie popped off the yellowed rubber head. She placed the length of the baton on the wood floor, stomped on the end and flattened it. Satisfied with the results, she returned to the trunk and needled the contrived implement under the latch and lifted.

It took two tries, but finally the stubborn apparatus yielded to the pressure and the lid released.

Joie sat in front, her legs crossed Indian style. Inside were three large plastic bags that zipped, each carefully labeled.

Leigh Ann—Karyn—Joie.

Curious, she lifted the bag with her name on it and slowly opened the zipper and peered inside at the contents.

Folded on top was a tiny pink nightgown, soft flannel with tiny white rosebuds. Beneath that, a crocheted pair of the tiniest slippers she'd ever seen.

There was more—dozens of little items. Baby apparel all carefully folded and tucked away for safekeeping.

Joie's breath caught as she lifted each item, held it to her nose. Even now, the faintest sweet smell could be detected on the garments, that of a baby and the scent of powder.

And that's when she noticed the envelope with her hand-written name neatly scrolled on top along with the date—a month before her mother had been transported to the hospital for the final time. While she didn't remember much about that night—or sadly, even her mother except for her hands and how they rubbed her back at night—Joie could close her eyes and still see the flashing red lights on the ambulance, feel the fear.

With trembling fingers, she turned the envelope over,

noticing the glue had browned with age. Her heart thudded with a strange mixture of anticipation and dread as she carefully tore open the end and slid a single folded sheet of paper from inside.

My sweet Joie—
It pains me terribly to know I'll be leaving you soon. The doctors try to give me hope, but my body is giving out. I know inside that it won't be much longer.

Your sisters will easily remember me, but I'm afraid in the years to come, I will fade from your memory. You're so little.

That's why I'm writing you this letter. I want to share some sentiments from my heart for you to tuck inside your own. I'm counting on you reading this . . . when it's the right time.

First, I want to tell you a little about the night you were born. We barely made it to the hospital in time. Unlike the long labors I had with your sisters, I simply woke in the early morning hours in pain. In the darkness, I fumbled for your father—told him we needed to go. By the time he got Sebastian up to the house to watch your sisters, my contractions were only minutes apart.

We did make it to St. Moritz though. You arrived in the midst of a flurry of frantic activity, taking everyone a bit by surprise at how fast you came and how loud you could scream. I looked into your tiny black eyes for the first time, and lost my heart to a little girl who I suspected would take the world by storm. There was little doubt those little dimpled fists would fight to make a place in this world—a unique place only you were meant to fill.

As a baby, you rarely cried—only when you were hungry. Even later, you would simply grunt when you got frustrated—as if deep inside your little spirit you knew you were destined for something special and didn't want to settle for anything less.

Even now, you barely have time for me to brush your hair. Often, it's a fight to get you in the bath at night. You are simply far too busy.

When I try to tie your shoes, you quickly demand, "Me do it myself." You dismantled your sisters' Easy Bake Oven so you could see how it worked. And when your father handed you girls dollar bills for doing your chores, you gave yours back and told him you needed a five on it.

Just imagine where that tenacity will take you!

Oh, how I hate to leave you, my sweet little Joie.

I long to cheer when you ace your school exams and high school track meets, applaud at your Christmas pageants and kiss all your skinned knees. Someday, you will no doubt fall in love. I ache inside knowing I will not be in the bridal room as you wait to walk down the aisle, or hold your hand on the day you give birth—or, see the look in your eyes when you first feel this kind of love for your own tiny infant.

Some will say I ran out of luck. I still count myself one of the luckiest women ever. I was a wife and mother. I was your mother.

Oh, my sweet darling child, you are deeply loved. More than you'll ever know. I would write this story differently if I could. I'm not sure what awaits in heaven, but nothing can keep me from peering through the veil at the ones I had to leave behind.

I'll be watching. ~ Mommy

JOIE SAT stunned and struggling for breath, her hands holding the sheet of paper like it was made of gold dust that might scatter with the slightest jar. After several minutes, her fingers fumbled as she tried to fold the letter. Unable to return it to the envelope, she simply held the paper against her heart.

She felt tears filling her eyes but was powerless to stop them. Years of loss and emotion crashed against the walls of her heart as she crumpled to the floor sobbing—deep, gasping howls that tore at her throat and hurt her chest with their force. Tears scalded her eyes and rolled down her face, laced with pain she never realized was inside her.

Her mom . . . her baby. Everything blurred.

That is how her Dad found her.

"Joie?" he said, rushing to her side. "Baby, what is it?" He knelt beside her, pulled her against him.

She buried her head against his chest, crying uncontrollably.

Smoothing her hair with calloused hands, he rocked her gently back and forth, his quiet strength filling the raw void inside her. When her tears began to subside, he tried again. "Joie, honey," he said in a soothing voice. "What's the matter?"

She took a deep breath, swallowed painfully. She pulled her head back and looked at the open trunk filled with baby clothes, then back at him, her throat again tight with tears.

"Daddy, I—I'm pregnant."

12

Karyn arrived at work early, eager to ensure everything at the lodge was just right prior to the arrival of Robert Nygard and his film team from Tanasbourne Media. According to her research, Mr. Nygard was well known in entertainment circles, had produced several successful independent films, two of which were nominated for Oscars. He had a reputation for being eccentric, and demanding. There were also rumors he had a penchant for women—which could answer why he was on his fourth wife.

She reminded herself it was not for her to judge. Her job was to make sure everything ran smoothly and that the entire crew felt like honored guests at the Sun Valley Lodge.

Jon Sebring, the resort director, was a little on edge about the whole thing too, she could tell. He'd cancelled a trip to Hawaii so he could be available should any issues arise. Grayson thought perhaps Jon wanted to snag a small part in the film, but Karyn didn't think that was the case. Jon was far too pragmatic to run after that kind of notoriety.

As soon as the black stretch limo pulled up into the portico, she realized she might have miscalculated the situation.

Jon nearly knocked over the doorman as he pushed through the front doors to greet their distinguished guests, which was odd. It wasn't like the lodge hadn't hosted celebrities in the past, including Oprah Winfrey, Jeff Bezos and members of the Kennedy family. Even Supreme Court Justice Sandra Day O'Connor had been a frequent guest.

Jon extended his hand. "Welcome to the Sun Valley Lodge. We're so, so very happy to have you with us," he gushed.

Mr. Nygard wore a pair of chinos and a leather jacket, with a pair of Panthère De Cartier sunglasses nested on top of his collar-length-jet-black hair. He shook Jon's hand. "Good to be here."

Jon motioned in her direction. "This is Karyn Macadam, our director of hospitality. She has been charged with making sure you and your crew have everything you need during your stay."

Mr. Nygard took her hand. "It's a pleasure. I was a huge fan of your husband. Uh—former husband. We certainly lost him far too soon." He studied her. "You have lovely bone structure. The camera would love you. Ever consider a career in film?"

Karyn shifted uncomfortably. She gently retracted her hand. "Goodness, no. I hate that sort of thing."

His eyebrows shot up. "You hate the movies?"

Her face flushed. "Oh, no. I love the movies. I'm just not the sort to be on stage." In an attempt to disguise her discomfiture, she chuckled lightly. "I'm much more comfortable behind the scenes."

Jon nodded. "We're extremely lucky Karyn agreed to join our team. She has consistently elevated the guest experience here at the Sun Valley Lodge."

Karyn grabbed onto that notion and went with it. "I think you'll find our accommodations rival any five-star hotel. We've booked you into the Marilyn Monroe Suite. You'll have an excellent view of Baldy."

A second limo pulled under the portico and parked.

Mr. Nygard pointed. "Ah, that must be Mia and Rick. Their plane was scheduled to land just after mine."

Security officers stood nearby in plain clothes ski gear, looking inconspicuous as the celebrated actors climbed from the car with the help of the doorman.

Security was only one of the many details Karyn had to attend to earlier. She'd spent hours with Amelio and Jess planning special menus to suit the meal preferences she'd been provided. The Duchin Lounge had been stocked with Mr. Nygard's favorite single malt scotch. Florals had been ordered and placed in all the rooms.

No expense would be spared. Not only had the film company rented the entire lodge for their extended stay, but the money flowing into Sun Valley from the movie remake would be a huge boost to the local economy.

"Hey, Karyn!" A thin-framed woman with short spiky white hair and red glasses strode across the lobby, unabashedly waving in their direction.

Jon's eyebrows immediately shot up. No doubt, he wondered why Dee Dee Henderson was heading their way. Only employees and those with delivery privileges had access to the lobby this morning.

She leaned to her boss and whispered. "Floral delivery."

He nodded, still not happy. They both knew how star struck Dee Dee tended to be.

Karyn quickly excused herself and moved in her direction, hoping to head off her friend before she arrived at her destination. "Sorry, Dee Dee. The lobby is off limits this morning."

"But, I just wanted to meet the director. And Mia Larimore. Don't you think she'll play a great Marilyn? And if Robert Nygard knew how talented I am, then—"

Karyn gave her a look of feigned sympathy, took her elbow and turned her around. "Look, the filming crew will be here for several weeks. Perhaps later you might—"

Dee Dee's breath caught. Her hand went to her mouth. "Oh my—I suddenly don't feel very well."

"Dee Dee? What is it?" Karyn asked. "Are you all right?"

"No—I don't think so." Suddenly, Dee Dee's eyes rolled to the back of her head and she crumpled to the floor.

Karyn sank to the floor next to her. "Dee Dee?" She quickly glanced around. "Someone call 9-1-1!"

Everyone rushed and formed a tight circle around the woman on the floor, including Mr. Nygard, Mia and Rick.

Mia's hand went to her chest. "Oh no! Is she all right?"

Jon held out his arm. "Stand back, everyone. Give her air."

At that moment, Dee Dee sat up. With a wide smile, she scrambled to her feet and held out her hand to Mr. Nygard. "That is only a sample, sir, of the method acting I'm fully trained to execute. I took a course over the internet, in my spare time of course, and made very high marks." She looked at all of them confidently. "In fact, the instructor said I'm a natural."

LEIGH ANN HELD the door to Pete Lane's Mountain Sports store. "Are you kidding me?"

Karyn moved inside. "No, I'm not kidding. The entire situation was humiliating. I thought the lodge was secure, never expecting anyone could possibly breach the measures we'd put in place." She shook her head and groaned. "What a great first impression."

Leigh Ann followed her inside. "Well, Dee Dee can be pretty inventive when it comes to celebrity sightings. Remember that time she dressed up like a waitress and photobombed Jared Padalecki's wedding reception?"

Karyn cringed. "Well, she is the self-appointed head of the Gilmore Girls' fan club. She even created a Facebook group. At last count, there were nearly fifteen thousand active members."

"Look, just consider the incident couldn't be helped and move on. No harm—no foul." Leigh Ann made her way to the counter.

Karyn trailed behind, not so sure. "Hope Jon and Nola Gearhart see things that way."

A young guy with scruffy hair stepped up to the register. "What can I do for you ladies?"

Leigh Ann smiled back at him. "I'm here to check on my new bindings. Pete said they'd be done in plenty of time for the torchlight parade."

"Okay, sure. Let me check." The clerk told them to wait while he headed for the back room.

As soon as he disappeared, Leigh Ann turned. "You did call and tell Joie to meet us for lunch, right?"

"Left her a text." Karyn scanned a publicity poster for the upcoming Valentine's Day torchlight parade. "I wonder if Grayson would like to do this?"

"I'm sure he would. Why don't you ask him to join us?" Her sister pulled a jacket from a nearby rack of ski parkas. She held it up to her in front of a mirror.

Karyn tilted her head. "Hey, that's cute. I like the color."

"Yeah, me too. Mark will kill me but I think I'm going to get it. It's not often you find a Lolë down coat thirty-five percent off." She grabbed a nearby sweater, then another.

The clerk reappeared. "Looks like we'll have your skis ready by tomorrow afternoon, Mrs. Blackburn."

Leigh Ann handed him the jacket and the sweaters. "Great!" She fished for her credit card. "I'll have my husband pick them up. By the way, do you have any ski pants to match this jacket?"

He confirmed he could have a pair overnighted and would deliver both items to her house.

Leigh Ann stuffed the receipt in her wallet. "You ready?"

Karyn nodded. "You do know that buying all that stuff isn't going to fix your problem?"

Leigh Ann frowned as she headed for the door. "What do you mean?"

"I mean, you have a new daughter-in-law sitting at your house and you haven't even brought it up."

"Oh that." Leigh Ann marched down the sidewalk, her arms overloaded with bags. "Let me drop this stuff off at my car."

Karyn dutifully followed on her sister's heels as they made their way to the parking lot. "You want to talk about it? I mean, how's everything going?"

Leigh Ann opened the trunk of her car and let her parcels topple inside. "Everything's fine." She slammed the trunk shut.

Karyn wasn't so sure. "I bet it's hard. I mean, you two barely know one another. What do you talk about? Besides missing Colby, I mean."

Leigh Ann brushed past and started walking toward the lodge. "I encouraged her to look into some line of employment. Colby agrees. She can't simply sit around the house all day. That isn't good for anyone."

Karyn nodded. "Yeah, you're probably right about that."

"She's doing some research, making a list of her options," Leigh Ann continued. "I thought retail might be an option, and since I know many of the retailers here, I could help her."

"But?"

"But, she declined. Apparently, she's reluctant to promulgate the illusion that retail consumerism is good for society."

"I'm sorry, but what does *that* mean?'

Leigh Ann huffed. "Exactly!"

Karyn couldn't help but chuckle.

"What do you find so funny?" her sister demanded.

She shook her head. "I'm just looking ahead and wondering how the two of you are going to do the holidays together."

Leigh Ann squared her shoulders and walked with determination. "Well, all I can say is that—"

"Hey, you guys!"

They both turned to find Joie jogging toward them. "Hold up," she called out.

They waited for her and when she caught up, each gave their younger sister a hug.

"I don't have much time today," Joie reported. "Things are really starting to pick up at the office."

Karyn looped arms with Joie as they approached the frosty-edged pond located in front of the lodge. "We can't wait to hear all the details."

Karyn had reserved a table at Gretchen's, one overlooking the outdoor skating rink. While they were waiting to be seated, she glanced at her watch. "I'm going to be a little short on time today as well. We have our quarterly inspection with the fire marshal in a little over an hour."

Leigh Ann pulled a compact from her purse, checked her lipstick. "Listen up, you two. It's not about having time, but making time." She snapped the compact shut as they followed the hostess to their table.

Joie slid into the chair opposite Leigh Ann's. "You find that on your motivational calendar this morning?"

Karyn quickly opened her menu. "Amelio is running a special today—a Reuben sandwich with bacon cheddar tots. Of course, you can sub out for a salad."

Leigh Ann held up open palms. "Yikes, pass. Even with the salad choice, the sandwich is laden with calories. None of us is getting any younger and those pounds don't come off easily. Just ask my gal at the gym." She squeezed some lemon into her water glass. "Joie, I can never thank you enough for introducing me to Ariana over at Zenergy. She's fabulous." She placed the used lemon wedge on the edge of her bread plate. "By the way, I hope you're not skipping the gym. Not to hurt your feelings, but you look like you're putting on a little weight."

"Leigh Ann!" Karyn scolded.

Her older sister waved her off. "Oh, don't get all crazy. She knows I don't mean anything by that. Don't you, Joie?" She looked across the table. Their sister was staring blankly out the window at the skaters. "Joie?" She exchanged glances with Karyn. "Honey, you okay? You have dark circles under your eyes. Are you getting enough sleep? You can't let that job—"

Joie nodded. "Yeah, I'm good."

Leigh Ann wouldn't give up. "You didn't look like you were feeling well the other night either. No doubt, you're working yourself to death, starting that law practice, and all." She nodded in Karyn's direction. "You're not the only one battling job issues." Leigh Ann tucked the linen napkin across her lap. "Did Karyn tell you about that stunt Dee Dee Hamilton pulled?"

Karyn told the story again, this time finally able to see some humor in the event. "I wish you could have seen the look on Robert Nygard's face."

Joie gave her a weak smile and fingered her silverware. "Yeah, I saw Miss Trudy in the parking lot earlier and she told me all about it."

Karyn and Leigh Ann exchanged another set of confused glances. It wasn't like Joie to be so distracted.

"Well, we want to hear all about your new job. Spill," Karyn urged.

Joie's face brightened a bit. "I love it," she said. "Working with Maddy Crane is amazing. I've never encountered anyone who makes being ambitious so okay. She's smart, and strategic and never accepts defeat."

Karyn grinned. "Sounds like a match made in heaven."

The waitress appeared at the table, and they placed their orders. Karyn ordered a bowl of minestrone soup, which would leave ample room for the apple crisp she'd had her eye on since she'd spied it in the kitchen earlier that morning. Leigh Ann made it clear she would only allow herself a cobb salad, dressing on the side and no bacon. Likely out of spite, Joie ordered the Rueben, with extra dressing.

Leigh Ann's perfectly arched eyebrows shot up. "Are you sure you want to do that?" she challenged. "I'm not kidding about the fact you are looking a little heavy these days. Maybe you should be more careful."

Without a moment's hesitation, Joie drew a deep breath and responded. "That's supposed to happen. I'm pregnant."

13

L eigh Ann tucked a stray piece of hair underneath her scarf and headed for her kitchen.

There were few things she hated more than a mess.

She flung the pantry door open, parked her hands on her hips and stared inside with disgust. How in the world did everything get so disorganized?

Because no one bothered to follow her neatly organized system and put things where they belonged—that's how.

She rolled her eyes and started at the top shelf, pulling down boxes of rice and cereal, crackers and baking mixes. When the shelf was successfully emptied, she moved to the second shelf and started on the cans of corn, olives, beans and beets. She removed spices and soup mixes, bottles of olive oil and vinegar.

A half hour later, the shelves were cleared and her counters were cluttered with the contents of her pantry. She swiped a sleeve across her forehead and headed for the sink, filled a bucket with sudsy warm water and went to work scrubbing the shelves.

"Leigh Ann? What are you doing?" Mark stood at the doorway. "Don't we pay someone a lot of money to do all that?"

She pulled her head from the pantry. "If you're referring to Isla, I gave her the day off."

Mark frowned. "But can't this wait until she returns to work?"

"Not possible," Leigh Ann explained. "I'm not able to stand this mess another minute." She chewed at her chapped bottom lip and returned to her task.

She heard footsteps, felt Mark's hands on her shoulders. "Honey," he said, then turned her gently around. "We both know all this isn't about a little flour spilled on your pantry shelves."

She hated when her eyes teared up—hated when the flood of emotions burst through her carefully constructed dam.

She buried her head against his chest and in a muffled voice admitted how pained she felt. "Oh, Mark. First Colby—now Joie."

Mark gently tugged the scarf from her head and smoothed her hair. "Everything is going to be all right, Leigh Ann." He pressed his lips against her forehead. "You'll see."

Leigh Ann sniffed and slumped on the floor, pulling Mark down to sit with her. She leaned against the pantry door. "I know everyone thinks I just want to dictate the details of life." She lifted her shoulders in a weak shrug. "I do know what is best for the people I love, and I only want them safe and secure—happy. You know what I mean, Mark?" She knew she was blabbering, not even making sense entirely.

Her husband nodded and wove his fingers with hers, gave her hand a squeeze. "Yeah, I know. It's just that sometimes people have to make their own way. You know that, Leigh Ann."

"No, I'm not sure I do know that. Was it wrong of me to push Colby to excel in school? To train for a career that would provide all the comforts, and give him a lifetime of open choices?" She stared at the ceiling. "What kind of mom would I be if I didn't guide him into the best choices?"

"Oh, don't get me wrong. I feel very much the same about what Colby did, Leigh Ann," Mark admitted. "I mean, I lie awake at night and worry about what his future will hold. Serving this country holds a lot of honor, but with that honor comes incredible risk. Military service can be very dangerous." He looked at her, his eyes filled with a sadness that matched her own. "I wouldn't have chosen that for Colby. Like you, I want him safe."

They sat there saying nothing for several seconds before Leigh Ann broke the silence. "Why do you think he would fall for someone so very different than—" She paused, unable to finish her sentence. It felt like saying what she'd been thinking aloud would somehow be too much.

"Neither did he want a career anywhere near his father's," Mark reminded. "Does that mean he doesn't respect me, or what I do for a living?" Now it was his turn to stare at the ceiling. "I just have to keep telling myself that his recent choices don't necessarily mean he doesn't love and appreciate us."

Leigh Ann let out a heavy sigh. "I suppose you're right." She thought a minute, then suddenly blurted, "And then there's Joie. That girl needs orange warning cones placed around her life."

Mark pulled his attention from the ceiling and drilled her with a look. "The key phrase being *her* life."

Leigh Ann was too tired to argue. Instead, she simply rubbed at the dull ache pulsing in her temple. "Mark, I was so hopeful lately. Seemed she just turned an important corner. She's practicing law again, is a partner in her own firm. And now she's pregnant?"

Her husband pulled his hand from hers and lightly placed his fingers against her abdomen. "Our story was not so different. We made it just fine."

Leigh Ann would never admit to anyone that she still carried a level of shame deep inside—even all these years later. She struggled for years wondering if Mark only married her because a baby was on the way.

Of course, Joie would face something entirely different. And more difficult.

"Yes, but we had each other," she reminded him. "Joie is

alone. This baby won't have a father. You and I both know that isn't good."

Despite living in a more open-minded society than her parents' generation, she was still very old-fashioned. Especially when it came to raising children.

"Joie's baby has a father," he pointed out. "Neither of us knows what role Andrew Merrill will want to play in helping to raise this baby."

The pain in Leigh Ann's temple intensified. "I don't think what that jerk wants will be the question."

Mark frowned. "I'm not following."

"I could be wrong," she added in an acid tone. "But I'm pretty sure *Mrs.* Merrill will want to have a say in the matter."

14

Joie took a deep breath and knocked on Maddy's office door.

"Come in," her voice rang out.

Joie swallowed. She turned the knob, pushed the door open.

Maddy sat behind her massive glass desk wearing a light yellow sweater trimmed in leopard-print fur at the scooped collar. She looked up, pulled the reading glasses from her face. "Well, darlin'—you're just in time. That little investigator we hired just reported in." She leaned back in her white tufted leather chair. "Apparently, Quinn learned another large block of stock was purchased earlier this week. A company called Equity Capital Group, incorporated in the state of Delaware."

Joie perked up, momentarily forgetting the reason she'd come to Maddy's office. "Good! That's a strong lead. Of course, identifying the actual principals could still prove tricky. Corporations often simply choose Delaware for the tax advantages and are really located elsewhere."

Maddy stood, came around the desk. "Yes, true. The original filing listed a law firm out of San Francisco as the registered agent. A small boutique firm, as far as I can tell." Her partner grinned. "I'm putting Quinn on a plane. I want her to go to the Secretary of State's office and research all the corporate filings made by that law firm in the past twenty-four months."

Joie beamed. "I think I see where you're heading. Whoever filed those corporate documents has a connection to the entities buying up the stock. If we piece together who the firm is working for, some common players may become apparent and we could possibly find the name behind the corporation."

"Exactly!" Maddy's eyes twinkled with excitement. "That is, if we're lucky. It seems we're hot on the trail of whoever is working to diminish the value of Preston, USA. Right now, we don't even understand why, but I can make a good guess. A person's actions tell all you ever need to know about their motivation. Just pay attention."

"Are you sure Quinn needs to go to San Francisco? That information is on-line," Joie reminded.

"Yes, I considered that. But I want no digital trace of our snooping around. No ability to connect our ISP address to any of this."

That was one of the reasons Joie loved Maddy Crane. She was always thinking twelve steps ahead of her opponent.

Maddy turned to the tray on her credenza. "You want some tea, sweet thing?"

"No, thanks. I just finished a soda." She fidgeted in her chair. No more stalling. It was time.

Joie's heart pounded as she forced her mouth open. "Maddy, I have something I need to tell you."

Her partner picked up the tea pot and filled one of delicate cups. "I'm all ears, darlin'." She turned to face Joie.

Joie had imagined this moment, had dreamed a thousand scenarios. Never did she estimate it would actually be this hard. She took a deep breath and began. "I, uh—"

Maddy motioned to the crème-colored damask sofa near the

window. She sat and patted the cushion next to her. "What is it, sweet thing?"

The way Joie figured, it was easiest just to say it. "I'm pregnant." She held her breath waiting for Maddy's reaction—waiting for the disappointment to appear in her new law partner's eyes.

Her partner surprised her by clapping her hands with excitement. "That's wonderful." She set her tea cup down. "I knew you'd tell me when you were ready."

Joie's eyebrows lifted. "You knew?"

Maddy's eyes grew immediately thoughtful. "I suspected." She studied Joie. "But—you're not happy about it?"

"I—I'm not sure." She shrugged and met Maddy's eyes, desperate for a lifeline. "I mean, sometimes life throws a curveball you don't see coming. But you adjust, and—"

Without waiting for her to finish, Maddy enveloped her entire torso in a hug that squeezed the air right out of her lungs. "Oh, Joie. You're having a baby. This is *good* news."

Joie couldn't hide her smile as she tried to process what had just occurred. This was not what she'd expected. "I was afraid you'd be upset."

Maddy looked appalled at the thought. "Upset? Because you're going to be a mother? Not in the least." She beamed. "Just the opposite. I'm thrilled for you." She took Joie's hands in her own, gazed in her eyes. "Darlin', I know that look. A thousand thoughts must be circling. But don't let fear rob you."

"I—I'm not sure I know what you mean." Joie's voice snagged and tears sprung to her eyes. She had no idea how her emotions had crept so close to the surface, and she struggled to get a hold of herself even as Maddy passed her a box of tissues.

"Listen, like me, you're independent as a hog on ice," she said, laughing quietly. "And that serves us well—until it doesn't."

Maddy's expression grew wistful. "I was far too cavalier over the years, always believing I had time. Hayden—he was my fourth husband—well, he desperately wanted a child. Kept pushing me until I finally gave in. We were trying to get pregnant when he had his first heart attack. After he recovered, he was all ready to try again. But knowing that his health was precarious, I decided I just couldn't face the possibility of having to bring up a child without him. I loved Hayden more than anything in the world, and oh, how I wanted to please that man. I ran from the idea of being a potential single parent out of fear. It was a deep disappointment to Hayden—and frankly, to myself." Her eyes dimmed. "Darlin', it is the only thing in my life that I will always regret."

Joie swallowed against a knot building in her throat. "Oh Maddy, I had no idea."

Outside the window, snowflakes softly drifted to the ground.

Her partner traced the rim of her tea cup with her manicured finger. "What I'm telling you is don't let fear keep you from something that can bring you much joy." She paused. "You're going to need help, no doubt. The road ahead isn't going to be entirely easy. Thankfully, you have your family. And you've got me," she said adamantly. "You've got me."

15

Karyn shut down the budget program and stared at her computer monitor. Nearly every expense category had doubled in recent days. Especially laundry and water. It seemed the Tanasbourne Media guests liked to take very long showers.

On the other side of things, publicity relating to the remake of the famous movie had done just what Nola Gearhart had hoped for—created a media frenzy and increased the bottom line for not only the resort, but the local economy.

Still, she'd hoped things would settle down after a few days, but it had only gotten worse. And by worse, she meant *bad*. Despite her best efforts to maintain normalcy here at the lodge, a slight level of chaos reigned.

Yesterday, Mr. Nygard and his crew returned from scouting a potential film location. When he stepped from his car underneath the portico, a woman suddenly appeared and pushed her two young daughters in front of him.

"Go ahead, girls," she urged. "Sing for the nice man."

In unison, the two blonde tykes broke out in song—off key, and very loud. *"The sun will come out tomorrow!"* Before they'd finished even a few notes, the mother joined in the act, tap dancing like something out of an old Fred Astaire movie.

Karyn had to call security, and apologize once again to Mr. Nygard. Thankfully, he was gracious about the intrusions, but she took her inability to control these situations personally—especially given how much Nola Gearhart and Jon were counting on her.

She'd tried to get Leigh Ann to commiserate with her on the phone, but her sister didn't seem to fully appreciate her angst. "That's just how people are, Karyn. Everyone wants in the limelight," she'd said. "There's only so much you can do unless you completely block off the lodge from the public. It's already been proven determined people like Dee Dee Hamilton can find a way to breach the security parameters. We're talking potential movie fame, Karyn."

"I know, but this is getting ridiculous. Did I tell you about Aggie?"

"I thought you talked to your former mother-in-law and she agreed to back off a little?"

Karyn sighed patiently. "Yes, she has. At least when it comes to hovering above my personal life. I mean, she's doing pretty well—for Aggie. But I'm talking about what she recently pulled relating to this whole movie business." A strange noise came through the phone. "What's that commotion?"

"I'm baking," Leigh Ann explained. "A cake, without refined flour. Colby's new wife believes in healthy eating—gluten-free, free-range, msg-free and no refined sugar."

"Yikes."

"I know. Don't even get me started on her anti-inflammatory turmeric bombs."

"Her what?" Karyn laughed.

"Oh, yes. Honey works synergistically with the properties in turmeric so she rolls the mixture into little balls and eats them. Leftovers are stored in glass, never plastic which emits unhealthy chemicals into the food." Her sister paused. "I'm sorry, I digress. What were you saying about Aggie?"

Karyn took a deep breath. "Well, where do I start? Aggie shows up at the lodge fresh from getting her hair done, her nails done, her face botoxed. She makes a bee line for the gift shop where she mills around browsing."

"The gift shop?"

"Oh, yes. But she doesn't know I'm watching. I hurry to end my conversation with our night clerk, fully intending to go see what she's up to—I mean, she never just shows up at the lodge like that unless she is meeting someone for lunch, and it's far too early in the day for that. I am on my way to her when Mr. Nygard steps from the elevator. He stops at the concierge desk where I'm standing, asks us to arrange for a private dining room that evening for a meeting he needs to hold with some union reps from the actors' guild. Anyway, before I can confirm that we'll take care of everything, Aggie rushes over and butts in, hands me a stack of envelopes she claims is my mail."

"Your mail? How'd she get your mail?"

"Apparently, she went to my house and took it out of my mailbox," Karyn patiently explained.

"That's outrageous, even for Aggie! I doubt she retrieves her own mail, probably has some staff person do it for her."

"Connect the dots, Leigh Ann. She notices Mr. Nygard, rushes over and starts gushing about what an honor it is to meet him, how she's loved all his movies."

"Wow," Leigh Ann said. "So, your former mother-in-law commits a federal crime to bring you some bills in order to orchestrate running into Nygard?"

Karyn sighed. "And some coupons from Popeyes. Worse, her little scheme worked! Somehow Aggie charmed herself into an invite and will be attending the filming of a key scene as an extra —one where the main characters meet in a diner. She was thrilled, of course."

"Of course. Hey, I hate to change the subject," Leigh Ann told her. "But I think we need to talk about Joie. She's planning a trip to Boise to break the news to Andrew."

Karyn put her phone on speaker as she shut down her computer. "Yeah, I know."

"She told you?" Leigh Ann sounded surprised.

Karyn stood and grabbed her coat from the hook on the back of her office door. "Yes, she told me." She slipped her arms in the sleeves. "I hate that she has to face that guy again, after all he put her through in the first place."

"If it were me, I'm not sure I'd even tell him."

"Oh, Leigh Ann. Of course she has to tell him. Andrew's the father and has a right to know."

Her sister sighed on the other end of the phone. "That's what Mark said. All I know is he'd better not hurt her any further. He's a married man and that creates a lot of volatility, if you know what I mean." Her voice grew anxious. "That's why I called. We need to go with her."

Karyn paused. "I agree. Unfortunately, Joie is very private when it comes to her personal life. I'm not sure she'd want us along."

"Joie doesn't know what's best. She needs our support. End of discussion."

"So, you talked to her already?"

There was a slight pause. "Yes," Leigh Ann admitted. "She said no. But maybe you can talk to her and convince her to change her mind."

Her older sister could be a dog with a bone. Fact was, Joie could be just as stubborn. "Are you sure it's a good idea to push?"

"Just talk to her—she'll listen to you."

"Okay, yeah. I'll try and mention it to her tonight at the torch light parade." She paused. "But I wouldn't hold your breath."

～

JOIE CLIMBED from her old jeep and lifted her face to the falling snowflakes. It wouldn't be long before she'd need to trade her beloved set of wheels in for a more sensible vehicle. She wasn't sure about a lot of this mothering stuff, but she was pretty sure she'd need a heater that consistently worked.

She felt a tightening at the back of her throat as she walked toward the large group of skiers gathered outside the Dollar Mountain day lodge. Truth was, her entire life was about to morph into something unrecognizable, and despite all the reassurances from Maddy and her family, she was fearful she might lose herself in the process.

"Hey, there you are," Leigh Ann waved. "Over here."

Colby's new wife stood near, her hair tucked up inside a knit cap that looked homemade. In her hand, she held two flares—a pink and a red one.

"Hey," Joie said as she approached. She pulled her scarf a little tighter around her neck before giving her sister a hug. Then, Nicole. "I see you're all set to go."

"Yeah, this whole torch light parade thing looks pretty cool." Her breath rose in visible puffs in the cold night air.

"It's tradition," Leigh Ann explained. "Every year on the weekend before Valentine's Day, the locals gather and ski down Dollar Mountain with the flares, making a serpentine of glowing red light down the face of the mountain. It's really beautiful to watch." She looked at Joie. "You'll take pictures?"

Nicole frowned. "You're not going?"

"No, I—"

"Yoo-hoo! Girls!"

Joie groaned as Penny Baker approached, another one of the Bo-Peeps. "Hey, there. I was hoping to run into Edwin. Is he here?" The slightly built woman adjusted her ill-fitted furry hat to keep it from sliding over her eyes.

Leigh Ann didn't try to hide her amusement. "He's up on the hill with my sister and husband."

"We'll tell him you were looking for him," Nicole offered.

Joie gave her a subtle jab with her elbow.

"What?" Colby's wife said frowning.

Leigh Ann hoisted her skis over her shoulder. "C'mon Nicole, we need to get going. Tradition never waits."

"Where's Karyn?" Joie asked. "And Mark?"

"We'll all see you at the base when we get done. The Women of Sun Valley group is furnishing hot chocolate and donuts." She pointed to a refreshment stand set up near the entrance to the tram. "Let's meet there afterwards and watch the firework display together."

Joie nodded and watched them take a place in line.

"Well, if you see your dad before I catch up with him, will you tell him I have homemade chocolate-covered cherries in the car for him?" Penny grinned. "For Valentine's day."

Joie assured her she'd pass along the message and waved as the woman sashayed off, still fighting the oversized hat.

Overhead, the bullwheel ground as an empty chairlift swung from the conveyer.

It felt odd not to participate in the annual event. She'd not missed a single year since she was twelve, the minimum required age. She was an excellent skier and wouldn't likely take a fall. But she couldn't take that chance. She had to be responsible now.

Fighting boredom, Joie wandered across the area to a bench on the observation deck. She brushed the seat off and sat with her phone ready to capture some photos. Overhead, streetlights grew misty as snowflakes pranced in the frigid air. The freezing chill brought a crispness to everything, especially the frost that crunched underfoot with every step.

Joie sat taking in the quiet beauty of it all when she heard a familiar voice.

"Hey, there." Clint smiled. He wore jeans, cowboy boots and a down jacket. No hat.

"Hey," she answered. "I wondered if you would show up."

"Yeah, well—everyone warned it was a sight not to miss."

"I'd have to agree with that." She patted the seat next to her.

He sat with his elbows on his knees and watched the mountain. "I'm surprised you're not up there making the run."

"Not this year." Joie tilted her head and gazed at the spray of brilliant tiny lights piercing the night sky. "I can't believe how pretty the stars are tonight," she said, purposefully changing the subject.

"Hmmn."

She could feel him studying her. "I mean, you just can't look at that inky canopy and not think there's something really—"

"Big out there?" he finished.

She smiled a tight little smile. "Yeah . . . big." Her hand involuntarily went to her stomach as she felt the baby move. "So, why aren't you up there on the mountain?" she asked, keeping her voice light.

"I planned to, but we're boarding a mare that looked like she had an eye infection developing and I had to meet with the vet."

Joie immediately grew concerned. "I hope the vet gave you some Terramycin ointment. That stuff works wonders."

"Yeah. Ended up a clogged duct, nothing serious. She should be good to go in a few days."

Clint nodded in the direction of the refreshment stand. "You want some hot chocolate, or something?"

She nodded. "You buying?"

Before he could answer, Maddy Crane appeared on the scene. "Oh, heaven's no! Your law partner is buying." She wore a white fur coat with matching hat and boots. Her gloves were black leather, as was the large bag she carried. "Happy Valentine's Day —well almost!" She paused, looked Clint over. "And who is this?" Maddy gave her a wink.

It dawned on Joie that she assumed Clint was the father and quickly shook her head. "No, we're not—"

"Just friends," Clint clarified. His eyes met Joie's and held them as he stood and pulled his wallet from his back jeans pocket. "Appreciate the offer, but this is on me."

The three of them made their way to the booth. Inside, Trudy Dilworth was busy filling Styrofoam cups. Ruby manned the cash register. "Well, hello," the sisters greeted, nearly in unison, as they approached the window.

"Hey, ladies." Clint said. "We'd like three hot chocolates." He turned. "Donuts?"

Joie shook her head no.

"Just hot chocolate, darlin'," Maddy told him. With a sly smile, she pulled a jewel encrusted flask from her bag and poured a generous portion into the cup Clint handed her. When he'd finished paying, she offered the flask up to him. "A little something to keep you nice and warm?"

He laughed. "Nah, I'll pass."

Joie allowed herself to exhale. Clint was hard to read, but there was no discernable change in his expression, no indication he noticed Maddy did not offer her the flask.

Maddy's face lit up. "Oh, my goodness. Look!"

A line of bright red and pink lights snaked down the side of the mountain, winding back and forth. From this distance, the sight reminded Joie of flowing lava.

The crowd *ooh'd* and *ah'd* at the beauty as bell chimes rang out over the entire valley. A few short minutes later, a whistling sound pierced the night air followed by a loud crackling pop. The darkness burst into sprays of color overhead."

Only feet away, a little girl perched on her daddy's shoulders clapped her hands. "Look at the fireworks, Daddy!"

Joie shared her enthusiasm. The entire experience was magical.

She looked over at Clint and caught him watching her. He studied her until she grew uncomfortable and had to look away.

"I agree with the little one," Maddy exclaimed. "That was an amazing sight." She turned to Joie. "You're right. I would have hated to have missed this."

Her sisters returned then, out of breath and filled with excitement. Even her dad had a big grin on his face.

Karyn pulled the knit hat from her head and shook out her hair with her fingers. "Oh, man—that was fun!"

"It sure was!" Nicole agreed. "What a rush."

Leigh Ann couldn't contain her smile. "One of Sun Valley's finest events."

Despite the late hour, they all agreed to go grab a bite at Louie's Pizza, a charming Italian restaurant housed in a converted church located in the center of Ketchum. Mark and Grayson planned to meet them there, and after a little urging by Leigh Ann, Clint agreed to join them as well.

Maddy passed on the invite. "Every woman raised south of the Mason-Dixie knows how important it is to get her beauty sleep."

Inside the restaurant, they were hit with a delicious smell that left Joie's stomach growling—a combination of garlic, tomatoes, baking bread, and hot cheese. It seemed like she was starving all the time lately, and tonight especially.

Even though Valentine's day was officially days away, the place was packed with couples celebrating. After a rather lengthy wait, they were seated at a large table draped with a red and white checked cloth near the front of the restaurant.

"I love this place." Karyn slid into her chair underneath the stained-glass arched window. At the neighboring table sat a couple of guys wearing ski sweaters. "It was so clever of the owners to convert this church. I hear they're doing so well they are opening a second restaurant in Boise."

Leigh Ann scanned the wine menu. She paused, looked over at Joie. "Speaking of Boise—Karyn wanted to talk to you about that."

"Yeah, we'd be willing to go with you," Karyn mentioned, as casually as possible.

"That's not necessary." Joie gave them both a pointed look, cutting off the discussion. She glanced across the table at Clint, who was busy breaking a warm breadstick in half. He waited for the steam to subside and then shoved one end in his mouth.

Leigh Ann held up her hands. "Fine. We'll table this discussion—at least for now. Until you hopefully change your mind."

Mark scanned the large wall-mounted menu. "Anybody up for sharing a spicy sausage pizza?"

Leigh Ann elbowed her husband. "You'll have heartburn."

Grayson draped his arm around Karyn's shoulder. "You choose. I'll eat whatever."

Nicole surveyed the large wooden beams overhead draped with strings of lights. "This place reminds me of that scene in Lady and the Tramp. You know, the one where the dogs share a spaghetti noodle and finally end up kissing?" She giggled. "I love that scene." She turned to Leigh Ann. "Do you think they serve gluten-free pasta?"

Grayson lifted a bread stick to Karyn, and she took a bite. "Ooh—hot!" She waved at her mouth.

When she'd finished chewing, she reported that Robert Nygard and his crew intended on filming a scene at Louie's next week. "Unfortunately, the place will be closed for two days just to get three minutes of film in the can." Her face broke into a wide grin. "In the can. That's Hollywood lingo."

A waiter appeared wearing a white chef's apron tied at his waist. "What can I get you folks tonight?"

They took turns placing their orders, procuring enough food for a party double their size. No doubt they'd all be boxing up left-overs. Mark ordered two pitchers of beer.

"How many mugs?" the waiter asked.

Not wanting to raise questions, Joie nodded that she wanted included.

That invited an immediate stink-eye from her oldest sister, which she ignored, praying her sister wouldn't open her big mouth with a dose of that cautionary advice she loved to dole out.

Thankfully, Leigh Ann kept her mouth shut. Especially after Joie let the mug be filled, and simply never took a drink.

Perhaps it was silly not to just come clean about her situation, but it was still too early. It was hard enough sharing the unexpected news with her dad and sisters. She suspected both Mark and Grayson had been told. Everyone else would know soon enough.

Unfortunately, she faced *soon enough* a little earlier than she expected when that *everyone else* asked her to drive him back to his car.

It had started to snow again, lightly.

She slid into the driver's seat and waited while Clint circled the back of the jeep and climbed in the other side. He blew on his knuckles. "Man, the temp sure dropped."

Across the parking lot, a couple kissed, oblivious that anyone watched.

Clint saw them too. "Looks like someone is celebrating a little early."

Joie had never been the sentimental type. Still, a lump formed in her throat. Would she ever get her life together? Ever have *that*?

The answer was likely no. How many men would scramble to take on a ready-made family?

Joie thought about the little girl on her daddy's shoulders, how the exploding lights in the sky thrilled her. It hit her again that she would soon be a single mother, and all that meant.

"You okay?" Clint asked.

She nodded. "Define okay." The minute the words were out of her mouth, she regretted opening what could easily morph into a can of worms. "I mean, yeah—I'm good. Never better," she lied.

Clint said a thousand words with his silence. Finally, he leaned forward. "Do you mind?" He placed his fingers on the radio knob.

She shook her head. "Nope, go for it."

He switched the radio on and dialed in a station, leaned back. "So, you're going to take a trip to Boise, huh?"

Joie shrugged. "Yeah, tomorrow. Just thought I'd get out of town for a while, maybe take a drive." She pulled out of the parking lot and headed down Sun Valley Road.

"A three-hour drive?"

She punched the gas pedal and speeded up. "It's nothing really. We both know I get carried away sometimes."

"Clearly." He paused, keeping his eyes on her like he was trying to decide how hard to push. Despite a volatile start, Clint had turned out to be one of the good guys. She didn't make friends easily. But he was definitely that—her friend.

It was hard to tell him what was going on without feeling like she would somehow tarnish the way he saw her. He'd already seen her in—well, not at her best. She hated to admit the full extent of the mess she'd made. Even so, she had to come clean before he found out from someone else. Take tonight, for example. One of her sisters could easily have slipped and let the cat out of the bag.

She pulled up to the intersection at Dollar Road. While waiting for the red light to turn, she kept her eyes down, afraid to meet Clint's gaze. Goodness, he always seemed to be watching her.

"I'm pregnant," she blurted, trying to sound casual, as if it was the most common thing in the world. "Yeah, I'm going to have a baby. In July. I'm going to be a mother." Her hormones betrayed her causing her eyes to tear up. "And I don't know how I'm going to do that—be a mother, I mean. There's far too many times I don't even feel grown up myself. I know what everybody says, but how in the world am I going to be trustworthy enough to care for a tiny infant who needs fed every few hours, and immunized? Or, a teenager? What am I going to do with a teenager? I'm sure that old adage will come true. You know, what goes around comes around? I suppose I would deserve that. But still, I'll have to do this all alone and—"

Someone honked in the car behind them.

"Okay, already!" she yelled at the impossibly impatient driver who couldn't give her just one stinking moment to see the light had turned. She thrust her foot down on the gas and made a sharp turn onto Dollar Road. The tires screeched a little as she pulled to the side of the road underneath a street light.

His face closed a little. She could see it, like a door shutting behind his eyes. She shouldn't have been crushed, but she was.

"Say something," she pleaded, tears now flowing freely. Dang her emotions.

"Are you crying?" he asked her.

"I'm not."

"You are. Why are you crying?"

She looked over at him miserably. "What? I need to explain? I've made a mess of everything—confirmed what everyone believes. I'm a walking tangle of wreckage. Hardly, mother material. Besides, being knocked up could not have happened at a worse time—just when I returned to the practice of law."

Clint's face broke into the weakest of smiles. He reached across the seat, took her gloved hand and squeezed. "Joie, be happy. This is a gift."

He grew quiet. She was quiet. The radio remained playing in the background, and she could hear Ed Sheeran sing her favorite song, *Perfect*.

She chewed at her bottom lip. "Did you know?"

He lifted his shoulders and shrugged. "I kind of suspected."

Joie shut off the ignition and stared out the car window at the ground blanketed in snow. The ice crystals looked like little diamonds in the light. "I don't think I can do this," she admitted. "I'm really scared."

Clint didn't say anything right away. He simply followed her gaze and stared outside at the tentative snowflakes making their way to the ground. Then he cleared his throat. "Never underestimate the beauty of being afraid."

She looked at him confused, and a little mad. "I'm not sure I follow."

"It's okay to be scared," he told her. "Just when we think we've figured things out, life throws us a curveball. So we have to improvise. We find happiness in unexpected places. Maybe we find our way back to the things that matter most. Life is funny that way—sometimes it just has a way of making sure we wind up exactly where we belong."

At that, she let herself smile. Clint Ladner was far more than straight fire, with a nice set of biceps and a bear tattoo. He was showing himself to be a good friend.

That notion was proven again the following morning.

Filled with dread about the trip to Boise and all that lay ahead, Joie grabbed her jacket and keys and opened the front door to find Clint leaning against her jeep with a thermos in his hand.

"This isn't up for discussion," he said, his voice ringing out in the dark, quiet morning hour. "It might snow and I don't want you driving to Boise alone."

K aryn arrived at the lodge early. Her desk was piled high with items needing her approval—dietary requests, staffing overtime, even special brands of toiletry items—all stemming from hosting their special guests.

She'd mentioned the extraordinary expense items to Jon and had been assured he approved her fulfilling all requests, so long as they were reasonable. That was the rub—reasonable was subjective and still required her judgement.

Karyn rolled her eyes. Was bar soap that had to expedited from Italy at a cost of nearly $80 per bar reasonable? And what would happen if she denied the expense?

She rubbed at the spot between her eyes. Before she could tackle the pile, she needed some coffee.

The lodge lobby was nearly empty, except for Melissa at the registration desk and a doorman who stood at the entrance, ready to assist arriving guests not likely to show up at this early hour. In the distance, she could hear the drone of a vacuum.

Near the concierge desk stood a hospitality table, with large silver urns of coffee and platters filled with pastries.

Karyn helped herself to a steaming cup of coffee. Savoring the quiet, she decided to wander down to housekeeping, check and see how everything was going.

She moved past the closed gift store, and its glass display window, showcasing souvenirs, high-end sunglasses and several pieces of gorgeous jewelry, and wandered down the hallway leading to the spa.

The wall was lined with framed photographs. Gary Cooper and Ernest Hemingway chatting circa 1940. Lucille Ball and her children. Marilyn Monroe filming *Bus Stop* in 1956. And several shots of the Kennedys who frequented the Sun Valley area in the sixties.

Near the end of the hall was a framed image of an elegant gentleman dressed in vintage ski gear and poised at the top of a snow-covered hill.

"I'm told that's Averill Harriman, the founder of Sun Valley."

Startled, she turned to find Robert Nygard. His collar-length black hair hung in loose waves. His cocoa eyes radiated uncompromising intelligence, yet were filled with amusement.

"Yes, you're correct. Mr. Harriman wanted to replicate a ski resort he'd visited in Switzerland."

All of a sudden, Mr. Nygard was standing close. Too close. She could smell that he'd recently taken a shower.

"I want to commend you and your staff for the excellent service our entire company has received." His shoulder brushed against her own.

She took a slight step away.

"I fully intend to make my satisfaction known to Nola Gearhart and Jon Sebring." He reached and boldly ran his finger up her arm.

"Excuse me?" Karyn frowned, rebelled against his inappropriate advance and moved back. "I need—uh, I need to go."

She turned to leave, but he caught her arm. "I thought you might want to show a little appreciation for giving your mother-in-law a part in the film. She really has no talent, but I've worked with much worse."

She ripped her arm out of his hand. "I'm afraid you've sorely miscalculated the situation!"

It was as though the temperature in the room dropped twenty degrees. Nygard froze in his tracks, his eyes cold as opals. He stared at her. "I just thought—well, given the fact you are a widow and all. I figured you might be lonely."

It took everything within her not to haul off and slap that smug grin off his face. She whirled and marched away, fuming.

"If you change your mind," he called out after her. "You know my room number."

17

L eigh Ann pulled the egg carton from the refrigerator and set it on the counter next to the link sausages. She rarely cooked breakfast, but Mark mentioned he might not get a chance to eat lunch. He and Andrea DePont were taking a charter flight to San Francisco to meet with the Equity Group board members.

According to Mark, the hush-hush plans to purchase Preston USA were progressing nicely, but not without minor snags. While he wasn't free to share details, he was hopeful collective minds would come up with ways to relieve these hurdles. "When we're finally able to put this baby to bed, Leigh Ann, we'll be able to build that second home you've wanted. What do you think of Puget Sound? Or maybe Monterrey?"

She cracked the eggs into a bowl and whisked them, then placed a frying pan on her Thermador induction stovetop and turned it on. She didn't have the heart to tell him her duties at the tourism council were not conducive to spending time out of state to manage a second home. He'd argue she was a volunteer, could leave at any time. That wasn't the way it worked. Just because she didn't get paid didn't mean she could just walk away any time she chose.

"Hey, Mom." Nicole wandered into the kitchen, her arms stretched high above her head in a yawn.

Leigh Ann still couldn't get used to someone other than Colby calling her mom. "Good morning, Nicole. Hungry?"

The sleepy redhead shook her head. "No thanks. I'll just have a kale shake."

Leigh Ann pointed to her Keurig coffee maker. "Can I interest you in a cup?

Her daughter-in-law wandered over to the pantry. "Sure, but I'll use the French press. This is where you keep it, right?"

She sighed and nodded. They couldn't even agree on which coffee maker to use. "Did you enjoy last night?" she asked, trying to make conversation.

"Yeah, the skiing thing was great. And so was that old church. But I have a question."

Leigh Ann put a pat of butter in the fry pan and grabbed a spatula from the drawer. "What's that?"

"Is Joie pregnant?"

Her breath caught. She dumped the eggs into the pan, keeping her back to Nicole so she wouldn't catch the surprise on her face. "Why do you ask that?"

Nicole shrugged as she measured out the coffee grounds into the French press. "She didn't drink her beer. She didn't ski. And her head turned every time someone with a baby entered the restaurant. So, I figured—bingo—the gal's knocked up."

Ignoring the crass way the girl who was currently dropping coffee grounds on her expensive tile flooring had just referred to the sacred state of being with child, Leigh Ann turned the eggs—gently, so as not to toughen the proteins. "Well, you are very observant."

"So, is she?"

She took a deep breath. She'd have to reveal the situation sometime. Might as well be now. "Yes, Joie is due in July."

Nicole lifted the tea pot and poured steaming hot water over the coffee grounds. "I knew it! I wonder if she'd be interested in letting me be her doula? I mean, I'm not officially qualified yet, but I've always been extremely interested in the whole birthing process. Ina May Gaskin is my hero. I've read every one of her books, front to cover. Some of them twice." She pressed the lever down slowly, then filled her mug.

"A doula?" Leigh Ann slid the cooked eggs onto a waiting plate, realizing she'd gotten flustered by this conversation and neglected to cook the links. *Oh, well,* she thought, and tossed the package back in the refrigerator. Mark could have toast instead.

"Mark, breakfast," she called up the stairs.

Nicole carried her mug to the table. "A doula supports the mother during the entire birthing process."

Leigh Ann frowned. "In the hospital room? She's there when the baby is born?" She'd heard of such things, but thought the entire movement a bit odd. "I wasn't sure I even wanted Mark in the delivery room when Colby was born. I can't imagine having some stranger watch something so private."

Her daughter-in-law took on a look of patience. "Actually, birth can be a euphoric experience, a way of accessing a uniquely female power. Birthing an infant is a normal life experience, not a medical event to be feared." Nicole slipped into a chair at the table. "Doulas and midwives help put the birth experience back in women's hands and show them their true power."

Leigh Ann had to bite her tongue. Let's see if this naïve little girl held to these silly ideas when she was the one with her feet in the stirrups. "Well, I think nurses and doctors are more than qualified to assist at the birth of a child. I'm not sure they really need any help."

Mark entered the kitchen, straightening his tie. "Morning, you two."

Leigh Ann chastised herself. Now, she'd neglected to put bread in the toaster. "I cooked you some eggs."

"Just eggs?" he asked, taking the plate from her.

"Let me get you some fruit." She buried her head in the refrigerator, scouring for the bowl of remaining peaches she'd cut up earlier in the week.

"Morning, Nicole." Mark took his place opposite her at the table. "Did you sleep well?"

She assured him she had. "Well, until Colby called so early this morning."

Leigh Ann pulled her head from the refrigerator so quickly she nearly banged her head. "Colby called?"

Nicole nodded. "He finally earned phone privileges, and his drill sergeant granted permission for him to call home."

"And he called you?" Leigh Ann failed to measure her words. Mark gave her the *look*—the one meant to remind she'd neglected to recognize her son was now married, that he had a wife. "What did he say? Is he okay? What about basic training? Is it hard?"

Mark held up his hands and laughed. "Whoa, Leigh Ann. Slow down."

Inside, she railed against the comment. Colby was her son—her only child—she'd never gone this long without talking to him. She worried whether he was sleeping well, what he was eating and if he was getting along with all his army buddies. She hoped his drill sergeant wasn't like those she'd seen in the movies. She didn't want someone yelling obscenities in her son's face!

He'd called Nicole—not her.

Yes, she realized that was how things were supposed to be, but her heart still had a hard time adjusting.

"Sorry," she said, her eyes growing misty. "I just miss my son."

Mark stood, placed his hands on her shoulders. "I know you do, babe. He'll be back home before we know it."

"Of course, then he'll ship off to who knows where." their daughter-in-law stated.

Mark and Leigh Ann glanced at one another, then at her.

"What?" Nicole said. "Did I say something wrong?"

18

W hen driving north on Interstate 84, there's a point where you go around a bend and in the distance, the dry vistas dotted with sagebrush turn to a vast landscape of trees nestled up against rolling foothills, the capitol building dome visible in the center—a scene that used to send a little thrill running through Joie. But today, as the city of Boise came into view, a wave of nausea rolled across her gut that couldn't simply be attributed to her pregnancy. Dread had every nerve ending tightly tuned to what lay ahead.

Clint looked across the seat. "You okay?"

She took a deep breath, swiped her palms across the top of her pants as she stared out the window, "I will be—when this is over."

She couldn't help but wonder if she'd made a severe miscalculation on the benefit of simply showing up without forewarning. Perhaps she should have texted Andrew, given him some sort of heads up.

Of course, any unexpected communication would have met with more questions. She'd have tried to be evasive. He would have continued to hound her, trying to learn the truth of her visit, which was comical given Andrew had already proven he was the one who had a loose hold on the truth.

He hated the words *lies* and *truth*. In the courtroom, there was only the story. Winning was more than facts and law, it was all about persuasion. A great litigator knew the practice of law was never simply black and white.

Neither could her current situation be painted so starkly.

One thing Joie was sure of—she did not want her looming pregnancy to be viewed as an invitation back into her life. No guilt trip, no amount of persuasion would change her mind.

Clint beat his thumb against the steering wheel. "You know, you're not the first person who tried to get rid of a hole in her soul, and filled it with the wrong thing."

Joie rolled her eyes. "Please, I don't need any advice."

"I'm not offering any," he told her. "But you might lighten up, give yourself a break."

"Meaning?"

"The fact this Andrew guy turned out not worthy of your trust is more a reflection of him, not you."

Joie rolled her eyes. "Yeah, I know. I'm a good person. I mean, it's been ages since I stole a Christmas goose from a crippled child."

That made Clint laugh.

She smiled too. "Glad to entertain you."

Andrew lived in a gorgeous historic home located on Warm Springs Avenue, an area synonymous with local wealth and elegant architecture. Joie had only been inside his home one time at a Christmas party he and his wife had hosted for the firm's attorneys.

By then, they'd been seeing each other for several months. She was crushed to learn he was married, of course, and filled with guilt—emotions she'd tried to push to the recesses of her mind by telling herself all the lies people need to justify their affairs. The problem was, she just couldn't do it. Deep inside, she knew what they were doing was wrong, and she ended it.

Unfortunately, the decision ended her career at the firm as well.

She packed up her deflated pride and moved back home, never intending to tell another soul that she'd crossed the sacred line. That is, until he showed up in town.

He was attending a bar association retreat in Sun Valley and searched her out, lured her back into his arms with more lies— this time assuring her that he'd left his wife. Another lie. She discovered the truth and sent him packing a second time.

She wished she could pack up the pieces of her torn heart as decidedly.

Her hand went to her stomach. Turns out what Father John preached on Sundays was true—if you're not careful with your choices, you can easily fall into a pit. And often you can't climb out without a little help.

Joie glanced across the seat as they pulled up in front of the Andrew's address. "Thank you for driving me," she said.

Clint shrugged as he surveyed the neighborhood. "No problem." He turned to her, his eyes filled with encouragement. "I'll be right here waiting for you."

She gave him an apprehensive nod. With a deep breath, Joie opened the car door, forced herself from the seat and climbed out onto the curb.

Andrew often described his home as being western colonial in style, boasting its symmetrical layout, dark gray hues, white trimming and wooden shingles with crossed windows that gave the bungalow-styled house a quaint appearance despite its size. The house had been featured in an architectural magazine. A framed copy of the article hung in Andrew's office.

With determination, she swallowed and pushed the doorbell.

The door opened, and the man she'd once known so intimately stood there, his masculine elegance, and long lean-muscled body stiffening. Andrew hated to be surprised.

He wore a pair of chinos and a white-button down shirt, both pressed into crisp precision. His jet-black hair was a picture of dignity and good breeding, except for one lock that fell carelessly over his forehead, betraying the carefully cultivated look.

"Joie? What are you doing here?" He glanced up and down the street, spotted her jeep with Clint inside. His grin instantly turned to a frown. "You're not alone."

She shook her head. "No."

Seconds passed in tense silence. "May I come in?" she asked.

Andrew continued to stare at the jeep, took a step back. "Uh, sure," he said, waving her inside.

Joie let the door fall shut behind her, and stepped into the center of the elegant room. Hand-scraped hardwood floors gleamed rich and smooth as honey, upholstered couches looked as if they'd been delivered only minutes ago. Every detail of his home—all stepping stones on the path to the holy grail of American ethos: prosperity, success, upward social mobility. A star in the courtroom, he had earned it all.

"Can I get you something?" he asked, with the politeness of strangers, not of someone who had—

She closed her mind to the images, the memory.

"No, I'm good."

"Take your coat, then?"

She nodded and slipped her arms from her jacket and went to hand it to him, then changed her mind. "I'll hang on to it. What I have to say won't take long."

That brought another scowl as they moved to one of those pristine sofas and sat.

That's when he noticed—his eyes catching sight of her slightly expanded middle. "Why are you here, Joie?" he pushed.

"I'm pregnant," she stated, simply and without emotion.

His eyes traveled to the window and her jeep outside. "Mine?" he asked, as if there was a question.

She instantly angered. "Yes," she told him with gritted teeth. "I'm due in July." She rushed to clarify. "And I want nothing from you except for you to waive all parental rights."

He stood, his face darkening. "I don't think that's a good idea," he said, pacing across the imported rug protecting that hardwood floor.

Her heart lurched with instant terror. Surely, he didn't want to be involved in any of this.

Her qualms were instantly squelched when he strode through French doors leading to his office. He opened the drawer and pulled his binder of checks out, grabbed his Montblanc pen. "I have money," he told her, scribbling furiously. "Surely termination would be—"

She stood, clasped her coat to her belly. "I won't be terminating, and I don't want your money, Andrew. I don't want anything from you. I don't even want to ever see you again. I simply need you to sign this." She reached in her bag and pulled out an envelope and thrust it in his direction.

"I'll draw something up."

"No," she said firmly. "Sign it. I'm sure anything you might be concerned about is properly addressed." She paused. "I'm not here to mess with you, Andrew, or to cause you any harm. I simply want you out of my life—and out of my child's life."

"Forever," she added.

He tentatively took the three-page document and began reading it.

Joie couldn't help but wonder about his wife, felt sick inside over the pain caused by her indiscretions and outright stupidity. She glanced around. There was no sign of her, no photos. Nothing that would imply he was still married. Perhaps his wife had finally had it and ended the union.

Andrew sunk to the sofa, bent over the coffee table and

signed the release. "I'll want a copy," he told her as he thrust the document back into her hands.

"Of course." She pulled a second copy from her bag and handed it to him.

Their eyes met. For an instant, unbidden images passed through her mind—tousled sheets, murmured promises, late morning breakfasts in bed. She pushed the painful thoughts to the back of her mind to examine later, at a time where she didn't feel like a thousand pin pricks were piercing every nerve beneath the surface of her chilled skin.

She pulled her coat up, slipped her arms into the sleeves. Andrew moved to assist her but she shook her head. "I need to go."

He nodded and followed her to the door, neither of them saying anything more.

Suddenly, the door swung open and a familiar blonde entered the room—a paralegal Joie recognized from the real estate department of the firm. Wendy Riggins' eyebrows raised in surprise. "Joie? Hey, what are you doing here? It's good to see you." She reached and gave Joie a fragile hug.

"Hey, Wendy."

The girl glanced between Joie and Andrew. "Are you coming back to the firm?"

Joie shook her head. "No."

Wendy stared, shamelessly. "Oh. Well, good seeing you." She leaned and gave Andrew a prolonged kiss on the cheek, her ambitious breasts pushing against his chest.

Joie simply peered at them in disbelief. Her former boss and his new lover barely had the decency to look embarrassed.

Struggling to breathe, she walked out the door.

At the car, she threw her purse into the backseat, then climbed inside. Clint reached for the ignition. "You okay?"

She leaned against the headrest, fatigue settling in. "Yeah, I'm fine."

She placed her hands protectively across her growing belly feeling shaky and unsteady, not at all herself. She bit at the inside of her cheek to gain control, hating that her emotions were as fragile as soap bubbles.

Fine.

It was a lie. He knew it. She knew it.

She rehearsed the scene that had just played out, struggled to gain some perspective. She supposed there was no use trying to figure out *might-have-beens* or *wish-I-hadn'ts*—so why even try?

Truth was—she *was* fine—and she mentally assured herself of that. She could still function, even when her heart had been torn to shreds.

Ever since learning she was pregnant, she'd been moving in slow motion, waiting for the inevitable ax to fall on her failings. But now, she felt herself waking.

The fox remained in the chicken house. But that was that other chicken's problem now. On the flip side of the story, she was ready to move on, ready for the future to unfold and anxious to embrace a new destiny.

Outside the car window, snow started to fall, like a blessing falls on a prodigal when she's finally admitted she's ready to return home.

Joie straightened, lifted her chin.

She had her life back.

19

K aryn stood in her doorway and waved at her guests. "Goodnight, everyone! Thanks for coming."

Joie waved a tiny dime-store trophy over her head. "Sure thing. Kicking your butt at Monopoly was worth the trip."

Her dad playfully punched his youngest daughter's shoulder. "Rematch next month. We'll see if you can hold on to the coveted title."

Leigh Ann called over her shoulder, "Let's leave the competition at the game table, you two."

Karyn gave a final wave, and slid the front door closed.

Grayson folded his arms around her. "Boy, your family is cut throat when it comes to playing games."

"Yeah," she agreed. "It's been that way since we were little. You should see all of us when we get out the dominoes."

He took her hand, led her into the kitchen. "Well, I think the losers deserve a bit of wine. Perhaps in the hot tub?"

She nodded. "Sounds like a great plan."

Minutes later, they languished in bubbling steaming water, wine goblets in hand.

"Joie sure seems happy, don't you think?" Karyn murmured, enjoying the blanket of stars in the night sky.

"Yeah, seems so. I mean, I still don't feel like I know her all that well, but being pregnant seems to agree with her."

"I know, right? Joie has never been one to open up completely, but I've really noticed a change. It's as if she's finally content to live in her skin—know what I mean?" She leaned her head against Grayson's bare shoulder. "I never expected she'd be this excited about being a mom."

"I don't blame her."

Karyn lifted her head and looked at him. "Yeah? What do you mean?"

Grayson took the bottle and filled his wine glass, then hers. "I don't know. I guess I always wanted to be a dad. In fact, I'd urged Robin to consider making the jump into parenthood. She kept putting me off. Finally, she agreed and we tried, but nothing ever came of it." He sighed. "And then, well—then the end came and she left me for that other guy."

"Yeah, sometimes things don't work out the way we hope." She'd wanted to have babies with Dean, then—well, then the accident happened. She pushed the sad thought from her mind, squeezed his hand. "You'd make a great father."

He smiled and took a sip of his wine. "Yeah, I suppose I would. I mean, I can't wait to play ball with my kid." He laughed. "Or build a playhouse, if I end up with a girl."

She smiled at him. "Maybe you'll be having both."

"Yeah, maybe. All I know is, your sister's lucky. Sure, her situation has its challenges, but she seems happy. I think that Clint guy has something to do with her happiness."

"Clint?" She looked at Grayson like he was half crazy. "I'm pretty sure they are just friends. Especially under the circumstances."

Grayson kissed the top of her head. "Sometimes friends make the best lovers."

"I'll drink to that." She clinked her glass against his, then took a sip. "Man, this pinot noir is really good. It's from the Argyle Winery in Dundee, Oregon. Have you ever been on a wine tour in the Willamette Valley? I'm just saying, if not, you're missing out on a really great—"

She paused, smiled. "What are you looking at?"

"You," he told her. "Do you know how beautiful you are?"

She was thankful for the darkness that hid the heat building on her cheeks. "I think you've had too much wine."

"Perhaps," he admitted. "But that doesn't change the fact that I am one of the luckiest men on earth." His finger slowly traced her jawline. "I'm so thankful I met you, Karyn. I hope you know what you mean to me."

A pool of yearning settled in the bottom of her stomach, surprising her. "I'm lucky too," she whispered.

He set his wine glass down on the edge of the spa, turned and grasped her face in his hands, pulled her toward him. He closed his eyes as his mouth found hers and he kissed her, slow, easy, as if they had all the time in the world.

She touched his face, the rough growth of beard she suspected appeared only hours after he'd shaved. She sensed something wash over her, something having to do with yearning and desire and . . . need.

Her legs turned liquid and moved beneath the water as she sought to draw closer to the intimacy she suddenly craved.

The years after Dean died were filled with an unbearable aloneness, an ache that seemed to crush her very soul. If it hadn't been for meeting Grayson, she might not have survived the loss.

In the past, anytime anyone suggested a healing so complete that it led to this kind of happiness, she'd resisted. She thought that pushing past that season meant forgetting Dean, forgetting the darkness of the loss and the journey of the healing, which are things she never wanted to forget.

But she could see now—it wasn't about that. The truth was

that she could no longer recall the truest sorrows of widowhood. The dark nights, the aching pain, the endless breaking. She remembered them as a vague shadow, no longer a searing, white-hot flame.

Because of Grayson.

Taking the next step in the relationship held risk she wasn't entirely sure she was ready for. Yet, the insistence she now felt as his body melted into her own sent another message, a promise that made her lose her breath. And she wanted that—to be so filled up she couldn't draw air.

She reached behind his neck and pulled his kiss deeper. There was nothing else to be done but this. He released her and she leaned into him. "Please don't let go, just keep holding me."

"Follow me." His voice was soft, commanding as he took her hand and helped her from the spa. She had no choice but to follow him as he made his way back inside. Everything around her clarified—the black of night, the brilliance of the stars, the chill in the air and smell of distant pine.

So this is what it meant to live in the moment, absorbing nothing but what was before her—giving in to a pull she couldn't fully describe—to destiny.

She laughed as they trod across her kitchen floor, dripping wet, and headed for the bedroom. Over her shoulder she could see Grayson grinning. "You seem very pleased with yourself," she teased.

"I am." He held out his hand. "I made you smile. I am more than pleased with myself."

Suddenly, he stopped. He took her shoulders, turned her to face him, lacing his fingers in her hair. "Karyn, I love you." His voice was raw and deep.

Her heart welled. "I—I love you too," she admitted, barely able to point to the exact moment when she'd fully released her connection to Dean and embraced a new direction—with Grayson.

He reached for her hand, and she eagerly placed her palm in his, ready to unearth the love inside her that had been buried for far too long.

It was at that moment the doorbell rang.

She looked in that direction, confused. Who would have the nerve to show up at her house this late?

Grayson's eyes told her the same thought ran through his mind. "Are you going to answer that?" he asked, his tone evidence he'd prefer her to ignore the intrusion.

She, too, was torn by the instant shift as she returned to the present. "I—uh—the lights." She shrugged. "Whoever it is can see the lights are on." There was something in her that always focused on what others wanted, what they thought and needed from her. "I'd better see who it is."

Grayson groaned. "Yeah, I suppose so, but—."

Karyn's hands went to her hair, straightening the damp tendrils as she grabbed her cover-up from the back of the sofa, slipped it on. The doorbell rang again. "Coming," she called out.

Grayson knotted a towel at his waist.

She peeked out one of her side light windows. Her breath caught when she saw the identity of her late-night visitor. Shocked, she pulled the door open. "Mr. Nygard? What in the world are you doing here?"

"You're kidding, right?" Leigh Ann pulled a peachy-looking shade from the rack of nail polish. "I can't believe he showed up at that hour? And how did Robert Nygard even know where you live?"

Joie rolled her eyes and leaned forward for a better look before reaching for a bottle of nail lacquer—a shade called Holy Pink Pagoda. "Geez, Leigh Ann. Could your interrogation get any more enthusiastic?" She followed her sisters to the back of the salon.

"Oh, hush! Karyn, none of this is normal. I mean, he's a big star and all but that doesn't entitle him to bad manners."

"What did Grayson do?" Joie asked.

"Well, he was as surprised as me to see Robert Nygard standing on my doorstep. Even though Robert claimed he needed to make arrangements for rooms for extra crew members showing up—that I wasn't answering my phone—I think Grayson suspected something else was up. So did I." She slid into her pedicure chair. "The guy's definitely a player."

Joie lifted her eyebrows. "You think he was hitting on you? He just showed up expecting—what? That you'd melt into his Holly-wood arms? What arrogance!"

Leigh Ann removed her shoes. "Yeah, that's creepy!"

"He thinks I might be a lonely widow," Karyn admitted, stop-ping short of telling them the full extent of their encounters. She planted her feet on the edge of the basin waiting for it to fill with warm water.

"What?" Leigh Ann said. "Oh now, that's definitely creepy!"

Karyn pushed the buttons on her chair, started the massage rollers. "Don't worry. It's handled. I have no intention of playing the lead in his fantasy." She leaned back, enjoying the feel of the rollers. "Goodness, I could get used to all this pampering."

June, the spa manager, had been urging her to make use of the services at the lodge spa which were complimentary to employees. As director of hospitality, she'd been able to extend that offer to her sisters, so long as she booked a time not slotted for guests.

Joie leaned back into her chair's massaging rollers. "Agreed. This is wonderful," she said, her eyes closed. "My back has been killing me lately."

"Just wait until you're further along in your pregnancy," Leigh Ann warned. "You have all kinds of things to look forward to—

inability to sleep, urgent need to find a potty when you're out shopping, waddling like a duck and your clothes never fitting, even the maternity tents."

"Oh, goody." Joie pressed a button on her control box. "By the way, do you think I can buy one of these chairs for at home?" She grinned. "I'm serious."

Karyn laughed. "Ha—I'll see if I can get you a discount."

One of the pedicurists displayed a tray with tiny bowls filled with scented creams. "Do you want lotus flower, honeysuckle or lavender vanilla?" she asked them in broken English.

Each of the sisters made their selection before dipping their feet in the azure-blue tubs of bubbling water.

"I hear pregnancy massage relieves many of the normal discomforts experienced during pregnancy, such as backaches, stiff neck, leg cramps, headaches and encourages blood and lymph circulation," Joie lifted one foot from the water and placed it in the waiting hands of the woman kneeling at her basin.

Leigh Ann rolled her eyes. "Who told you that? Nicole?"

Before Joie could answer, Leigh Ann continued. "I'm really working to have a relationship with that girl, but it's slow going. I mean, she has the strangest ideas. She's taking an online course to be a doula—even suggested she attend the birth of your baby, Joie. Can you even imagine?"

Karyn pondered the idea. "I don't know. I think that whole birthing experience thing is gaining popularity. I have several friends who have chosen alternative birthing."

Leigh Ann huffed. "Well, I find the whole notion ridiculous. Inviting a stranger to serve as some sort of birthing assistant who only gets in the way of the real medical professionals seems ridiculous to me. Unsafe, even."

They both turned to Joie, who held up her hands in surrender. "Don't look at me. I'm doing good to get through my work day without falling asleep at my desk. No one told me how exhausted you can get."

Leigh Ann waved off her comment. "You're nearly past the worst part of that, well—that is, until the end. The end is grueling in terms of fatigue."

"Oh, yay," Joie responded with a groan.

Karyn gave her sister a sympathetic look. "Speaking of work, how is everything at the firm? Is it everything you'd hoped?"

Before Joie could answer, they heard a commotion in the area down the hall from the front area. Miss Trudy emerged, wearing a white spa robe. "Well, hello girls," she said, wrapping the tie into a bow. "I'm heading in for one of those hot stone massages. I hear the feel of the smooth warmth against your skin sends you to heaven and back." She wiggled her fingers. "Well, ta-ta!"

They smiled and waved. "Enjoy!"

"I will," she assured them.

When Miss Trudy had exited the scene, Karyn again turned to her younger sister. "The firm. How's it going?"

"I love it. We're really busy. Of course, Maddy's reputation and incisive litigation skills draws a lot of clients."

"That's wonderful, Joie." Karyn was sincerely pleased for her. There was a time not so long ago when their entire family had worried about the reckless way Joie lived, and particularly her drinking. No doubt, Andrew's betrayal had a profound effect on the decisions she now made, but more so this pregnancy.

In a few short months, her little sister was going to be a mother. She would be an aunt. The idea of a tiny baby in the family made them all ecstatic.

She thought again of Grayson, how he'd shared his desire to be a parent. Her heart broke thinking about how his ex-wife's indiscretions had crushed his dreams of throwing a baseball with his own son.

She couldn't help but smile inside. After last night, it was entirely possible their relationship might progress to the point of the big next step—and after that? Who knew? Maybe even marriage. She knew it might be premature to consider all that, but she couldn't imagine a man she'd rather have father her children. Grayson was kind, patient and dedicated—perfect parent material.

"What are you grinning about?" Leigh Ann asked her.

"Huh? Oh, nothing."

"Nothing, my foot," her sister chastised.

The petite Asian woman looked up with concern. "*You* foot? *You* foot, okay?"

Leigh Ann nodded. "Yes, thanks. My foot is fine."

The woman bobbed her head and smiled, continued her clipping.

"It seems our younger sister isn't the only one who looks happy these days," Leigh Ann noted. "I take it you had a good time with Grayson last night?"

"Well, I did," Karyn told her. "Until Robert Nygard showed up at my door." She relented, decided to tell them the whole story. She glanced around the spa, lowered her voice even though they were nearly alone. "You know, he's a bit—well, I think he's trouble."

Leigh Ann scowled. "What do you mean?"

She told them about the encounter in the hall, the way he'd run his fingers up her arm, the threats he'd made about Aggie before he offered to remedy her loneliness."

"Are you kidding me?" Leigh Ann's eyes turned hard. "I hope you told him where he could place that remedy!"

Joie agreed. "You need to tell Jon."

"Oh, I don't know. I'm afraid that would only cause trouble. Nola Gearhart made it clear she expected this movie project to bring prosperity not only to the resort—but the entire valley. I don't want to create any issues. People are counting on that money. Besides, Aggie is scheduled to be an extra in the big parade scene. In the 1956 version, that scene was filmed in Phoenix but the update has the parade going right down Main Street in Ketchum. Dean's mother would be heartbroken if her debut on the big screen fell through. I just couldn't do that to her, you know?"

Joie nearly climbed out of her chair. "That's ridiculous! You can't *not* tell. If he did that to you, he's pushing that nonsense on others as well. You need to nip this horrible behavior in the bud." She paused. "Or, give him the knee."

"Joie!" Leigh Ann gaped at her sister. "Not everything can be solved with vulgar retorts."

"Bet me," Joie said. "Just ask Steve Wade. He learned that lesson behind the high school bleachers a long time ago."

Leigh Ann held up her hand. "Okay, I don't even want to know."

Joie shrugged. "Just sayin'."

Leigh Ann scowled and drilled her with a look. "But what did Grayson say about all this?"

"He didn't like it," she admitted. "After Grayson learned of the incident Robert Nygard pulled in the hallway, he grabbed his jacket and threatened to go teach *that Hollywood goon* a lesson."

Leigh Ann switched feet, smiled at her pedicurist. "So, then what happened?"

"In the end, I helped him see reason. It took some effort, but I convinced him that roughing up a Hollywood producer would only make things worse—and might land him in jail. Grayson warned me to never be alone with Robert Nygard, and said if he crossed the line again in any way, he'd make sure his face was no longer photogenic. He also made me promise I would file a report with Jon. And I will eventually, when it's a good time and won't wreck everything."

Leigh Ann nodded with satisfaction. "Good. That's exactly what needs to happen. And I don't think you should wait."

Joie shrugged, nested her arms on the rise of her growing stomach. "You know this is a power thing. Until you show him *you're* the one who's boss, he'll try again. I can tell Maddy, maybe a letter threatening legal action might—"

Karyn shook her head. "No. I'll handle it." Her sisters gave her the look. "What? I will."

Even as she said this, something inside told her Robert Nygard would show his colors again. When he did, she had a plan—but it didn't include telling Jon. At least not right away.

20

There were arguments to be made for the best month in Sun Valley, but March often made Leigh Ann's list. Think two words: spring break. If history was any measure, crowds of ski enthusiasts would soon pour into the area from Seattle and San Francisco, skipping southern beaches, instead opting for America's premier ski runs.

A late season vacation in the Idaho mountains meant warm, sunny days under bright blue skies, snow that turned into delicious corn on the slopes by mid-morning, après ski on the deck of the Roundhouse at the top of Baldy—not to mention a romantic sleigh ride across a glistening blanket of snow to a beloved log cabin restaurant where you could dine in front of a roaring fireplace.

Leigh Ann put the final touches on the tourism counsel's press release which touted all these amenities and pushed send. Sometimes her job was far too easy.

A light knock at her office door interrupted her reverie. "Hey, you're early," she said when she saw Mark standing there, smiling.

"Couldn't wait to spend time with my favorite girl."

"Is that the best line you've got?" she teased. "Because you're the third guy to stop by today. Granted, the others had different motives than the one displayed on your face, but I'm just saying."

"Is that so?" Her husband grabbed her jacket from its hook and held it while she slipped her arms inside the sleeves. "Did the others pack up a picnic and your swim suit so he could surprise you with a little drive?"

She turned, grinned. "No! Are we heading up to Frenchmen's Bend? We haven't been there in—well, probably ten years."

Mark patted her on the butt. "We won't be able to drive all the way in. You up for some cross-country?"

Leigh Ann looked out the window at the skis mounted on top of his SUV. "You thought of everything!"

"I did," he told her, satisfied he'd sufficiently prepared for their outing. She could tell he was pleased with himself. She could barely believe this was the same husband she was married to last fall, when they'd had their blow-up.

She leaned and kissed him on the cheek. "You're a keeper!"

Frenchman's Bend was located about ten miles outside Sun Valley. Hushed, snow-laden evergreens surrounded a natural hot spring bubbling up from the east bank of Warm Springs Creek where icy currents rushed past a wall of stones built up to contain the steaming spring water, creating a favorite bathing spot for locals who knew how to find the outdoor pool.

With the aid of their four-wheel-drive, Mark and Leigh Ann drove a little more than half way in before the snow-covered roads forced them to pull over.

Pines lined the road, their bows still drooping under the weight of heavy snow. It had been a good snow year with lots of moisture-filled snow pack, providing for an even better spring ski season than in prior years.

The mood in the car was quiet for several minutes, each of them enjoying their own private winter nirvana. Finally, Leigh

Ann broke the silence. "Oh, Mark. I've seen these winter scenes thousands of times and they still take my breath away."

Her husband reached across the seat and threaded his fingers through her own. "Yup, never gets old." He gave her hand a squeeze. "You ready?"

She nodded and climbed out, her sweater on over thermals, ski pants, her parka and hat hung tucked in her arm. She put her skis and boots on, stabbed her poles into the crusty spring snow and gazed up at the robin-egg-blue sky.

Mark secured the backpack filled with their picnic lunch onto the place between his shoulders and fastened the buckle.

"Did you bring sandwiches?" she asked him.

"Uh-huh."

"And something to drink?"

"Got it."

"Hot soup—that'd be nice up here. Did you think to bring a thermos of—?"

Mark shook his head. "Yup. With hot chocolate."

"How about marshmallows? I had some homemade ones on the top shelf in the pantry, in the airtight plastic container. It was labeled."

He laughed, scooped up a handful of snow and tossed it at Leigh Ann. "Give it a rest, Martha Stewart."

She grinned and brushed herself off. "Oh, stop. Besides, I'm much prettier."

"Not going to argue with that." He tilted his head in the direction of the road ahead. "C'mon, let's head out."

She pulled her hat in place and pushed off, following him across glistening virgin snow. "Looks like we're going to be all alone today," she hollered, nearly breathless as she drew in the frosty, chilled air. She stabbed the snow with her right pole and glided her skis forward at a brisk pace. Then the left pole. Stab . . . glide. Stab . . . glide.

They reached their destination in less than thirty minutes.

Feeling invigorated, Leigh Ann stood on a rock and stripped off her gear, donning her swim suit as quickly as she could. Despite the sunshine, the air was frosty.

Laughing, she raced to plunge in the steaming water to ward off the cold. "Hurry, Mark!" she called to her husband.

"Hold on, let me get us some of that hot chocolate first. Oh, and I may have spiked it with a little Bailey's Irish Crème."

Minutes later, they were nestled together against the rocks, relaxing in the thermogenic pool of water.

"Mark?"

"Yeah?"

"You know I've tried to get to know Colby's wife, make her feel like part of the family. Really, I have. But that girl is strange." She wrapped her hands tightly around the cup of hot chocolate. "Beyond the fact she doesn't wash her hair with shampoo and doesn't shave—I mean, really, can you believe the girl doesn't shave? Anyway, Nicole is determined she wants to be some sort of birthing coach. Her room is stacked with books and instructional DVDs."

"You went into her room?"

"To change her bed," Leigh Ann responded, without missing a beat. "She asked me to approach Joie and see if my sister would agree to let her attend the birth. Never mind she's not yet certified, or whatever it is those people do for training, but she says there are no regulations that cover family situations. Of course, I'm not about to ask Joie to accommodate her request."

She paused, the Styrofoam cup inches from her mouth. "As you can imagine, Nicole's request puts me in the middle of a bad situation. I don't want Colby to think I'm not being kind to his new wife." She turned to her husband. "Did you know Colby calls her nearly every day? Never mind that his time is limited and I don't even get a chance to talk to him. Goodness only knows what she might be telling him about us." She took a sip of the hot chocolate, sighed. "Perhaps I'm worrying too much. I mean, I've really made an effort to be friendly."

"You? Worry?" Her husband chuckled, then placed his finger at his lips. "Shhh—look." He pointed.

An elk stood at the edge of the water. The majestic bull lifted his rack and watched them for several seconds before he dropped his head and took a drink from the ice lined creek bed.

"Isn't he beautiful?" Mark said in a hushed tone, echoing her own thoughts.

She took a deep breath of pine-filled air and leaned forward for a better view. "Oh, Mark. You're right," she whispered back.

Snow fell from a branch in the distance not far from where the elk stood, his regal head poised, puffs of breath coming from his nostrils. Leigh Ann found herself wanting to stop time as they watched in silence until the elk eventually moved past the creek and then sauntered up the hill out of view.

Mark squeezed her bare shoulder. "I'll get out and start a fire so we can eat our picnic, then we'd better head back."

A rock cropping provided the perfect spot, and minutes later they were dressed with their hands warming out over the fire. Mark unpacked a sack from Main Street Market—chicken waldorf sandwiches with arugula, pine nuts and shaved parmesan, and individual cups of quinoa salads. For dessert, they enjoyed large brownie squares topped with frosting.

When they'd finished, Mark handed her a napkin. "Babe, I've got something I wanted to discuss."

Leigh Ann dabbed the corners of her mouth. "What's up?"

Mark paused as if he didn't know how to start.

"Wait!" She dropped her hand and grinned. "This isn't one of those bad movies that are so popular? The ones where there's a couple all cozy and in love and then one of the spouses goes all diabolical on the other one? I really hated that *Gone Girl* flick." She shuddered. "And the book our club read last month was a similar story—bam! The wife didn't even see it coming."

Mark laughed. "No, Leigh Ann. I didn't bring you up here for dubious purposes. I just wanted to update you on the business deal with Equity Capital. I think our project is about to take a very positive turn."

"Yeah?" She picked at the remaining brownie crumbs from the wrapping paper and slipped them into her mouth. "Well, let's hear it."

Mark looked like a kid in Santa's lap. "Well, it's like this—after returning from San Francisco, Andrea DuPont reports we're ready to move forward with our purchase of a very large block of stock in Preston USA."

Leigh Ann didn't know much about the intricacies of corporate acquisitions, stock dividends and deferred annuities. All she knew is that the expression on Mark's face was pure delight.

"I take it that's a good thing."

He nodded with enthusiasm. "A very good thing. We stand to make a lot of money, Leigh Ann."

"That's wonderful, Mark. But about that second home—"

He waved off her comment. "No buts. We should have the entire deal wrapped up by mid-summer, and we'll be in a position to do a lot of things, financially speaking. We can buy two vacation homes if we want. Or, maybe we can take a trip. I've always wanted to visit Bali."

"We can talk about that." She didn't want to completely burst his bubble, but Joie's baby was due in a few short months, and she planned on being there to support her sister. "That sounds wonderful, honey. I mean, Joie's baby is due this summer. And I've got a lot on my plate at work. I'm not sure I want to juggle house-hunting and planning a trip abroad in the middle of all that. Perhaps we can put some of those plans off until fall?" She started gathering the lunch remains in preparation of heading home.

She turned away from the disappointed look in her husband's eyes. "I know compared to what you do, my volunteer responsibilities at the tourism council are a bit inconsequential, but people depend on me. Same with my family." She bagged the trash, then leaned over and kissed his cheek. "Let's just let the dust settle a bit before we race off and spend our newfound riches." She tweaked his earlobe. "Regardless, I'm thrilled for you, babe. And proud. I know how hard you've worked."

"Well, I suppose it's useless to try to get you to change your mind. But we are going to do those things—so you'd better keep those plans on the horizon, and in your planner. In the meantime, you're going to have to at least let me buy you some expensive trinket—maybe a yellow diamond ring from Holli Jewelers— a piece that says *Mark Blackburn took a huge risk and it paid off big.*

Mark let the disappointment slide from his face. He loved to impress her . . . and he loved to make money.

Leigh Ann didn't know what to say. She and Mark had a stunning home in one of the best neighborhoods. They drove nice cars, and Mark made sure she didn't want for much. Still, people who showed off their wealth were considered garish—even in the tightest circles. "We'll see," she promised.

On the way home, Leigh Ann mentioned she thought that rather than buy a vacation home they might only use a few times a year, perhaps they should consider buying a belated wedding gift for Colby and Nicole, a house in Sun Valley. "Maybe something up Warm Springs," she told Mark. "Not that those two deserve such an extravagant gift after they robbed us of seeing them say their marital vows. I'm still really mad."

"How mad?"

"Don't tease me, Mark. I'm serious. We raised Colby to be more thoughtful. I'm sure we're not the only ones who felt slighted. What about Daddy? And Karyn and Joie? I mean, family is everything, and that stunt communicated loud and clear how insensitive Colby has become since meeting that girl." She leaned down and rummaged in her purse for a stick of gum. "By the way, we're going to need to head back to the office and pick up my car. Unless you want to take me to work in the morning." Mark reached and patted her leg. "Whatever you want, but you'd best get over being so mad."

"Why's that?" Distracted, she pulled the gum from her purse. Mark turned into the driveway. "Because it looks like basic is over and our boy's home."

21

L eigh Ann squealed and scrambled from the car. Rushing past her son's car, she bolted inside and quickly hollered. "Colby?"

He appeared from the kitchen, Nicole on his arm. "Hey, Mom."

She made her way to him, slapped at his shoulder. "Quit with the surprises already." She pulled him from Nicole and into a tight hug. "I'm so glad you're home."

Mark wasn't far behind. "Good to have you back, Son." Colby was still dressed in his camo fatigues. Mark patted his son's stomach. "Looks like the army fed you well."

Nicole leaned against their son's shoulder. "I hope you told them you were vegan. I mean, they have to honor that and not feed you any murdered animals."

Leigh Ann rolled her eyes, finding it hard to hide her impatience. "I'm sure Colby had to do what he was told."

Mark picked up his son's duffel. "Well, whatever they fed you, you look great."

Colby grinned. "I ate a lot of pasta. Faster than meat." He thought to look at Nicole. "And healthier."

"Are you hungry now? I can cook something." Leigh Ann moved for the kitchen.

Nicole took off her headband and shook out her hair. "No need. I already fixed him something."

Leigh Ann lifted her nose. "What did you fix? I don't smell—" Mark touched Leigh Ann's arm. "Well, how about a drink? We're anxious to hear all about your experience, Son."

"Sure, Dad. I'll take Maker's Mark on the rocks."

So, her son had graduated from blended margaritas and daiquiris to what Mark called a *real-man's* drink. That wasn't the only noticeable change. His upper body had a new bulk, his upper arms muscled. His facial features were now lean and chiseled. Gone was the boy who had hugged her goodbye only a few weeks earlier. A man had returned in his place.

From Mark's expression, he'd noticed as well. The only difference was he was no doubt happy about the change.

Mark knew he was supposed to provide emotional support, but failed to fully understand her feelings, had even chided her for packing up the framed childhood soldier drawings. She simply couldn't bear to look at them while her baby boy was off playing army.

Colby took a seat on the sofa with Nicole next to him. "All-in-all, basic was a great experience. Not much like all the rumors you hear about." He chuckled. "Oh, there are some ass—uh, mean drill sergeants who make a real point of trying to get under your skin. Soon you realize that's just their job and let that junk roll off." He grinned at Nicole. "Basically, we ate, slept, got shots, went through briefings and learned exercises that helped prepare us for our units. Your body is in a constant state of exhaustion. You never know how strong you are until you're training to become a soldier."

"Well, your mother and I are proud of you, Colby."

"Thanks, Dad." He took a sip of his drink. "That means a lot."

Nicole reached and swept a stray lock of his hair back in

place. "So, baby—what's next?"

Colby jiggled the ice in his glass and downed some more bourbon. "I'm only here for a couple of days, then I have to report back for AIT—Advanced Individual Training—and then I deploy."

A wave of disappointment washed over Leigh Ann. "A couple of days? That's not long enough." Her voice broke. She knew she sounded like a child, but he'd just returned and was expected to just turn around and go back so soon?

Mark, Nicole and Leigh Ann all looked at each other, and in that look they each revealed their fears, their worries.

Mark leaned his elbows on his knees and looked at the floor. "That soon, huh?" He looked up. "Do you know where yet?"

"Where?" Leigh Ann asked, confused.

"Do you know where you'll be deployed?" Mark clarified.

Now it was Colby's turn to look at the floor. "Yeah. Got my orders before I shipped home."

"And?" Leigh Ann urged.

Her son knit his fingers and twiddled his thumbs. "I'll be stationed in South Korea."

She drew a sharp breath, felt something inside her break. "Oh, no! No!" She stood. "You are not going somewhere only miles south of a lunatic dictator with a penchant for testing nuclear weapons." She shook her head adamantly. "No, sir. Huh-uh."

Mark also stood. "Son, I'm with your mother on this one. South Korea is a dangerous place right now."

"Dad, you know I don't have any say in this. Besides, that schmuck makes one bad move and we'll take him out."

Leigh Ann buried her face in her hands. "You've drunk the Kool-aide." She looked up at her son, desperately wanted to talk some sense into him. "I only have one son and I'm not willing for you to risk your life. Let someone else go play army. I want you to do whatever it takes to get out of this. Do you hear me?"

Nicole frowned. "I don't think—"

Leigh Ann jabbed her finger in the air. "I don't really care what you think. Colby is my son. He's not going. And that is that!" She grabbed the drink out of her husband's hand and downed it in one swallow, then stormed out of the room, slamming her bedroom door behind her. "There must be a way for him to back out," she told herself.

If anyone would know the laws and how they might apply to this situation, it would be Maddy Crane.

"I'M SORRY, sweet thing. There's nothing that can be done." Maddy Crane folded her manicured hands and placed them on the desk. "Short of being diagnosed with a terminal disease, no legal options exist that would allow for your son's honorable discharge from the army."

"What about dishonorable?" Okay, yes—she was pushing it. But she was desperate.

Maddy pushed her chair back and stood. "I know how you must feel, darlin'. As his mother, I'm sure you are agonizing over the possibilities this deployment presents. Let me assure you— my own daddy was an officer. The United States Armed Forces are the best in the world. They take the safety of their recruits very seriously. All necessary precautions will be taken to ensure your son's safe return."

Joie nodded. "None of us want Colby in the middle of a risky situation, but we don't have any choice but to pray for the best."

Leigh Ann tried to swallow. This news was not what she'd hoped to hear.

Of course, she'd pray. How many Sundays had she sat on a pew at Grace Chapel and listened to Father John's sermons on prayer? She believed she could take her concerns to the good

Lord. Problem was, Jesus couldn't always be counted on to respond to her exact marching orders.

"So, what now?" she asked, hating how timid her voice sounded. Colby needed her to be strong—needed her to be a lioness willing to take any measure to protect her cub.

Joie touched her arm. "You go home. Colby will be leaving soon and you don't want to waste what time you have banging your head against walls you can't bring down." Her sister guided her to the door.

Maddy followed, her taffeta skirt making swishing noises. "Again, I'm so sorry, darlin'. Even a blind hog finds an acorn now and then. But not this time." She shook her head. "Wish there was something we could do to change all this—there just isn't."

"Well, I appreciate the information." Feeling defeated, Leigh Ann gave her sister a weak hug on the way out. "Talk to Dad lately?"

"Yeah, he's having some issues with predators. Not sure if wolves or coyotes, but he's taking precautions to keep them out of the lambs."

Leigh Ann nodded. "And how are you feeling?"

Joie smiled. "Now that I'm past that nasty morning sickness business, I feel great. I'm hungry all the time, though. And I'm craving the strangest things. Last night, I couldn't sleep until I had some garlic bread."

"Garlic bread?"

"Uh-huh. Had to get dressed and make a run to Atkinson's." They hugged, and Joie turned back and headed for her office.

Leigh Ann remembered her own cravings, her worst being a yearning for jelly beans which added pounds to her pregnancy weight. Many women hated losing their shape during pregnancy, but that was a small sacrifice.

She loved being pregnant, had been pregnant four times.

Being pregnant and having Colby was such a joy, she talked Mark into trying again very soon after. Colby was not even a year and a half old. They told everybody, everywhere, right away. The baby was due on Father's Day. But at nearly twelve weeks, they went in for the first ultrasound and learned the baby had no heartbeat.

She remembered lying on the crumply paper as the doctor delivered the devastating news, and sobbing—Mark bending down and whispering a promise in her ear. "We'll try again, Babe."

When she was pregnant the third time, they didn't want to tell anybody. In fact, she didn't even tell her dad and sisters until she was showing symptoms of a second miscarriage. She remembered weighing the words in her head, "The good news is I'm pregnant. The bad news is I'm bleeding."

Two days later, she and Mark held hands as they scanned the ultrasound screen, hoping against hope for that blinking white light that would assure them of the baby's heartbeat.

There was only stillness. The technician said, "The doctor will give you the results soon," and he left the room. And Mark said, "I'm sorry, sweetheart." Because he knew.

They decided not to try again. You can only get your hearts broken so many times.

Leigh Ann knew she was a bit over protective of Colby— always had been. But he was her only child. He meant everything to her.

Now he was going to go serve his country in some dangerous place. She could hardly bear the idea of him risking his life in a country projected to be the next hotspot for a breakout of war.

She'd always honored the servicemen who had given their lives—had even headed up a committee to place wreaths on the graves of the lost every Christmas. How foolish of her not to recognize there also needed to be monuments to the mothers of those dead soldiers. Certainly, their sacrifice was just as great.

Those thoughts plagued her mind as she headed into the lobby where an elegantly thin woman dressed in a tailored black suit sat talking on her cell phone. Leigh Ann didn't mean to snoop, but she couldn't help but overhear the conversation while she put on her coat.

"Yes, I'm here at Crane and Abbott. Our attorneys are working to pierce the corporate veil to find out who the real players are." The woman paused, listened. "That may be true, but time is of the essence here. Our largest supplier of acetal resin has increased their prices by well over double in the past two months alone. Same with the supplier of the heel base plates for our bindings. The investigator has learned both of these companies have something very important in common—a recent stock purchase by the same company."

The woman got up, paced the floor. "We're in the middle of a hostile takeover. Whoever is behind this activity plans to gain control and then dismantle our company and sell off the assets. A lot of money can be made in the short term by scalping potential long-term growth. Not only will we lose as current owners, but our stockholders and every employee and supplier will suffer. Let alone the local economy here in Sun Valley."

The woman noticed Leigh Ann by the door and hushed her voice as the conversation continued.

Hanging back so she could eavesdrop would seem too nosey, so Leigh Ann quietly buttoned her coat and slipped outside, glad she didn't have that woman's problems.

No doubt she'd seen her somewhere, but where? A fundraiser, or perhaps at a party?

She shrugged. Didn't really matter, she supposed. There were a lot of part-time residents who lived in New York or California who used their home here as a get-away from the hustle and bustle. She was likely one of them.

Leigh Ann pulled her keys from her bag and moved for her car. That's when she noticed another car in the parking lot—a slate grey SUV with a company logo emblazoned on the sides. *Preston, USA.*

22

After sixteen solid weeks, the final day of filming finally came for Robert Nygard and the production team at Tanasbourne Media. Late May in Sun Valley could still be unpredictable, but weather reports hinted they would be enjoying bright sunny days in the weeks ahead, the kind of welcome days filled with warm, lilac-scented air and freshly sprouted green grass. Certainly, today looked to be perfect conditions for filming.

The final shoot was scheduled to take place along the road leading to the Trail Creek cabin. Unlike much of the earlier filming, today would be open to the public. It seemed everyone had taken Mr. Nygard up on the invitation, not only locals, but people had travelled in from the surrounding counties, hoping for a close-up glimpse of their favorite stars—or better yet, a bit part as an extra.

Karyn rose before dawn and chose her clothes carefully—a light sweater in a pretty shade of blue and gray pants. She passed over her cute new booties with the four-inch heels for a pair with sensible structure, plain and nothing eye-catching. No need to draw attention to herself. Not today—and not with Robert Nygard around.

Orange cones blocked the lanes from traffic. Law enforcement staff stood at the entrance point and were positioned in strategic locations to manage the crowds now heading toward large white tents up ahead.

As director of hospitality she could certainly have finagled a ride with the production crew, possibly even one of the actors. But she couldn't risk getting stuck riding with Mr. Nygard. Not after that stunt he'd pulled in the hallway that day—and him showing up at her house.

She'd made her point. Without question, she was not interested in any proposition he had to offer—on camera, or off. Since then, there'd been no incidents, just an uneasiness that crept up her spine whenever he was around. Which is why she kept her distance whenever possible.

"Hey, Karyn—isn't this exciting?" Dale Lochin, the airport manager, waved. "My girls are going to be in the restaurant shot. They could barely sleep last night."

She smiled. "That's wonderful. I'll be watching for them." Dale and his wife had darling twin girls who were cheerleaders at the local high school.

Dale wasn't the only local resident who had left work to take part in the big day. Karyn spotted the guys from Crusty's—Joie's friends, walking toward all the activity from the main parking area. Close behind, Larry Harshbarger, the piano player at the Ram Restaurant, and Tessa McCreary, Grayson's realtor, chatted as they made their way to the filming location.

Of course, Dee Dee Hamilton and her husband were among the crowd as well. Since that first day in the lobby, Dee Dee had been banned from getting anywhere near where Mr. Nygard was filming, but today was open to everyone and Dee Dee was taking full advantage of the fact.

As Karyn neared the tent, Rory Sparks, the local sheriff held up the palms of his hands. "Whoa, Karyn. I need to see your badge."

This is where her sisters would roll their eyes and call him Barney Fife under their breath. She simply gave him a sweet smile and held up her credentials.

Rory nodded. "You're good to go." He waved her on.

A red carpet led to the white tent, where pockets of media with cameras crowded in as a sleek black town car pulled up and the stars of the film emerged.

"Ms. Larimore! Over here!"

An older woman with frizzy lemon-colored hair let out a shrill scream only steps away. "It's Rick Hudson. Oh, my goodness! It's really him."

Karyn had to work at not rolling her eyes. Why did anything connected to Hollywood make people act so crazy? Of course, Dean used to tease her unmercifully about her infatuation with authors of her favorite books, so she supposed she shouldn't judge all these groupies too harshly. She'd have gone weak-kneed if she'd ever gotten the chance to meet Pat Conroy before he passed away.

"Hey there, sweetheart."

She turned to the familiar voice. "Dad? What are you doing here?"

Her father stood with his hands buried deep inside his jeans pockets, a sheepish grin on his face. "Oh, just thought I'd come check and see what all the chatter is about."

"Yoo-hoo. Edwin!" Penny Baker scrambled across the parking lot to join them. "I was wondering if you'd be here," she said, nearly out of breath.

Karyn couldn't help but smile. Despite her slight build, that woman could move.

A gentle smile pushed through her dad's leathery wrinkles. "Morning, Penny. I sure enjoyed that cobbler you made. Not often I get marionberries."

Penny beamed. "My sister lives in Oregon and she brought them to me. I have several packages in the freezer. Perhaps you could come over sometime, and I'll make homemade ice cream topped with those berries. You will think you died and landed in heaven."

"I can only imagine," he told her, his eyes meeting Karyn's. They both knew he wasn't likely to head over to Penny Baker's house any time soon.

The Bo-Peeps were lovely women, if not a little pushy, but her dad hadn't been interested in anyone romantically since her mother died a very long time ago. She and her sisters had urged him to at least consider the possibility of a new relationship, but he always shut them down saying, "This 'ole sheepherder hung up his shepherd's hook a long time ago."

"Look, I need to find Jon," she said, giving her dad a quick hug. "I promised I'd meet him here. Apparently, someone from Ski Resort magazine is going to show up today. They want to do an article about all this."

"Okay, honey. We'll catch up later."

She waved and left him to face Penny's continuing chatter, then headed in the direction of an area filled with trucks and trailers she'd learned was known as the *circus*. One was a makeup trailer. Another a wardrobe trailer. There were equipment trucks and grip trucks and portable tents that housed rushes runners, editors, and a myriad of production assistants.

As Karyn neared, a trailer door opened and her former mother-in-law emerged. "Karyn! Look! I'm playing an extra in the diner scene—the one they're filming in the kitchen here at Trail Creek." She shoved her copy of the call sheet into Karyn's hands. "See, that's me circled in red. Right there on page fourteen."

Only then did Karyn realize Robert Nygard stood only feet away. "We're finding that Aggie is very talented. We just ran through the blocking and she was spot on every time." His wide smile made her mother-in-law puddle like a teenage girl who'd just been invited to the prom by the cutest boy in class.

"Oh, Robert! You make everything so easy." Aggie's open hand went to the neckline of her pomegranate-colored blouse. "You are a wonderful director. Did I tell you I studied Theatre Arts at Brown University when I was a girl? I was told I was pretty good."

A man with a scarf tied at his neck poked his head out of the trailer. "Ten minutes to roll."

Robert boldly planted his hand on Karyn's shoulder. "Well, looks like I've got to run. Are you sure you don't want a part? It's not too late to squeeze you in."

She nonchalantly stepped aside so that his hand was forced to drop. "No, I don't think so."

A leopard never changes its spots.

From the expression on Aggie's face, she clearly couldn't believe Karyn would turn down such an opportunity. "Oh, honey. Are you sure, dear? There's nothing to fear. Those of us with experience are more than willing to help you novices."

She loved Dean's mother, but Karyn didn't know whether to sigh in frustration or move aside to make room for Aggie's pride.

"By the way, dear—where's—I'm sorry. What is the name of your new—uh, friend?"

"Grayson? He had a last-minute obligation at the airport. He'll join me when he's finished."

"Bert was tied up too. He's on a health kick and works out every morning—no matter what." She rolled her eyes. "No number of chin-ups is going to keep him from growing gray hair."

A young guy who looked eerily like John Denver walked by carrying a small megaphone in one hand and an electrical cord in the other. He wore a jacket with lettering on the back that read Assistant Director.

"That's the AD," Aggie said. "I've got to go."

Karyn gave her a quick hug. "Have a good time."

"I plan to," Aggie wiggled her fingers in a wave, then turned and trailed the John Denver look-alike in the direction of the historic Trail Creek Restaurant.

Inside, Karyn groaned. This day could not get over fast enough. Soon everything would be back to normal.

Despite a myriad of issues, she'd worked hard to meet Nola and Jon's expectations and play host to the production company. She'd supplied extra towels, ordered special brands of cream cheese, installed darkening curtains, removed curtains, spent a fortune in flowers for the rooms. The finish line loomed just ahead.

Turning away, she went over to a table and sat down. She pulled out her phone and texted Jon, the one person who didn't seem to get caught up in all the Hollywood hype. *"Where are you?"*

He quickly texted back. *"I'm afraid I'm going to miss our meeting. Robert offered me a walk-on roll today with a speaking part! If anything critical comes up needing my attention, let me know."*

"My, Karyn. You look like you just swallowed a small artichoke."

She looked up. Miss Trudy and her sister, Ruby, stood there. Miss Trudy was dressed in flowing trousers and top in a tropical print that included parrots and brightly-colored flowers. Ruby's outfit was far more sedate—black pants and a pretty blue sweater. Both wore concerned looks on their faces.

Karyn tried to smile, but it wasn't the real thing. "Hey."

Miss Trudy slid into an empty chair at the table. She placed both of her hands, covered in silver and turquoise rings, on her arm. "Karyn, dear—what's the matter?"

"Yes," her sister said, joining her. "You look like you're carrying all the world's troubles on your shoulders."

For the briefest of seconds, Karyn considered unloading her experience. She wanted to tell a sympathetic ear how overwhelming this whole film experience had been, and especially with Robert Nygard—how he seemed to undress her with his eyes—and how he believed his hands had the right to land on her arm or shoulder, lingering until she moved away. She'd never done anything to invite that behavior. She knew it. Had even made it clear his advances were unwanted—but nothing seemed to work. He still crossed all appropriate boundaries.

But she couldn't tell them—not if she didn't want the situation broadcast all over town.

"I'm fine," she fibbed.

"Well, maybe you need more rest. You young people never get enough sleep." Miss Trudy leaned forward. "By the way, have you heard the news?"

Ruby's expression turned enthusiastic. "Oh yes, tell her Sister."

Miss Trudy glanced around to make sure no one overheard. "Well, there are folks here from a big national magazine—what was the name, Ruby?"

"*Ski Resort.*"

Miss Trudy nodded. "Yes, that right. *Ski Resort Magazine.*" Her eyes gleamed with excitement. "Anyway, they stopped by the Painted Lady—a man and a woman—and they interviewed me."

"They dropped by the Opera House earlier. Took my photo and everything," Ruby added.

"Yes, the magazine contacted me as well," Karyn told them.

"You will like them. They were such nice folks, very complimentary of our area. Did you know the magazine is distributed in twenty-eight countries? Anyway, they posed so many questions. I guess they thought Ruby and I knew a lot about the area." Her face took on a more somber look. "Although, some of the things they were asking puzzled us a bit, didn't they Ruby?"

Karyn watched in the distance as a boom with a camera moved into place. "Yeah?"

"They asked a lot of questions about your brother-in-law?"

She pulled her attention from the filming. "Mark?"

Miss Trudy bobbed her head. "About some of his business dealings."

"And about Preston USA," Ruby inserted into the conversation. "They wanted to know about all the people who were employed there and how it might affect our economy if there was a huge lay-off."

Miss Trudy's eyes narrowed. She leaned forward. "What do you suppose is going on with Mark and Preston USA?"

"Do you think it's connected?" Ruby wondered out loud.

Karyn didn't know the answer to that question, but she wasn't about to get drawn into any more drama—especially anything concerning Mark's business dealings. She had enough on her plate.

Her phone dinged. Karyn glanced at an incoming text from Grayson.

"Sorry, Karyn. I'm not going to be able to make it today. I'll call you tonight."

Miss Trudy lifted her eyebrows. "No trouble, I hope?"

"No—no trouble." Karyn stood and gave them each a brief hug. "But I do have to get going. You girls have a good time today."

Ruby laughed. "We will—but if you hear anything juicy out there, let us know!

JOIE WALKED—WELL, waddled—down the hallway toward Maddy's office. Now well into her third trimester, she often felt like a penguin with a law degree.

Truth was, this part of the pregnancy had been amazing.

She lightly rapped on the closed door.

"Come in," Maddy called out.

Joie peeked her head inside. "You needed to talk to me? Said it was urgent?"

"Yes," Maddy quickly confirmed. "Sit down, we've had a break in Candy Tubbs' case."

"Yeah? That's great!" She wedged herself into Maddy's guest chair.

Maddy folded her hands on the top of her desk. "I'm afraid the news isn't great, darlin'. It concerns your brother-in-law."

She stood and came around her desk, sat on the corner and folded her arms. "Have you ever heard of greenmailing?"

Joie nodded. "Sure. You buy stock in a floundering publicly traded company, then threaten a take-over which prompts owners to buy back the stock at a premium. Companies often have to sell off assets at garage sale prices to raise cash, and sometimes they lose the entire company. Many times, the corporate raid costs thousands of employees their jobs and threatens the local economy." Her heart began to thud against her chest as her mind rehearsed what she knew about Candy's situation and her company. "And you think Mark is involved in—"

Maddy turned grim. "Yes, darlin'. I'm afraid so."

"Picture up." The John Denver look-a-like held both arms high. "Quiet everyone."

Karyn stood still, watching as the camera man swung the boom into place. A woman crouched took the arm of the clapper and slapped it shut. "Action," she yelled.

Robert Nygard stood, his sunglasses nested in his hair. "Roll."

Rick Hudson slipped a cowboy hat from his head. "Well, I've been thinkin' about them other fellas, Cherie. And well, what I mean is, I like you the way you are, so what do I care how you got that way?"

Mia Larimore turned, her eyes filled with dramatic tears. "Bo! That's the sweetest, most tender thing anyone ever said to me." She folded into his embrace and they kissed.

"Cut!" Robert Nygard clapped his hands and grinned. "That's a wrap, folks!"

Applause broke out on the set and in the extended audience watching.

Despite her earlier sour mood, Karyn couldn't help but smile. The process of creating a film for the big screen was indeed fascinating. She couldn't believe how many takes just to get a few minutes "in the can" as they say.

She turned to leave and immediately planted her nose into Robert Nygard's chest.

"So, Karyn—you ready to pack up and move to Hollywood?" he asked, his tone low and suggestive. "Land of the stars?" He was standing so close she could smell his cologne. A sure sign of trouble.

She took a wide step back. "I'm afraid the only stars I'm likely to hang with are the ones dotting the night sky," she said as politely as she could muster.

She sidestepped to leave, only to realize he'd cornered her out of sight of most of the crowd. Only a few milled around in the distance, and no one seemed to be paying attention. "You'll have to excuse me. I have an appointment."

He grabbed her wrist. "What's your hurry, Karyn?" His spa-pampered face twisted into a sneer. He stared at her, with eyes cold and taunting. "I'd really hoped we could be better friends. Especially when I took the time out of my busy schedule to pay a visit at your house."

Now she got mad. "I said I have an appointment." She yanked her hand, but he wouldn't let loose. "Hey—let go! I mean it, or I'll—"

Robert cut her off by grabbing her head with both hands. He pressed his lips against her own, hard and demanding. She wiggled to free herself but she was no match for his strength.

Suddenly, a masculine hand grabbed her arm—wrenched

her free from the unwanted embrace. A fist sliced the air and hit its target. Bones crunched and blood spattered.

She screamed.

Robert Nygard buried his face in his hands. "What the hell —?" His head bolted up to face his attacker. "You asshole! You broke my nose!"

Her rescuer stood rubbing his fist, a man who looked to be in his late forties with careless black hair and warm brown eyes.

"You okay?" he asked. A slow grin played at his mouth as he straightened his jacket.

Before she could answer, media swarmed with cameras flashing.

Karyn audibly groaned. After everything she'd done to avoid it, this creep had still landed her in a huge mess.

Robert bent and gathered the pieces of his expensive sunglasses from the ground. He straightened, jabbed his fingers toward his nemesis. "I'll sue! I don't care who you are. When I get done, you won't have a pot to piss in!"

Indifferent to the threats, the dark-haired stranger rubbed his swollen hand, then raised it in a tiny salute before simply turning and jogging away.

23

L eigh Ann strode through her front door, flung her purse on the sofa. "Mark? You home?" she called out as she headed for his office.

"In here," he called back.

She marched to the doorway, crossed her arms and met Mark's surprised gaze.

"You're home early," he said. "I didn't expect you back until late this afternoon."

"Are you planning a corporate raid of Preston, USA?" she demanded.

His expression turned to one of confusion. "What?"

"Are you and Andrea cooking up a plan to force their stock prices down so you can manipulate the value, buy the company and sell off all the assets?"

His eyes narrowed at her tone. "Where did you hear that?"

The fact that he answered her with a question set her teeth on edge. "From the horse's mouth—in this case Candy Newberry Tubbs. I overheard her talking on the phone in Joie's lobby and then I saw her car in the parking lot. I jotted down the license plate number and stopped by the county office."

Mark bolted up from his desk. "In Joie's office? What was she doing there?"

There he went. More questions.

She had a brief flash of memory from last fall—the credit card being denied, his drinking. All seemed to resolve when he met Andrea DuPont. After months of late nights spent in his office, stewing, her husband had suddenly become a new man nearly overnight. He walked with a spring in his step, a smile on his face.

She'd mistakenly believed he was having an affair. Of course, that pathetic assumption was quickly corrected when she was introduced to his new business partner. Apparently, a business partner who might make him financially successful, but at a horrible cost.

"You are, aren't you?" she challenged. Long ago she'd learned to trust her gut—and her gut was telling her she'd trusted her husband far too much in the financial arena of their lives. "Oh, Mark—do you even know what destroying Preston USA will do to the entire Sun Valley area? People will lose their jobs—their livelihoods." She paused, the air heavy with tension. "And what about me? I'm the director down at the tourism offices. Did you stop to think about how this will affect *my* job and our standing in this community?"

Mark jabbed the air with his finger, his face dark with anger. "Your job? You mean the volunteer position that brings in no money?" He ran his fingers through the top of his hair in frustration. "Do you have any idea what I've been dealing with? No!"

He paced. "While you plant flowers in the front yard, I see our accounts dwindling. You have no understanding of the cash flow it takes to maintain this house and your lifestyle."

How dare he!

"*My* lifestyle?" she shouted. "I'm the one with the garage filled with fancy cars and motorcycles? I'm the one who dreams about buying vacation homes in Monterrey?" She took a deep breath, rubbed at her forehead. "Mark, I don't get you. Why would you do this?"

Mark slumped into a nearby chair, his elbows on his knees, his head hanging. "Do you have any idea what it's like to face financial ruin? To know that if you don't find a solution quick, everything you've worked for your entire life will circle the drain?" He looked up at her. "Do you?"

Leigh Ann couldn't bring herself to respond. She simply stared at the man she thought she knew.

He rubbed at his eyes. "Don't look at me like that," he muttered, with a weariness she'd never heard in his voice.

She sensed a rupture in his commitment to his plan and folded to her knees in front of him, covered his hands with her own. "It's not too late. You can back out."

He shook his head, smirked. "Yeah? And get sued for breach of contract? Now that's a plan."

"Think of all those people, Mark. Can you really fix our situation by destroying their well-being?"

The look that crossed his face told her she'd gone too far. He stood, brushed her hands aside. "That's not fair!"

She remained silent, knowing her remark splashed vinegar on his already nicked conscience. The truth of what she'd said no doubt stung.

"There is no winning here, Leigh Ann. If I pull out of this deal, Andrea DuPont will make sure I pay. She'll go forward with the takeover and people will lose their jobs regardless." He looked her straight in the eyes. "The only question remains—will we go down with them?"

24

Joie unloaded the Amazon boxes from the closet and stacked them next to the crib in her new nursery. She'd had a horrible day at work after learning about Leigh Ann and Mark, and the only thing she wanted was to quit thinking about the situation and her impossible role in the whole mess.

Normally, she'd have stormed right over to Leigh Ann's and confronted her—given her a piece of her mind. I mean, really— all those years of living under her constant critical eye, never measuring up. Her sister always lived above the line—Joie was destined to slither below.

Truth was, Leigh Ann earned that position. She had impeccable ethics—or at least that's what Joie had believed. Wrongfully so, it now seemed.

Regardless, she had a client and was bound by attorney-client privilege. She'd have to proceed very carefully.

Joie sat cross-legged on the carpet, took the box cutter and slashed open the seal on the first box. Inside was a set of light blue sheets. She ran her hand over the clear plastic wrap, still in absolute wonder over the notion that in a few short weeks she'd be mother to a tiny little boy she'd decided to name Hudson.

The doorbell rang and she struggled to get up. Before she could raise entirely to her feet, she heard the door open. "Joie? It's me—Karyn."

Both of her sisters had keys to her new place, and they weren't afraid to use them.

"In here," she called out.

Karyn appeared in the doorway, looked around at all the boxes. "Goodness, what's all this?"

Joie rubbed at her back. "I've been so busy at the firm, I've barely had a minute to get this nursery ready." Her sisters had helped paint several weeks ago, but she'd never had a minute to fill the bureau drawers or make up the crib.

"Ah—" Karyn nodded. "I sure love how this room turned out."

"Me too," Joie agreed. The walls were painted light gray. The curtains were sheer and matched the cream-colored crib, wardrobe and changing table. In the corner, a nursing chair and ottoman in a navy print tied the look together.

By far, her favorite element was the calligraphy print on the wall above the crib—*Hudson* in navy letters—all thanks to Leigh Ann. Her gifts extended beyond bossing people around.

"Here, let me help." Karyn reached for the box cutter.

"So, I thought you were headed over for dinner with Grayson tonight."

Karyn pulled a tiny onesie from the box. "I was, but I begged off. I had a horrible day." She held the tiny garment to her cheek. "The fabric is so soft."

Joie scowled. "Bad day? What happened?"

"Huh?" Karyn shrugged. "Oh, it's a long story."

The doorbell rang again.

Joie pulled a tiny pair of booties from inside a box and laid them on the floor next to a stack of disposable diapers. "Who can that be?"

Karyn folded the onesie and placed it neatly inside the open drawer. "It's Leigh Ann. She texted and said she was on her way over. Her life is falling apart."

"Hello?" Their sister's voice called from down the hall. "It's me."

"We're in the nursery," Karyn called back.

Leigh Ann's tear-stained face caused Karyn to scramble to her side.

"Oh my goodness, Leigh Ann—what's the matter?" Karyn asked. "Are you okay?"

Their sister shook her head. "No, I'm not okay. It's Mark. He's involved in something awful." She gave Joie a severe look, one that clearly communicated she was not happy.

With effort, Joie lifted from the floor. She held up open palms and headed for the door.

"Hey, where are you going?" Karyn asked.

"I can't listen to this."

"What do you mean you can't listen? To what?" She glanced between her and Leigh Ann. "What's going on?"

"You knew?" Leigh Ann challenged. "And you didn't tell me?"

Now it was Karyn's turn to hold up her hands. "Wait, what are talking about? What didn't Joie tell you about?" She turned to Joie. "What didn't you tell her?"

"Nothing. I only learned the details this morning. Again, that's all I can say—or hear. I'm not going to risk my license over another of Mark's stupid—and greedy—business schemes."

Leigh Ann parked her hands on her hips. "Now wait a minute, you're out of line!"

Joie whipped to face her. "I'm out of line? Oh, that's rich, given what you guys are doing."

Karyn wedged herself between them, held her arms out like a wrestling referee. "Stop, you two. I mean it! I don't have a clue what you're talking about, but both of you need to quit this before one of you says something you can't take back!"

Joie couldn't believe her quiet evening had morphed into this match of wills. She was done—and she said so. "I'm going to go make a sandwich. Either of you want anything?" She turned to Leigh Ann. "You have exactly ten minutes to spill your guts to Karyn, with me out of the room." She looked at Karyn. "And good luck with what you're about to hear."

She marched out, leaving her sisters to talk without her violating any duty to her client.

In the kitchen, she slapped a piece of ham between two slices of bread and shoved the corner in her mouth and took a bite.

Despite legal ethics, she'd love to be a fly on her nursery wall to learn how in the world Leigh Ann could justify this business deal.

～

THE MINUTE JOIE shut the door, Leigh Ann fell to tears. "Oh, Karyn. She's right. Mark has done something awful."

Karyn's arms folded around her older sister. "Honey, it can't be that bad. I mean, nobody died." She hesitated, knowing that comment was insensitive in some measure. Just because her sister wasn't a widow like her did not discount her pain. "I'm sorry. I didn't mean to—I mean, I'm listening. Tell me what's wrong."

Leigh Ann looked at her miserably as she recounted the entire story, beginning with what she'd overheard in Joie's lobby to what Mark had confirmed when she'd challenged him. "Say something," she said when she'd finished.

Karyn pulled her hand from her mouth. "I—I'm not sure what to say."

"I know—right? If Mark goes forward with this plan, we'll be as welcome in this town as the Ebola virus."

Karyn couldn't believe Mark hadn't realized the position he'd put Leigh Ann in. "What are you going to do?"

Leigh Ann shook her head miserably. "According to Mark, there is no winning on this. If he backs out, we'll get sued. And the deal will still go forward, regardless. The bottom line is Preston, USA is at risk of being torn apart and that will severely impact so many families." She stomped her foot. "I'm so mad at Mark, I could just spit."

Karyn handed her the box cutter, pondering whether or not to add her own woes to the evening, when Joie pushed the door open. In her arms, she carried packages of cookies, chips and candy.

"What?" she asked when they both stared at her. "If we're going to have one of *those* nights, clearly we're going to need sustenance."

JOIE LEANED against the changing table, empty boxes and wrappers scattered on the floor. Her hands rested on the top of her belly. "I shouldn't have done that," she said, feeling so full she could pop.

Leigh Ann chomped on a piece of red licorice. "Don't know about the two of you—" she said with her mouth full. "But empty calories make me feel better."

Karyn nodded. "Well, at least a little."

Joie brushed a few stray crumbs from her shirt. "I'm sorry, Karyn. You said you had a horrible day and—"

Leigh Ann straightened. "You did? Why didn't you say something?"

Against her better judgment, Joie reached for another cookie. "She mentioned it before you got here." She turned to Karyn. "But not the details. Now, spill."

Karyn lifted her shoulders in a shrug. "It's nothing, really. I mean—it was awful, but it's over. And my woes are nothing compared to—," she glanced at Leigh Ann.

Leigh Ann and Joie stared, waiting.

"Okay, well—here's the story." Karyn took a deep breath. "As you know, today was the last day of filming."

They both nodded, urging her to continue.

"Well, I thought I'd go on over to the film site. Part of my job responsibilities is to—"

Joie rolled her hand impatiently. "Yeah, yeah—what happened?"

Karyn dropped her gaze, grabbed a cookie and shoved it in her mouth. "Robert Nygard cornered me," she explained, her mouth filled with chocolate chip mush. "He forced a kiss on me."

Joie bolted up straight. "He what? Did you encourage him?"

"No!" Karyn said, offended.

"Then that's unwanted sexual harassment. That behavior is against the law."

"He's not my boss," Karyn argued.

Joie shook her head. "Doesn't matter. He has economic power over you and your job."

Leigh Ann lifted her hand, interrupting Joie's legal analysis. "What did Jon Sebring say?"

"You told him, right?" Joie asked.

"Of course I told him. And if I hadn't, he would have found out anyway." She groaned. "The media was everywhere. No doubt, there will be pictures on the news and in the papers. At the very least, the Dilworth sisters will spread the report."

Leigh Ann's hand went to her chest. "Karyn, that's awful. What did you do?"

"Well, I tried to shove him away, but I couldn't. He was too strong. All of a sudden some guy took hold of Nygard, and he punched him right in the face. I think he broke his nose." She allowed a grin. "There was blood."

Joie frowned as she slipped back to the floor. She rubbed at the small of her back. "And you reported this?"

Karyn rolled her eyes. "I told you I did."

"And what did Jon say? Did he make a formal report?"

"Both Jon and Nola Gearhart were very supportive. They provided formal statements to the media and promised to stand behind me. They have a no tolerance policy."

Satisfied, Joie leaned back and rested against the changing table. "Good. That's good to hear."

Leigh Ann tucked a strand of hair behind her ear and went for another piece of licorice. "What did Grayson say?"

Karyn sighed. "I haven't had a chance to tell him. But I will."

The doorbell rang.

"You expecting anyone?" Leigh Ann checked her watch. "I mean, it's pretty late for guests, don't you think?"

"What? I'm still in high school and have a curfew?"

Leigh Ann waved her off. "Oh, stop! You know what I mean."

Her sisters helped her to her feet and followed her down the hall. Before opening the door, Joie peeked out the window—and smiled.

She swung the door open. Clint stood on her porch holding what looked to be a handmade cradle.

25

J oie stood on her father's front porch, enjoying the warmth of the June sunshine and surveying the nearby mountainsides painted with blue lupines and yellow biscuitroot blooms scattered amongst the pungently fragranced sagebrush.

Her hand went to her very swollen belly. With only a little over a month until little Hudson was due to arrive on the scene, she couldn't believe there was enough room for him to grow more.

So much had happened in the past year. Was it only last summer that she was jumping out of airplanes and taking daring risks with little attention paid to the possible consequences? Or, spending most of her time down at Crusty's with the boys and living as if she had no one to answer to—not even herself?

Joie shook her head. She'd been in a bad place back then, in many regards. She'd been carrying the shame of a horrible mistake, one she would repeat. But then, how could she regret her bad choice? Reigniting a relationship with Andrew—even under his false pretense—had resulted in little Hudson.

It was true what her father always said—redemption can come from even our worst mistakes.

Besides, if she hadn't been hanging out playing pool at Crusty's, she'd never have met her best friend.

She knew it was rare for two people of the opposite sex, and especially two who were so clearly different, to gravitate to each other the way she and Clint had. Well, maybe not initially, but it wasn't long before she realized he seemed to really get her—and just when she needed a friend most. In her darkest hours, he'd been by her side with his unqualified support.

Her mind drifted back several weeks to the day he showed up on her doorstep with a cradle.

"What's this?" she'd asked, eyeing the beautifully handcrafted bed made of wood, glossed to perfection.

"It's a cradle," he said simply.

She rolled her eyes. "I know it's a cradle, but—"

"I made it." He thrust the tiny baby bed out in front of him, his face beaming with pride. "From that old tree back of the horse stables, you know—the one that got hit by lightning?"

Her throat grew tight. "You made this from a—a tree?"

Clint shrugged. "It was nothing really. You just need the proper tools."

"But—this project had to have taken you months." She ran her fingers over the intricate wood pattern he'd created.

He looked embarrassed then, shifted on his feet slightly. "Yeah, well—"

"Oh my goodness," Leigh Ann exclaimed as she burst onto the scene, pressing against Joie's back in order to get a better look. "Did I hear you say you made that?"

Clint nodded.

Karyn joined them at the door. "It's lovely. And so thoughtful."

Later, after Clint left, both her sisters immediately pounced on the idea that Clint had feelings for her—romantic feelings.

Joie quickly assured them he did not, restated for the umpteenth time that their relationship was purely platonic. "He's just a friend," she declared, a little more sharply than she intended. Then, more softly, "Albeit, a very good friend."

In the pasture, a rock chuck poked his head out of a cropping of black lava rock. He took a couple of tentative steps forward, then perched on his hind legs and assessed whether or not danger lurked nearby. Finding none, he skittered across the lavish green grass sending tiny yellow butterflies into the air in flight.

Today she was in such a good place—happy even.

"Hey, Sis."

Joie turned to find her dad standing next to her on the porch.

"Hey, Dad. I didn't even hear you come up."

He wiped his hands on a kitchen towel. "I have lunch ready. You hungry?"

She shook her head. "Nah, I stopped at Bistro on Fourth and had a cup of hot chocolate and a croissant with Nash Billingsley this morning. Truth be known, I can't wait until this little guy arrives on the scene so I can go back to drinking my morning coffee. Maybe then I won't feel so tired all the time."

Her father placed his leathered hand on her shoulder. "Your mother battled fatigue at the end of her pregnancies as well. Maybe you should just come in and lie down for a bit. I've got to head up the canyon leading to Gray's Peak. Sebastian called. He spotted a wolf. Damn predators! They got into Flat Top's band of sheep two days ago and took out over thirty head. Left half-eaten carcasses strewn all over."

It was no secret the livestock men in the valley detested coyotes and wolves. It was a constant battle to keep them out of their sheep and cattle.

Joie sighed. "I'd love to, but I have answers to interrogatories due in the morning and I should spend a few hours at the office."

Now her father placed both hands on her shoulders. "Listen,

honey. You know your 'ole dad rarely meddles in the affairs of his girls. But this lawsuit business has me a bit concerned. Nothing is worth risking your relationship with your sister."

Joie's heart grew heavy with the weight of his warning. "I know, Daddy. The problem is Mark and his business associates have been playing the Monopoly board with game pieces that aren't theirs to move."

Her dad's face took on an uncertainty, like he worried he might be crossing the line with what he was about to say. Even so, he was not deterred. "And you're determined to send Leigh Ann's husband to jail without passing go?"

She lifted her jawline. "I'm not sending anyone to jail. First off, I practice civil law, not criminal. I'm simply representing our client and helping her to save her company. And in the process, I'm saving the livelihoods of many families, our friends and neighbors."

Her dad tweaked her chin. "That's indeed noble, Sweetheart. But I worry the facts in this case will lead to a criminal action that might devastate Mark—and Leigh Ann."

Joie couldn't look him in the eyes. Instead, she quickly planted a kiss on his cheek. "I don't have any control over the consequences Mark may or may not pay for his actions. Regardless, I'm bound to represent the best interests of our client. The only other option is to recuse myself, and I'm sorry. I'm not prepared to do that. Not when this is the first big case Maddy has entrusted to me. Not after all the work our firm has put into breaking wide open the fact Andrea DuPont and her Equity Capital Group are pulling some underhanded business tactics."

Her dad sighed, resigned to the fact he wasn't going to easily change her mind. "Well, regardless—it won't hurt for you to take it easy. You don't want your body giving out. Eventually, you'll have to start your maternity leave, but with a little care, that can still be a ways off."

She knew her dad was right—on all counts. It didn't matter. She simply wasn't going to let Maddy down.

Mark was a big boy when it came to business. He'd have to roll with the punches. Sure, his name would be mud for a while, at least in business circles. But Mark was like a cat with nine lives. He'd proved before he could take his business licks and keep on kicking.

"I think I'll take you up on that offer. I think I'll slip onto your sofa and grab a few winks."

Her dad's face instantly brightened. "Good. Tell you what, call your sisters and have them come over for dinner. Elda Vaughn brought by a casserole that looks pretty good. In the meantime, I'll pack up my lunch and head up the canyon."

When her dad left, Joie grabbed the afghan from the back of his sofa and snuggled up. Despite her exhaustion, she couldn't seem to drift off. Her mind was filled with her dad's warning.

What if the consequences to Mark were more severe than even he could weather? And what would that do to Leigh Ann. She loved her sister. Could their relationship take the kind of hit that might occur if she and Mark tumbled financially because she wouldn't back down from this lawsuit?

She shook the thought from her head. Even if she recused herself, and she could—the key defendant was her brother-in-law—that would not stop the legal action or the remedies Candy Newberry Tubbs would no doubt seek.

Besides, as far as she could tell, Mark and Andrea had done nothing illegal. Their business maneuvers were indeed under-handed, but nothing that might land them in jail. It wasn't fair that Candy was having to sell off assets at basement bargain prices to raise cash to buy back shares to gain control back over her company.

Joie turned and punched the pillow, trying to find a more comfortable position.

It simply wasn't fair—not to their client, and not to the dozens of employees and vendors who depended on Preston USA for their financial well-being. She was on the right side here!

She squeezed her eyes shut, willing herself to sleep, wanting to take advantage of this precious time allotted for much-needed rest.

Maddy had a plan. With any luck, her strategy would stop the hostile take-over and restore control to Candy.

The trouble was, Leigh Ann was smack dab in the middle. If Mark got hurt, so would her sister.

JOIE WASN'T sure when she drifted off exactly, but she woke to a nightmare.

"Joie! Joie, wake up!" Leigh Ann shook her little sister's shoulders. "Wake up."

She pulled herself from a deep sleep, opening her eyes one at a time. She squinted against the light. "What? I was napping."

"This is no time to sleep," Leigh Ann scolded. "Not when you've ruined my life."

Joie sat up, now wide awake. "What are you talking about?"

Leigh Ann huffed. "Oh, don't give me that innocent look. You know exactly what just went down. We're ruined—Mark and I. Not only are we broke, but we'll never be able to face our neighbors again."

Joie rolled her eyes in an exaggerated manner. "Settle down, Drama Queen. Both of us know money can't buy happiness."

Her sister huffed and crossed her arms. "Okay, yes. I'm a drama queen. And, whoever said that doesn't know where to shop." She paused, stared. "Joie, you don't get what I'm telling you. We may have to sell our house."

Joie brushed aside the afghan. "Mark took that risk when he jumped in bed with Andrea DuPont."

Leigh Ann's eyebrows shot up.

"Metaphorically speaking," she quickly clarified, not meaning to bring up old baggage.

"I admit Mark made some bad judgment calls in this whole deal, but you could at least be on our side. I mean, we've got a son who will soon be in some far-away country carrying a gun, trying to stay alive, a daughter-in-law he will leave under our care, a household to maintain and—, she paused, unable to go on. "Mark—he's ruined."

Joie's head began to pound. "I'm sorry, Leigh Ann. Truly, I am. I don't mean to sound harsh, but this is the bed Mark climbed into and now it's his to make. I'm not his maid, and am not responsible for cleaning up his mess."

"I don't expect you to," she said, miserably. "But you and that crack-pot boss of yours didn't have to send me and my husband to sleep on the sofa, with no pillows." Fear, as unmistakable as it was brief, surfaced in her older sister's expression. "It's possible we'll never be able to recoup this time."

Joie rubbed at the place between her eyes. "What about Preston, USA, the shareholders and employees? What about them?" She took her sister's hand. "Look, it's possible you don't understand—"

"Oh yes, I fully understand." Leigh Ann's eyes narrowed as she pulled her hand back. "Preston USA just diluted their shares and offered them to existing shareholders at an even greater discount. That sent the company value plummeting, which left Equity Capital Group holding stock purchased far over value. Of course, their objective to take over the company was foiled in the process."

Joie took a deep breath. "Look, I'm sorry for how this all turned out. Truly, I am. Our firm represents Candy Newberry Tubbs, but the decisions surrounding her company's response to Equity Group's plan did not rest at our doorstep. The poison pill is a common defense to hostile take-overs. Mark should have known that was a possibility."

"Well, he didn't."

Perhaps, but Joie doubted very much Andrea DuPont failed to note the possibility. Andrea DuPont's long history of shady business maneuvers had been the subject of a three-hour meeting between Joie, Maddy and the client as they weighed options. Thankfully, Candy Newberry Tubbs had other liquid assets and the needed capital to fund such a risky defense move. And she had employees who were willing to liquidate their 401Ks and put up the funds to assist the maneuver.

Leigh Ann stood, looking even more miserable. "Well, word has already gotten out. Not only have the Dilworth sisters done their part in enlightening every resident within a hundred miles of Sun Valley, but lear jets are already landing at Friedman. CNN and NBC anchors will be swarming in no time, shoving microphones into the faces of anyone willing to talk. Of course, both Mark and I will be made out to be far more villainous than any Stephen King henchman. Just get the buckets of blood ready . . . it's prom night."

"Mark will recover. He always does." Joie challenged her sister with a look. "Perhaps what he and Andrea were trying to pull off was legal, but they fell short of ethical standards—by anyone's measuring stick." In an attempt to move on from the subject, she headed into the kitchen. "Dad said one of the Bo-Peeps left a casserole. He wanted me to call you and Karyn and have you come join us for dinner."

Leigh Ann squared her shoulders and followed. "I'm not sure you understand what is at stake for Mark and me. All this—"

Joie interrupted by holding up her open palms, hoping to skirt what had become a dangerous conversation. "Let's agree to just disagree. We're never going to see eye-to-eye on this one."

"Fine," her sister replied, in a voice that indicated it was anything but fine. "I already called Karyn. She'll be here soon. I'll just shove this in the oven and make a salad."

Barely able to walk for the chip she carried on her shoulder,

Leigh Ann pulled the lasagna pan from her hands. "Here, let me," she snipped. "Go sit down. You look like you're about to pop."

"Well, maybe not pop. But I do need to scoot to the potty before—"

Leigh Ann rolled her eyes. "Don't be crass, Joie. No one needs to know your bathroom habits."

Joie tried hard not to laugh as she waddled down the hall. "Now you're the potty police?"

"Be careful, or you might lose a babysitter," Leigh Ann called out.

Joie waved her off. "I don't believe that for a minute. We both know you'll never be able to stay away from this baby."

By six o'clock, Karyn had arrived and was busy making a coconut cake. Leigh Ann had not only assembled a salad, but had baked homemade biscuits and stirred up some honey butter.

"What time did Dad say he'd be back?" Karyn asked as she sprinkled white coconut flakes across her perfectly frosted cake.

"He didn't say," Joie admitted. "Only that he was heading up Gray's Peak to check on the sheep. Apparently, Sebastian spotted some wolves." She glanced at the wall clock. "That was hours ago."

Leigh Ann pulled a bottle of salad dressing from the refrigerator, checked the expiration date. "Then he should be here soon."

Two hours later, their father had failed to return.

"I'm worried," Leigh Ann admitted. "It's not like Dad to be gone this long."

Joie picked a piece of tomato from the salad and popped it in her mouth. "It's going to be getting dark soon, so he should be riding in to the ranch anytime now."

Karyn grabbed a bowl from the cupboard, and turned to Joie. "Well, looks like you're hungry. You need to eat something."

She wanted to argue, but her stomach had been growling. "Yeah, okay." She rubbed the top of her stomach. "Little Hudson knows it's past dinner time and he's been reminding me for over a half hour."

Karyn raised on her toes and peered out the kitchen window. She scowled. "Sebastian's back. And he's leading Dad's horse."

"What do you mean, he's leading Dad's horse?" Leigh Ann demanded.

Karyn headed for the front door. "Just what I said."

Joie and Leigh Ann scrambled to follow. Outside, they raced to meet up with Sebastian.

"Sebastian? Where's Dad?" Joie hollered, while trying to keep up with her sisters.

Sebastian wiped his brow with his arm. "I—I don't know. It was getting late, so I headed this way and came upon Edwin's horse, but no sign of him anywhere. I was hoping your dad might be here."

His response sent Joie's alarm meter rocketing. Her gut clenched with instant worry. "Something's wrong. He's still up there." Without a moment's thought, she headed for the barn.

"Whoa! Where do you think you're heading?" Leigh Ann challenged, grabbing her arm and pulling her back. "Surely you don't think you can get on a horse in your condition?"

"I'm not staying here! We have to find him."

Karyn chewed at her lip. "I'll go."

Leigh Ann nodded. "We'll both go. Sebastian, is there gas in the four-wheeler?"

He tossed his horse reins to Karyn. "I'll go make sure." He raced off to one of the out buildings.

Karyn ripped her phone out of her pocket. "I'll call Grayson." She glanced at the sky. "If he hurries, he can still catch enough daylight to go up in the plane."

Leigh Ann followed suit, quickly dialing a number on her phone. "I'll call Mark," she said, her face furrowed with worry. "Dad could be anywhere up there."

Joie turned for the house. "I'll notify Rory Sparks and get a search team together." She would also alert Clint, knowing he'd drop everything and join in the hunt for her dad.

By nightfall, their efforts had not been successful. The shadows of darkness creeping over the mountain tops served to remind each of them that danger lurked—bears, cougars and yes, wolves—were known to roam the surrounding high-mountain terrain.

Her emotions rising to the surface quicker since she'd become pregnant, Joie fought against panic.

She had to do something. She couldn't just leave her dad up there with no food or water. June nights could still get cold in the higher elevations of the snow-capped peaks. She tried to remember if he'd even worn a coat when he rode out in the morning.

It dawned on her then that his scabbard had been empty, meaning there was a good possibility her dad had his rifle with him, where-ever he was. At least that was some comfort.

Of course, there was no assurance of that fact.

A myriad of possibilities marched through her mind, an infantry ready to take aim and kill any peace. A heart attack? A fall?

She remembered an article she'd read last year about a search party in Canada who had discovered the partially consumed body of a twenty-two-year-old in the woods of northern Saskatchewan. The young man had gone out for a walk and had a fatal encounter with a pack of wolves.

She wasn't about to allow that to happen to her father.

While the others were discussing the strategies they would employ at dawn, she slipped away in the darkness undetected. No doubt, she'd catch hell from all of them, and especially her sisters, for pulling this stunt. She'd take that risk. If she disclosed her intentions, they'd stop her. That was not an option.

Besides, she'd worked at the stables for a living before returning to the practice of law. Her riding skill was above the average person. There was no reason to think she was putting her baby at risk, especially since she was weeks away from delivering.

In the barn, she saddled one of her dad's mares and led her to a feeding trough. Joie lumbered onto an upside-down bucket and carefully climbed up into the trough, holding the reins with one hand and the saddle horn with the other. "Easy girl," she said in a calming sing-song voice.

Even so, when she tried to slip her foot into the stirrup from that elevation, the horse backed away.

This was not going to be as easy as she'd first considered.

The effort took three more tries before she successfully hoisted herself and her considerable additional weight into the saddle. "Atta, girl." She rubbed the horse's mane before gently digging her heels in and urging the horse to the open door and into the darkness.

As far as she could tell, no one had noticed she was gone.

Thankfully, Joie knew every ditch, every fence line by heart. She'd ridden this ranch and every inch was committed to memory. She could ride across the acreage with her eyes closed, which tonight, was far too close to reality.

When she'd ridden enough distance to be out of sight, she lit the lantern she'd tied to the saddle horn and headed in the direction of the gulch leading to Gray's Peak, fingering the pistol she'd brought along for safety.

In the distance, a wolf's howl echoed in the darkness.

26

Morning, if you could even call this god-awful hour morning, arrived with the knowledge that Edwin was still up on the mountain. Worse, Joie was nowhere to be found.

Leigh Ann looked out the kitchen window at the thin line of pink threading across the horizon. She pounded her fist on the countertop. "I can't believe she was stupid enough to pull this. Does she realize she's carrying a baby, or does she just think someone pushed an inanimate basketball inside her belly?" She pounded a second time. "I could just throttle her!"

Karyn paced. There were not many occasions where she wholeheartedly agreed with her older sister's assessment of their youngest sister. But this time, she was fully on board with the criticism being levied against Joie's choices.

Not only that, she was worried sick.

Her father had spent the night on the mountain. The only reason he hadn't returned with his horse was the likelihood he was hurt up there somewhere. Despite her father's innate ability to track—he was like a human GPS when in the hills—even he could have gotten turned around up there and be lost.

Add to that scenario the fact Joie was up there as well in her condition—her mind could barely carry the weight of all the horrible possibilities.

Clint appeared in the doorway. No matter what they'd said to convince him to make use of the spare bedroom last night, he'd slept in his pickup, barely accepting the offer of a blanket. He swept his fingers through his already tousled hair, his face lined with concern. "I'm heading up," he announced. "I want to get a good start."

"It's still dark," Leigh Ann argued.

He nodded. "I'll be all right. Besides, I want to be in a position to start a serious search the minute it gets light enough." He tucked a topographical map in his back jean's pocket.

Karyn and Leigh Ann didn't argue. Grateful for his help, Karyn moved and gave him a tight hug. "Thank you," she whispered.

A half hour hadn't passed when Grayson also showed up. "Karyn, you want to come with me or stay? It'll be light enough very soon for me to get in the air."

She grabbed her jacket. "I'll come." She turned to Leigh Ann. "You okay here?"

Her sister nodded. "Yes, go. Be sure and radio in."

"I'll be in constant contact with the tower and they will alert you if we see anything," he told her.

Minutes later, Colby and Nicole arrived. "We brought breakfast," Colby said, holding up a bag from Bistro on Fourth.

Nicole slipped off her hand-knit cape, took the sack from his hand and moved for the counter. "Nash opened up early and whipped up the meal especially for you. Spinach and dried tomato frittatas made with eggs from cage-free chickens. Really healthy. Said to tell you everyone is in his prayers."

Leigh Ann moved to the cupboard, took out some plates. "That was nice of him—and you," she added, begrudgingly.

Despite the tantalizing smell of the food, she was far too

worried to have an appetite. On top of Mark's financial debacle, she now was sick with worry over the possibility that two of the people most dear to her heart were likely in danger up on that mountain. She wanted to believe everything would turn out fine, but her faith often waivered when it came to her loved ones' safety.

"I can't just sit here." Leigh Ann placed the plates on the counter and moved for the coat closet. "I'm going to help look."

Colby slid off the barstool. "I'm going with you, Mom."

Nicole glanced down at the frittata with a forlorn look on her face. She sighed. "Wait for me."

KARYN SAT NEXT to Grayson in his Cessna 206, peering out the window as a nearby plane touched down on the adjacent runway and trundled past them.

"Ready?" Grayson silently mouthed against the noise of the engine.

She nodded. The sooner they got up in the air, the faster they could scour the mountain for her father and Joie.

Grayson gave her an encouraging smile. He revved up, and announced their flight plan over the radio. After receiving the go-ahead, he worked the pedals to bring them into position on the runway. The blades on the propeller spun so fast they disappeared.

Minutes later they raced down the runway, speeding forward until they lifted off. The ground floated away beneath them.

Karyn adjusted her headphones.

"Don't worry. We'll find them," Grayson assured her. For extra measure, he reached and squeezed her hand.

On any other occasion, she'd lean back and relax—enjoy the whole *Out of Africa* experience as the plane tilted severely to the right, then righted and drifted over the green landscape. Not today. Her father and Joie could be in danger and every muscle in her body remained taut and on high-alert.

In minutes, they were positioned at the entry of the canyon leading up Gray's Peak. Karyn peered out her window at the landscape below. Everything looked so different from this altitude. The tops of the pine trees, the croppings of quaking aspens, the outlines of the tiny mountain lakes that dotted the canyon, still full from the snow runoff.

Grayson descended as low as he could, throttled the engine back to give them every advantage as their eyes combed the area below.

They spotted a doe and two fawns, bravely walking into a clearing. The sound of the engine caused all three deer to freeze. Seconds later, the doe pivoted on her back legs and darted back into the trees, her babies chasing close on her heels.

Up ahead, patches of blue camas and red Indian paintbrush blooms dotted the landscape. The sky was now bright blue.

Grayson pointed ahead. "See those clouds?"

"Uh-huh." She nodded.

He explained that clouds actually sit on columns of rising air. "I'm fascinated with weather patterns, how they change and what causes extremes."

Typically, she'd have engaged in the conversation. One of the things she loved about Grayson was his keen ability to see extraordinary details connected to ordinary things. He often had a perspective others lacked. He was interesting.

Not today. Looking for her dad and Joie captured her full attention.

Her silence failed to deter Grayson. "There's a favorite scripture of mine, '*The wind blows where ever it pleases. You hear its sound, but you cannot tell where it comes from, or where it is going.*'" He looked over at her. "Life is like that, I think. When unexpected storms blow in, I try to remember there's someone much bigger than me directing the flow."

She gave him a weak smile. Another thing she loved about him. He always seemed to find a way to look at every situation in a positive light. Even this.

Suddenly, Grayson's face brightened. He pointed. "Look— over there!"

Her heart lurched as she strained her neck to see what he had spotted. The plane dipped, giving her a better view.

That's when she saw it—a sight that thrilled her heart.

"Dad! It's Daddy!" Elation like nothing she'd known filled her soul. Her father was walking, making his way across a rock crop- ping. He was safe!

He saw them, waved wildly.

Grayson dipped the wings back and forth in an aviation wave of his own.

Karyn clapped her hands with excitement. "Oh my goodness. He's okay."

Grayson grabbed the radio and called their location into the tower. While transmission was spotty, he successfully got word to authorities that her dad was fine and where he could be found.

Suddenly, Karyn thought the sky was more blue, the ground colors more vibrant. Then she remembered they still had Joie to find and everything again dulled.

27

Torn pieces of sunlight whispered through giant ponderosa pines as Joie led her horse up a path of pine needles and twigs, picking her way through a large rock cropping lined with rotting logs. The elevation forced her to go slow. In fact, she'd had to stop every few feet to catch her breath.

Riding up here had been an unfortunate decision. She'd only made it to the first crest before jostling in the saddle became far too uncomfortable. She'd have made quite a spectacle maneuvering into a position that would allow her to slide from the saddle, if anyone had been around to watch.

The only thing she could think about now was how she'd neglected to bring any food with her, except for the cellophane bag of trail mix in her shirt pocket. A stupid move, for sure—but then, desperate measures had not allowed many options.

She stopped, leaned over and inhaled deeply, trying to catch her breath. At this rate, she'd never find her father.

Finally, she raised up. An eagle perched at the top of a pine tree watched her every move, majestic, yet wary.

"What are you looking at?" she said, unable to appreciate the grandeur of her surroundings, or the wildlife.

A tiny pain sliced across her back, telling her she'd jostled in that saddle much longer than she should have. Her hand instinctively went there and she massaged the spot, hoping to make it several more yards up the steep incline before she was forced to sit and rest.

All night and she hadn't seen a sign of her dad, even calling out. She'd considered shooting into the air, but knew the more likely outcome of that would be to alert anyone looking to find her. If they did, they'd force her to return home—she'd be back at square one. Her father would remain lost, and in danger.

Determined, Joie pushed herself to climb higher. She'd been up on this mountain several times with her dad, but the terrain was rugged and changed with every heavy winter. Avalanches often rerouted stands of timber and formed new crests and canyons.

The grassy bowls nestled at elevations up to ninety-five hundred feet provided lush feed and fresh, mountain water—a perfect place for sheep to graze.

Joie stumbled over something in the trail, an unyielding stone. Her leg wobbled and she fought to right herself.

That's when she spotted it—a small ring of rocks filled with blackened embers. Her heart skipped a beat as she scrambled toward her find.

As she drew closer, she could see the center of the makeshift fire pit was still wet. It appeared water had doused flames only hours before, if that. She surveyed the surrounding area and spotted a place under nearby pine tree where someone had gathered tiny pinecones and laid a thick layer of dry needles and earthy moss on top.

A bed!

Her dad had no doubt been here. Maybe even minutes before.

That meant one thing . . . her dad was okay. While it remained a mystery as to how he got separated from his horse, her dad was mobile. She glanced around. There was no evidence he'd been injured, no blood.

In all likelihood, he was making his way back down the mountain now. No doubt she'd simply missed him, their paths had crossed, which didn't matter really. What mattered was that he was safe.

Elated, Joie turned to the horse. "Well, girl—guess it's time to head home."

Suddenly, another pain hit. This time the pain was not sharp but an intense ache that started in her back and traveled forward to her abdomen. It felt like someone was taking a rolling pin to her gut.

Worry sprouted, causing tiny beads of sweat to break out on her brow as she considered the possibility of what these recurring pains might mean.

"No, it can't be—I'm still weeks from my delivery date. The books all warned about Braxton Hicks contractions, cramping that mimicked labor. Still, it was a good idea for her to get going.

She grabbed the reins and took only a few steps before another tiny pain tore across her stomach. She experienced a strong twinge between her legs followed by what felt like leaking.

Joie looked down and gasped.

I'm wet—it's all wet.

Her mind raced to find a reason why her pants were soaked, hoping beyond hope it didn't mean what she couldn't deny. Her water had just broke.

Now, she was scared.

Her eyes darted around, to the pines and sagebrush, the rock face in the distance, the blue sky overhead. She was alone and on the side of a mountain—and in labor.

LEIGH ANN NUDGED her horse up the tiny path no wider than a

good-sized cookie sheet. "I could just pop her head off for pulling this trick!" she grumbled, as she routed her horse around a clump of skunk cabbage. "Joie," she called out into the crisp morning air. "Did you hear me? I'm going to hunt you down like a Kate Spade purse, and when I find you—well, it ain't gonna be pretty."

Truth was, when she found her very pregnant little sister, she was going to finally be able to release the breath she'd been holding. She'd simply die if anything happened to her up here—or to her soon-to-arrive baby nephew.

Colby pointed up the mountain to a spot in a clearing of trees. "Look at that! I think it's Grandpa."

Leigh Ann whipped her attention to the position on the mountain side. A speck-of-a-man in the distance slowly descended going in and out of view as he criss-crossed the terrain. "Yes! It's him!" she cried. Her heart immediately filled with gratitude. She was so thankful to see her father safe and sound. She squinted against the sun. "He's walking. That's a good sign. Looks like he's okay."

"Dad," she called out as loud as she could and joined the others wildly waving their arms. Clint unholstered his Ruger pistol from its holster, aimed it in the direction of the cloudless blue sky and fired. "That'll alert him we're down here," he said.

Within only a few seconds, another shot rang out—this time from her father's rifle, signaling he'd heard.

When they finally met up, Leigh Ann climbed down from the saddle and threw the reins to her son. She rushed to her father's side. "Dad! What happened? We were so worried. Are you okay? You don't look great." She patted down his arms before moving to his chest. "Any broken bones?"

Her dad gave her a weak smile. "I'm fine Doc Blackburn. Just tired—and hungry."

She slapped at his chest. "This is no time to tease. I'm serious —are you all right?"

He nodded. "I'm fine, honey."

Colby joined them, tucked his hand in the crook of his grandfather's arm. "What happened, Grandpa? Did you get bucked off?"

"We were worried sick when your horse showed up with an empty saddle," Leigh Ann added.

Her dad ran his hand through his hair. "No, no accidents or anything. My horse got spooked when we'd stopped for a drink. She pulled the reins clean out of my hands and took off." His eyes grew serious. "Damn wolves, no doubt."

Leigh Ann looped her arm through his other arm. "Well, you look exhausted. We need to get you home." She remembered then that Joie was still on the mountain. "You—uh. You haven't seen Joie, have you?"

Her dad's head popped up. "Joie? No, why?"

Clint dismounted. "She went looking for you."

"Last night," Leigh Ann clarified. "A stupid move."

Her dad grew immediately worried. "We need to find her." He moved for Colby's horse, but Leigh Ann caught his arm.

"No, sir!" she said. "You need to get home and rest, get something in your stomach."

Clint agreed. "Don't worry, Edwin. I'll find her."

"Joie shouldn't be on a horse at this stage in her pregnancy, but she's a good rider. Guess there's no reason to borrow trouble." He rubbed the back of his neck. "Grayson's plane flew over a few minutes ago. He spotted me. Hopefully, he'll locate Joie too." He turned to Clint. "Son, I appreciate that you're willing to continue the ground search. I'm sure she's fine, but I'll feel better when I know she's not alone up here on this mountain. Especially with wolves roaming around. That, and I noticed some bear tracks up there over the ridge."

Nicole nudged her horse forward. "I'll go with Clint."

"Me too," Colby quickly added.

Leigh Ann rolled up her shirtsleeves. "I don't think that's a good idea," she told her son. "I need you to help me get your grandfather off this mountain."

"I'm fine, Leigh Ann," her father argued. "Let the boy go."

"Daddy, you've walked miles, slept on the hard ground all night and haven't eaten since early yesterday. I think that warrants a little special attention."

Colby nodded. "No, Mom's right. It doesn't take three of us to find and alert Aunt Joie we've found Grandpa. I'll head back with Mom and Grandpa. When we get down to the ranch, I can let everyone know that Grandpa is home and all right." He turned to his wife. "You okay with that?"

Nicole nodded. "Sure."

Edwin's face grew slightly sheepish. "So, guess the whole town is in an uproar, huh?"

Colby lifted the rifle from his grandpa's weathered hands and slung the strap across his own shoulder. "That's an understatement."

Leigh Ann patted her dad's back. "Okay, Little Boy Lost, let's get you home."

28

J oie lowered herself onto the makeshift bed her dad had made on the ground. There was no mistaking she was in labor. After her water broke, the pains immediately increased in strength and were coming more quickly, meaning she had no time to get off this mountain.

She refused to panic. Even so, she couldn't help wishing she'd taken time out of her busy law practice to attend birthing classes. Earlier, she'd downloaded some books to her phone. That didn't do her a lot of good up here where there was no cell service.

Weren't you supposed to breathe or something? That, and in movies they often called for boiling water, which again, didn't do her any good. It wasn't like she had a set of Calphalon cookware waiting for her on the next rock.

Another pain formed at her lower back and travelled forward to her concrete-hard belly.

Oh, God. Help me . . . this hurts.

Okay, yeah. She wasn't above calling on the sovereign maker of the universe. She needed his support. She deserved to be chastised, mentally and otherwise. Once again, her impulsive decisions had landed her in hot water. This time she'd put little Hudson at risk.

She took a deep breath. That kind of thinking was not help-ful. Not right now. Instead, she needed to focus all her energy on the task before her. She could do this.

Hoo-hoo-hee. Hoo-hoo-hee.

Joie squeezed her eyes tightly shut and mimicked the breathing she'd seen in the movies, surprised the exercise really did help.

When the pain subsided, she slowly opened her eyes and stared at the empty sky. No matter how brave she wanted to be, a lone tear escaped and ran down her face landing in her hair.

Her heart thudded against her chest. She didn't want to do this—especially not alone. Unfortunately, she had no choice.

It dawned on her then that she might want to consider disrobing. She lifted into an upright position, which actually felt much better. Her hands went to the buttons on her maternity jeans.

Suddenly, a chill ran up her spine. She wasn't alone—she could feel it.

Her eyes darted all around, taking in the surrounding area—the pines, boulders and sagebrush. A rustle from behind moved her to whip her head around. She squinted against the sun. That's when she saw what she'd earlier felt—several sets of eyes watching her from within the deep shadows of a thick stand of aspens and brush.

Wolves.

~

AGAINST THE DRONE of the engine, Grayson's voice crackled through Karyn's earphones. "Babe, we've been searching for hours. I think we should return to the airport and gas up."

She could hardly argue. "Yeah, okay," she said into her

headset microphone, wishing they could make at least one more sweep up the main canyon leading to the summit of Gray's Peak. Joie could be anywhere, of course. But likely, she'd taken the path leading to the bands of sheep grazing on the western slope—the same path her dad had likely followed.

Admittedly, she was anxious to check on her dad. He appeared uninjured, but he was a man in his senior years who had spent the night alone on the mountain. "Yeah, let's get back."

Grayson glanced at her, a look that told her he understood how torn she felt. He reached and grasped her hand. "We'll fuel up and head right back up if you want."

She nodded without taking her eyes off the landscape below, reminding herself that few individuals could ride a horse better than Joie. Her younger sister knew this terrain almost as well as their dad. That didn't mean she hadn't foolishly embarked on this ill-advised venture. Joie was pregnant, which added a layer of risk Karyn hated to even contemplate.

Eventually, Joie would likely make her way home just fine once she realized her dad had been found. The sooner they were *both* safely back at the ranch, the sooner Karyn could quit worrying about her.

"Babe, you okay?" Grayson asked through her headset.

She nodded. "Yeah, I'm fine."

Grayson banked the plane and pointed the plane in the direction of town before leveling out. They soared above the earth several thousand feet, the engine humming. Karyn sat in the cockpit quietly, aware Grayson watched her.

She tucked a strand of hair behind her ear. "What?"

He reached and lightly fingered her cheek, an unexpected move that sent a warmth through her, a comfort that diminished the tense concern she'd been carrying over the past hours. As difficult as seeing that empty saddle on Dad's horse was, of learning Joie had stolen off after him in the middle of the night— she couldn't imagine facing any of this alone. Truth was, Grayson had been right by her side, providing his unwavering support in both practical and emotional means.

She reached and caught his fingers, pulled them to her mouth and lightly kissed them. "Thank you," she said. "I mean it. This—"

"Shhh—," he interrupted. "Do you have any idea how much you mean to me? How beautiful you are?"

She felt heat rise in her face as her hand brushed off the comment.

"No, I mean it. I know I don't often say things—the things that are on my heart. But I've been thinking a lot about you lately. And us."

Karyn noted a flicker in his eyes. Nerves, perhaps?

"Can you hear me all right?" he asked. He lowered his fingers, trailed them down her skin, ran them over her collarbone.

She nodded, struggling to find her voice against his touch. "Yeah. I can hear you fine."

"Good. Because what I've got to say is important." He paused, returned his gaze to the instruments on the flight deck as if he couldn't say anything more while looking at her directly. "It's no fun having a clothes closet all to myself. I detest eating alone while looking at my phone, wondering if I'll interrupt something if I call you. I hate going to bed alone, waking alone—seeing only one toothbrush in the holder by the sink."

She swallowed, nodded. "Yes, I know what you mean."

"The thing is, we're going to grow into a couple of old, lonely people if we don't do something about that."

She looked at him, confused. What was he saying?

"Karyn, I love you. I think you know that." His gaze caught her own, held her captive. "Today's events only serve to remind that life can turn on a dime. It's critical that we say the important things. And I love you. More than that—I want to take our relationship to the next level."

"The next level?"

"Yes, I—I want more."

Even through the headset, she could hear the passion in his voice, the urgency. "What do you mean by more?"

"I don't want you to misunderstand and think I'm rushing things. I know we've only known each other a year, but I know what I want long-term. I want you." He grinned at her. "I want to come home at night and see you curled up on the sofa with one of those books you love reading. I want to grab a ball and a bat and head out in the back yard to practice hitting grounders with my kid. Or, have a tea party in the playhouse I built especially for my little girl. I want it all—the whole corny Norman Rockwall family portrait—especially the parenting thing." He hurried to add, "When it's time, I'll do this right—I'll officially propose and we'll make our plans. Until then, I need to know you want the same, that at least we're both heading in the same direction."

He grabbed her hand, held it tightly against his chest. "So, are we—heading in the same direction?"

Grayson couldn't have surprised her more if he suddenly grew an extra set of ears. She'd suspected he had serious feelings for her, but thought those emotions would develop and play out over time. Still, she'd be lying to say she hadn't thought of the future too. Truth was, she couldn't imagine that future without Grayson.

Karyn lifted her head, studied the horizon out the front of the plane, the bright blue sky. "I—I love you too, Grayson." She turned to see his reaction.

His face burst with pleasure. "And?"

"And, I want all that too." She took a deep breath. "With you."

He laughed then, reached for her. "I swear, if I could get this plane on the ground any sooner, I would. Because I'd like to—"

She slapped playfully at his arm. "You sure enjoy putting a girl at a disadvantage." She wiped at a tear forming.

"Are you crying?"

"Happy tears," she reported. "These are happy tears."

29

J oie froze at the sight of those eyes staring at her from the shadows. She'd never been prone to fear, but pure terror raced through her veins like boiling water, melting any remaining resolve.

A myriad of possibilities flashed in her mind, none of them good.

Her eyes darted to the gun she'd brought for safety, now leaned up against a rock several yards away. She swept her hand across her forehead to get rid of the sweat that had formed. Her mouth was dry and her entire body trembled.

Then another pain hit—hard.

Oh God, help me!

Joie bit the inside of her cheek, tried to blow through the pain but nothing worked. Worse, she grew vaguely aware of a rustling in the trees. They were moving—the wolves.

She swallowed and leaned forward, trying to assuage the fire ripping through her abdomen. It felt like she was breaking in half.

Her eyes filled with tears.

I can't do this. I—I can't.

Suddenly, she heard a low growl. A wolf stepped into her line of vision. One step. Freeze. Another. Freeze.

The wolf's shoulders hunched. The wild canine lowered its head and stared at her. From behind, three more wolves cleared the trees and joined in the showdown.

Hardly a contest—she knew who would be the victor in this match. And it would not be her, or her tiny Hudson.

He'd depended on her to bring him safely into this world. Once again, she'd let down a person she loved. This time her thoughtless impulses would kill her, and her baby.

She stifled a sob, while her mind raced to—

Joie grabbed a rock and lobbed it in the direction of her tormentors, giving the toss every bit of strength she could possibly muster.

Nothing.

"Leave me alone!" she screamed, at the top of her lungs. "Go away!"

Her voice echoed in the stifling air, weighted with the fact she was up here all alone, with no one to come to her aide.

She couldn't help it, she started to whimper as she felt another pain take hold.

Joie lifted her knees and grabbed them, leaned forward and tried to imagine herself somewhere else. But all she could conjure when she briefly closed her lids were those eyes—yellow and menacing.

Another growl.

Her eyes flew open to a nightmare. Comprehension dawned. They were circling her, like prey.

If she was going to have any chance at all, she needed that gun.

Despite the pain now subsiding, she maneuvered onto her hands and knees. She froze, waited.

The wolves watched, but did not advance.

Joie wouldn't kid herself, knew they could pounce and take

her down in an instant. It was only a matter of when. How long before their predatory instincts would kick in and they would attack? Wolves were not aggressors typically, but nature had designed them to hunt and kill for food and protection. Right now, she was vulnerable to both issues.

She drew a breath, ragged with fear.

Only a few yards separated her from the gun. She moved in that direction, which instantly proved to be a mistake.

As if on some unseen signal, the wolves collectively closed in —so close she thought she could smell their breath.

One step, two—now three.

She screamed.

A shot rang out, then another.

Instantly, the wolves froze, then turned and ran off in all directions.

Joie's head whipped around to the area where the shot had come from. Clint stepped into view from behind a large cropping of rock followed by Nicole. His hand rested at his side, holding a pistol.

Her head dropped with immediate relief. She folded onto the ground and openly wept.

Clint rushed to her side, his face peppered with stubble and dark circles under his eyes. "You okay? Joie, look at me. Are you all right?"

She raised her head miserably. "Do I look all right?" she managed.

Before she had a chance to say anything more, a contraction formed and immediately pulled her into another cycle of pain. She winced and grabbed for his hand, squeezed.

"Everything's going to be okay. I'm here." He scooped her up and returned her to the make-shift bed of pine needles, where Colby's young wife had spread her jacket as further cushion against the hard ground.

Nicole jumped into action. She quickly removed Joie's pants

and draped her the best she could with Clint's jacket. "Joie, look at me. Right here. Look at me." She positioned herself, placing both her hands on Joie's upright knees. "I know how to help you. You can trust me. Now, breathe through the contractions." She mimicked how, pacing her own breaths so Joie could follow the rhythm.

Joie tried, but the last minutes had simply been too much. "I —I can't," she sobbed.

"Yes, you can," her nephew's wife assured her. She turned to Clint. "Take off your t-shirt. We're going to need something to wrap this baby in."

He nodded and complied, unbuttoned his shirt and slid his shirt off over his head. At another time, Joie might have noticed his broad shoulders, his bear tattoo. But, not now. All she could think about was the way the contractions ripped through her gut.

"Don't push," Nicole warned. "Not yet."

The pain mounted, taking Joie to a higher level of anguish. "I —I don't want to go through with this. I want out. I can't be a— I'm not able to deliver a baby. Not here—not now. It hurts too much." She wailed. "And, I'm all alone."

Clint squeezed her hand, brushed the damp hair from her sweat-glazed forehead. "You are not alone, Joie. We're here—I'm here. You have me." He bolstered her with an encouraging smile, a look filled with promise. "I'm not going to leave you. We'll get this done—together."

30

K aryn gazed out the plane window, elated at Grayson's pronouncement that he wanted to move their relationship to the next level. The notion wasn't lost on her that there was a time after losing Dean when she didn't believe any of this was possible—wondered if that kind of love ever happened twice in a lifetime.

Despite the turn her life had taken two years ago, she wanted the happy ending—all of it, the house with the white picket fence, the adoring husband and precious little children she'd tuck in at night.

Dean's accident had dashed that dream. Fortunately, life had a way of resurrecting the heart's deepest desires—of restoring hope. What could she say? She believed in love—and as it now appeared, in second chances.

As they approached Friedman Airport, Grayson called in their coordinates in that official pilot's voice, which was a little deeper than his regular one, and then he maneuvered into the flight pattern for landing.

He pulled around to the left, then turned to run along the length of the runway before the plane descended to the ground.

Karyn felt more than saw the ground getting closer. Then a funny thing happened. As they were nearing the runway, the wings did a little waggle—dipping sideways a little and then levelling back up. It was over in a second, but Karyn's heart fluttered with a brief moment of fear, never the less.

She looked over at Grayson, her finger nails biting into the flesh of her palm. "What was that?"

"The wind shifted," he reported, his face stone still. Seeing the worry on her face, he quickly added, "We're okay. Just a little crosswind, that's all." As if to reassure her, he took his hand from the dials and squeezed her hand. "Don't worry. We're safe."

A breath of relief escaped her lungs. Of course they were safe. She was silly to worry otherwise. Grayson was piloting the situation. He wouldn't let anything bad happen.

Within minutes, the tires touched down on the runway, coming in straight and steady despite the momentary scare. When the plane came to a stop, Grayson shut down the engine. After climbing out, he handed off the keys to an attendant with instructions to gas up, then he moved to help Karyn out of the plane. "You okay?"

She folded her hands in his. "I'm fine, as long as I'm with you."

She followed him inside the terminal. "I'll meet you at the ticket counter," he told her before heading off in the direction of the men's room.

Karyn nodded and made her way through the modest terminal. She glanced sidelong out the glass panels of the automatic entrance trying to remember where she'd parked her car—her hands fishing her phone from her purse. She needed to make a quick call to Leigh Ann to report in.

Her sister picked up on the first ring. "He's here—safe and sound."

Karyn listened to the details and let out a breath. "That's good news. What about Joie?"

"Clint and Nicole are up there. They've no doubt found her by now. I expect to see them riding in any minute."

Karyn nodded. "Good, well—let me know. Grayson is having the plane gassed and we'll head back up if you don't hear from her in the meantime."

A man walked past, dragging a duffel on wheels. They exchanged courteous smiles.

"And, Leigh Ann?"

"Yeah?"

"Give Daddy a kiss and tell him I love him."

Leigh Ann promised she would, and they hung up.

Karyn looked around the small terminal. She'd stopped short of telling Leigh Ann about the conversation she'd had with Grayson. That kind of news deserved to be delivered in person. They would celebrate, of course. The three of them—Leigh Ann and Joie would both be delighted for her.

Grayson exited the men's restroom and stopped at a vending machine where he shoved a bill through a slot and pressed a button. A pack of gum dropped and he bent to retrieve it.

"They found Dad and he's home, safe and sound. Clint and Nicole are still looking for Joie."

"So, you want to head back up?"

Karyn quickly pondered the options before committing to the choice that made the most sense. "Yes, but let's wait a half hour. Leigh Ann seemed convinced they would all show up at the ranch anytime now."

"Sure, okay—but if you change your mind, just let me know." He leaned and kissed the top of her head, then tilted her face to his and grazed her lips. "Maybe we should catch a quick bite of breakfast—or, whatever." His smile turned into a grin. "Celebrate our decision alone—at my house."

"Maybe after we drive out to the ranch?"

He nodded. "Of course. But later—definitely later." He grinned and coiled his arm around her shoulder. Together, they headed through the terminal, past the chandelier made of elk horns and toward the parking lot.

This time it was her turn to smile. An unfamiliar giddiness enveloped her. How could one woman possibly grow to be this fortunate?

"Grayson?"

They both turned to face a woman heading toward them, a young toddler in her arms.

The woman looked vaguely familiar. Her eyes were so blue they seemed almost scooped from the sea—her skin pale against a dramatic short pixie bob, dark in the back and graduating to a platinum blonde front. She wore white jeans, a turquoise silk shirt, and open-toed short booties, with turquoise jewelry adorning her neck and wrists. Very chic, and intense style.

The little boy in her arms studied them, his thumb stuck securely in his mouth.

Grayson's arm dropped from around her shoulder.

Karyn glanced his way to find his expression had turned to stone—the first sign her life was about to go seriously off track a second time.

31

Despite her exhaustion, Joie gazed down at the face of her newborn infant with pure infatuation. How could something so perfect come from someone so flawed? Did God even know what he was doing when he chose her to be little Hudson's mommy?

The minute Nicole placed that tiny boy in her waiting arms, her entire world tilted. It was as if someone waved a magic wand in the air, and Cinderella traded in her torn and tattered wardrobe for an elegant ball dress.

She was a mother.

Joie leaned back into the padded stretcher, more content than she'd been in some time. Nothing—not even practicing law—felt like this.

The EMT held an intercom mic to his mouth as they pulled up to the hospital, "We're bringing in our out-of-hospital birth, near-term, baby weighing in at six pounds two ounces. Apgar score is nine. Mom's BP is one-thirty over eighty. Baby and Mom both seem to be doing fine."

The intercom crackled. "ETA?"

"We're arriving now," the EMT reported. The ambulance lurched to a stop and the doors flung open.

"Okay, young lady. Let's get you inside," a nurse said as they pulled the gurney from the vehicle.

Leigh Ann rushed forward, immediately appeared at her side, her face still flushed from the argument she'd gotten into with the EMTs when they refused to allow her to ride in the ambulance with them, even after she threatened to unleash demons they did not want to meet.

Her sister gazed at the little bundle in her arms with reverence. "Oh, Joie!" She looked down at the infant in her arms. "Oh, goodness. He's amazing."

She looked up at her oldest sister. "He is, isn't he?"

"Joie? Joie, we heard and couldn't get here fast enough." Miss Trudy lifted to her tippy-toes and waved from a nearby sidewalk.

"Congratulations, sweet thing!" Ruby added. "We were so worried when we heard the story. Thank goodness you're all right."

"Colby's wife delivered little Hudson," Leigh Ann volunteered proudly. "Right up there on the side of the mountain." She walked alongside the gurney. "Just like a pro."

The hospital doors slid open and they entered. Her dad, Colby and Sebastian all came racing over to meet her.

"Ah, honey—let's see our little man." Her dad lifted the blanket back and tears immediately formed. "He's a fine one. Look at that hair."

Sebastian grinned from ear-to-ear. "Congratulations, Miss Joie. That was sure something, having that baby up there on the mountain."

"It was a dangerous thing to do," Leigh Ann scolded. "Taking off on a horse at such a late stage in your pregnancy."

"But things turned out okay," Colby reminded.

"Yes, thanks to Nicole. I take back all those comments I made about all those birthing books she constantly pored over—well, almost everything." Leigh Ann glanced around. "Where is your wife, anyway?"

"She's with Clint. They were going to stop and pick up a quick bite to go—said they'd meet us here."

Joie swallowed emotion building in her throat. "I'm—well, very grateful—to them both." She reluctantly tore her eyes from little Hudson. "Seriously, I hate to consider what might have happened had Clint and Nicole not shown up when they did."

The nurse smiled at the small crowd. "Well, we'd best get this little lady and baby over to the unit so they can be checked."

"Well, there she is." Maddy Crane scurried toward them from the lobby, her arms loaded with a massive bouquet tethered with balloons. "Congratulations, sweet thing."

Joie grinned. "Thanks, Maddy."

Her partner neared the gurney wearing a lime green suit and matching heels. "Let me catch a peek at that darlin' baby." She leaned and pulled the blanket back. "Oh my goodness, isn't he something?"

Karyn bolted through the hospital doors. "Joie?" She rushed to her side, peered down at the bundle in her arms. "Oh my goodness, look at him! Hello, little Hudson. I'm your Aunt Karyn." She leaned and kissed Joie's cheek. "He's precious. I'm so happy for you."

Joie squeezed her sister's hand. "Thanks, Sis. I can't believe I'm a mother." She paused, looked into Karyn's face. "Are you okay? Is something wrong?"

Her sister took a step back, stared back with a blank look. "It's nothing, really. A little unexpected wind blew in is all."

Karyn hung toward the back as she followed the entourage down the hall. To steady her shaky mind, she focused on the portraits of the hospital's benefactors as she passed each framed wall hanging. Despite these efforts, images of that woman in the airport—Grayson's former wife—continued to barge into her thoughts.

Admittedly, in the past, she'd wondered about Robin Chandler occasionally—especially after her relationship with Grayson turned more serious. She'd imagined what his ex-wife might look like, if she was short or tall, if she was as pretty in person as the photograph Grayson had once shown her.

Karyn had never envisioned her looking like she'd just stepped off a movie set. Robin was one of those women who didn't have to try to look stunning, she simply was—even when she'd just climbed off a long flight from Alaska with a baby kid in tow.

And that little boy—

Karyn swallowed hard against the lump in her throat.

That was the rub—none of them had to say the words. One look and the situation had become apparent.

"Yes," Robin confirmed before Grayson even had to ask. "He's yours."

Grayson had a son.

Karyn's stomach knotted.

How could a woman have a baby and not alert the father? Even Joie knew withholding that kind of information was wrong. And, what did that mean—the fact that this little boy was Grayson's son? What did Robin want, exactly?

"What do you mean, he's mine?" Grayson rubbed at his jawline. "I—I don't understand."

Robin then landed another sucker punch. "I'm here because I made a horrible mistake. Grayson, I want you to be part of his life." Her eyes teared up, betraying her stoic stance. "I've made a huge mistake keeping him from you. I need you to forgive me—"

She tenderly swept a piece of damp hair off the little guy's forehead. "For his sake."

"What's his—" Grayson's voice was ragged with emotion. "His name—what's his name?"

Robin quickly glanced at Karyn, then back. "His name is Michael."

Grayson knotted his fist in front of his mouth, let out an emotion-filled cough. "My dad?"

Robin slowly nodded. "Yes—after your father."

Karyn felt something like fear come into her, sit down in her stomach. She swallowed, tried to breathe.

Her mind could barely wrap itself around any of this. Nor could she erase the look in Grayson's eyes as he gazed at that little boy.

Without any warning, this woman—this stranger—had delivered a sucker punch right to her gut.

She'd watched as Grayson reached and took the little boy from Robin's arms, the way he placed a kiss at the top of his head. Obviously, while shocked, he was in love with the idea of this little boy—his son.

Karyn stared at the two of them, perversely needing to imprint the scene on her brain.

She knew now, that was when the moment shifted. A key moment. One that spun her around and pointed her in a new direction.

Grayson Chandler—her Grayson—was a father.

She'd never planned on being a stepmother. Still, if she wanted to be Grayson's wife someday, and she did—she'd have to find a way past the fact she would not be the woman to make him a father, as heartbreaking as that was for her to grasp. One thing remained paramount—Grayson loved her. She loved him.

Karyn softened.

The most important thing now was to be supportive. Grayson

hadn't planned on his ex-wife showing up with a surprise announcement. No doubt, the news had rocked his world as well.

She drew a deep breath, knowing there was only one choice before her.

He'd need her, now more than ever.

32

J oie stared out the hospital window as darkness fell on what had been a mind-boggling and wonderful day.

Hudson's birthday.

While unexpected, Hudson's birth had gone well, considering she'd delivered on the side of a mountain. Even so, she'd no longer take any chances when it came to her baby boy. Which is why she'd so easily agreed to remain at St. Moritz overnight with him for observation. That, and she simply didn't have the emotional strength to argue otherwise with Leigh Ann.

A parade of visitors had shown up—Crusty and the boys, Rory Sparks, the sheriff, and several of her former co-workers at the stables. Candy Newberry Tubbs had gifted them with a well-funded college fund for little Hudson. Nash Billingsley named a new menu item after her son—the Hudson sandwich, teasing that it featured "mountains" of beef on a sourdough roll.

The Dilworth sisters hung around most of the afternoon, paying close attention to every detail of the story so they could adequately pass on the drama of little Hudson's birth.

"I'm so sorry I put everyone through all that worry," Joie said, apologizing to all of them.

Ruby waved her off with one of her movie quips. "No worries, dear. Love means never having to say you're sorry."

One-by-one, they each finally said their goodbyes and headed out, leaving a nurse as her only company.

"Honey, it's time for him to eat." She came over to the bed. "Let's raise this up and get you comfortable."

Joie looked over at her newborn son. He was wrapped up tightly in a soft blanket with blue and yellow boats all over it and he had a tiny blue cap on his head. She couldn't take her eyes off him.

The nurse lifted her baby boy out of the bassinette cart and gently laid him on her lap. "There you go. There's your mommy."

The nurse's words danced in her ears. She was a mommy.

Little Hudson's eyes peeked open, his tiny lips parted and he opened his little mouth and yawned big. A contented sigh escaped Joie's lungs.

The nurse puffed up the pillow behind her back and instructed her how to push the buzzer if she needed anything. Finished, she turned and headed for the hallway, pausing to smile at them before closing the door.

For the very first time—it was just the two of them.

Joie gazed down at his face. She gently removed the cap, bent down and kissed the top of his downy head. He smelled good— sweet, like baby powder. Her fingers slowly traced over each little eyebrow, then down his nose. She was looking at perfection wrapped in soft pink skin. His mouth opened and he began moving his head with his pink tongue extended like a little baby bird trying to catch a worm.

Joie smiled. So, this is what it felt like to be a mother.

She started to unwind the tight little blanket. "These nurses do a good job of this," she told her little son. "You're going to be in first grade before I get you unwrapped!"

She laid the blanket aside and lifted the little white t-shirt over his head. Then she unfastened the diaper and placed it next to the T-shirt and blanket.

There he lay—naked as the day he was born—because it *was* the day he was born! "Happy birthday, little one," Joie whispered.

Joie examined every inch of this little miracle, lightly touched the crusty remnant of the umbilical cord that had tethered him to her. She caressed his legs, the dents of the dimples at his knees. She again counted ten tiny fingers and toes before leaning down and bringing his little foot to her lips.

Oh, look! There were still traces of ink in the creases between his toes from the footprints they had taken.

People had told her it would be like this, but no words could begin to capture this feeling—the fierce love she had for the little human she'd carried inside her body. Without any doubt, she'd die trying to protect him, if necessary.

She couldn't help herself. She laughed out loud. Joy swept into the hole in her heart replacing years of feeling empty. It was nearly indescribable. She started to cry, giving her newborn son his first bath in her tears.

Suddenly, a yellow stream sprouted. She scrambled and quickly covered him with the diaper. "I guess I deserve that, after what I put us through," she told him, laughing.

A noise pulled her attention to the doorway. She looked up to find Clint leaning against the door jam, watching. "Hey," he said, his voice warm and steady.

Joie smiled. "How long have you been standing there?"

"Not long." He moved to join her at the bed. In his hand was a vase filled with tiny yellow rose buds.

"Those for me?"

He nodded and placed them on the bedside table beside several other bouquets. "Looks like a florist shop in here."

Joie grinned and pointed him to the guest chair. "Yeah, the little man and me have had a steady stream of visitors."

"No doubt. I almost didn't come. Thought you might want to be alone—"

She folded her hand over his. "I'm glad you're here."

He never said so, but she could tell he was pleased by her remark.

He leaned, placed his forearms on his knees. "You must be tired. That was something—up there on that mountain."

"I guess I should be—tired, I mean. But, I'm not. I'm still on a high like nothing I've felt." She cooed at little Hudson. He wrapped his tiny fingers around her own. "I can't stop looking at him."

After putting on a diaper, she snapped up the front of the onesie, then wrapped the matching blanket tightly and held the baby out in his direction. "Your turn. You want to hold him?"

His eyebrows lifted. "Me?"

Joie laughed. "Yes, you. Do you want to?" She gently placed little Hudson in his waiting hands. "Meet the man who saved us, Hudson." She looked into her friend's eyes, her own filled with gratitude. "I don't have the words to adequately thank you."

Clint flashed a grin, a wide smile that strangely made her heart beat a little faster.

"Hey there, little fella." In spite of his obvious discomfiture, he beamed. She doubted he held many day-old infants. Like her, he seemed fascinated with the tiny human in his hands. "I'm just glad everything turned out all right," he told her.

After a long silence, she narrowed her eyes and looked at him. "I don't have a lot of really close friends, Clint. Lots of buddies— drinking friends and such. But no close friends."

"What about your sisters?"

"They're family—they have to be in my corner." She paused, swallowed. "You're the best friend I've ever had. It seems I can always count on you," she muttered in a choked voice.

It was true. Despite their rocky start, Clint had become very special. Unlike Andrew, Clint was rock steady. He seemed to know her, not only the surface stuff, but the deep-down essence of who she was, how she thought and what she cared about most.

She paused, took everything in—the night in the stable when he'd shouldered up next to her and let her cry, the trip he'd made to Boise with no judgment, the surprise cradle he'd made, and the gentle, reassuring way he'd held her hand up on the mountain while telling her, *"You can do this, Joie."*

Suddenly, tears formed. She quickly wiped at her eyes, embarrassed. "Looks like the hormones have kicked in." For a brief moment, she dared to picture the future and couldn't imagine him not in it. "Seriously, you always seem to show up when I need you the most. Little Hudson wouldn't even be here if it weren't for you."

"I can't take the credit for delivering this little fella. Nicole took the stage on that one," he reminded her.

"Yes, but you saved our lives," she told him, her voice breaking. "I was so scared up there. I've seen firsthand what predators can do in these situations. All I could think was how I needed God to help me. Of course, I don't have a lot of clout with the Big Guy Upstairs. Not after all I've pulled."

"That's not how it works."

"Oh? And you know this for sure?"

He smiled and gently nodded. "I do."

She made her voice light. "Well, anyway—when you showed up, suddenly my life got a whole lot better."

Clint shrugged, grinned at her. "Rescuing horses, rescuing girls—all the same thing."

She laughed too, then poked him in the ribs. "Careful, or I'll cut off your babysitting privileges."

He looked down at Hudson. "Did you hear that, buddy? Your mommy is threatening to shut down our play dates."

In a single moment, anything bad and scary faded away. Everything was as it was meant to be—here with little Hudson and Clint.

Their eyes met. For one long moment, they stared.

Finally, Joie broke the silence. "I—I need to tell you—"

Clint nervously stumbled over her words with his own. "I guess I—"

They laughed—together.

Clint looked down at the baby. "He really is something, Joie."

"Clint?" What she was about to say came with considerable risk. She didn't want her motives misunderstood. Still, there was no denying what this guy with the bear tattoo and easy manner had come to mean to her.

"Yeah," he said, looking over at her.

"The baby—his name is Hudson Clint Abbott."

33

G rayson and Karyn walked silently down the sidewalk leading to Grayson's house, neither of them anxious to talk, at least not to each other. There had been a span of nearly two days before she'd finally heard from him—two grueling days of wondering what was going on.

She'd forced herself to pocket her phone numerous times after pulling it out to contact him. When his call finally came, her heart had nearly thudded right out of her chest the second she saw his name on her phone.

"Hello," she'd answered, valiantly trying to hide her irritation. It was not the time to lose her cool.

Grayson had been thrust into an impossible situation. Her reasonable self knew he needed space to sort all this out, even time to discuss the issues at hand with Robin privately. It wasn't every day you became a parent without any warning. Someone like Grayson couldn't simply brush off the fact he had son. He'd want to do the right thing.

"I'm sorry," were the first words out of his mouth. "I know I should've called earlier."

"That's okay," she assured him. "I knew you'd call when you could."

He took her to dinner at the Ram Restaurant, a poor choice in her estimation. Now, the site of their first date was marred with an evening of tense conversation, neither of them saying what was really on their mind. The evening started out with her telling him all about Joie's birthing experience up on the mountain, the danger she'd encountered and how Clint had showed up and fired his gun, scaring away the wolves. She chattered on nervously about how Nicole had showcased her knowledge of natural childbirth and had guided little Hudson safely into the world.

"He's so very cute," she told him, instantly realizing the topic was a hot button. Grayson had missed out on the night little Michael had been born.

"I'm sorry," she said flatly when sadness crossed his face.

"No, no that's all right. It's okay, really," he told her, in what they both knew was a lie. Especially when his voice cracked on the last word.

She'd learned Robin had discovered she was pregnant shortly after making the decision that was fatal to her marriage—the affair that had sent Grayson filing for divorce and fleeing to Idaho, leaving his former wife in Anchorage.

"She wasn't sure the baby was mine," Grayson explained.

Karyn asked the obvious question. "And she is now?" She fingered her hair. "I mean, she knows for certain little Michael is yours?" She held her breath, waiting for Grayson's response.

"Yes, there was a DNA test that ruled out the other guy."

Karyn slowly nodded, cleared her throat. "Okay, yeah. So, we're sure."

He'd purposely changed the subject then, reached across the table for her hand. "Let's talk about this later." He rested his elbows on the table between them. "When we're alone."

He wasn't himself the rest of the evening. He was shaken and distracted. Clearly he had a lot weighing on his mind.

She did as well.

She wondered where Robin was staying. Not at the lodge—she'd checked. How long did she intend to remain in Sun Valley? And what would her sisters say when they learned she and Grayson had made a commitment to move forward with their relationship, only to have the decision stymied by a surprise visit from his ex-wife?

All the way back to his place, she'd kept her questions in check.

Now, as they climbed the steps to his front porch, she could wait no longer for the answer she most needed to know. "So, what does Robin want?"

Grayson shoved the key in the slot. "What do you mean?"

"I mean, she showed up here with little Michael in tow. So, I'm wondering—what does she want?"

"You heard her," he said, a little gruffly, as he opened the door. "She wanted me to meet my son."

"She asked you to forgive her," Karyn reminded, as she followed him inside.

Without answering, Grayson made his way to the kitchen. "Can I get you something to drink?"

"Scotch," she said, focusing on the dark circles under his eyes. "I'll have a scotch."

He looked surprised. "Okay, sure." He retrieved a bottle from his liquor cabinet, filled two glasses with ice and poured a generous amount in each glass. She watched as he sliced a lemon and twisted a slice in her cocktail before handing it off to her.

She thanked him politely, headed for the door leading to the back deck. "Let's sit outside," she suggested.

"Are you sure? It's kind of cold."

"I'm sure." The truth was, the walls of the house were closing in a bit. She wanted to ask if Robin had been here earlier, or if they'd had their talk elsewhere. It was a first for her to feel like such an outsider, like he had a separate life she was not supposed to be a part of. Perhaps she was being silly, but to be honest, she felt like the *other woman* in this situation.

As if tuning in to her building insecurity, Grayson took her hand and led her outside. She loved the way he entwined her fingers in his and squeezed, appreciated the boost the gesture provided to her confidence.

The air smelled starkly of pine and wood smoke. In the distance, she could hear water tumbling over the rocks lining the bottom of the Wood River.

Directly overhead, the midnight blue sky seemed to be stitched together with waves of milky galaxies thousands and thousands of miles away. Clouds gathered near the crest of the nearby Pioneer Mountain range, threatening to snuff the stars' valiant attempt to shine.

"You want a fire?" Grayson asked. Without waiting for a response, he gathered several pieces of wood from a large jute basket and placed them in the outdoor fireplace. Within minutes, flames crackled and sparks escaped into the night sky.

He gave the fire a final jab, tossed the stick in the flames, then sank into the cushions of a wicker sofa and patted the spot next to him.

At no time did Grayson look in her eyes.

Karyn lifted her glass and took a sip, fought a grimace as the deep amber liquid made its way to her belly, leaving an unfamiliar trail of warmth. She sat beside Grayson, placed her hand on his knee. "The fire's nice." She took another sip.

In an unexpected move, he turned and fingered her hair. "Look, we need to talk."

The tone in his voice, his demeanor—all of it caused her stomach to cinch. Her emotions turned weak and wobbly. "Of course. Let's talk."

"Look, this entire situation is my fault," he began. There was hesitation. His own confidence seemed to fold in on itself. "A better man might be able to find words to explain."

The touch of his hand on hers was like an electric charge, unexpected. She could feel his hand travel to her arm, squeeze desperately. She turned and met his eyes. "What do you mean?"

His mouth opened and closed, but no words came out.

"Grayson? You're scaring me." For the briefest of seconds, she fantasized they were back in the air, gliding toward their happy future. Not here, struggling to connect.

"He's my son, Karyn."

Her fantasy landed with a thud. "Okay, I know that. I know you—how important this revelation is to you and how seriously you take your responsibility. And I'll support you in every way I can." She knew she was blathering. "We can do this—" She let the rest of her sentence fade like smoke when she saw his face reflected in the light of the fire.

He was crying.

Understanding suddenly dawned. "What? You—you're not considering going back to Alaska? To her?"

Grayson turned, deep sorrow in his eyes. "I—I'm not finished loving you," he whispered with desperation. "But, I can't stay here."

"Grayson, talk to me," she pleaded. "You can't just move back. What about us? Our plans?" She shook her head violently. She wanted him to love her enough to stay. "There's no reason you can't co-parent from here. People do the long-distance thing all the time."

The sky grew shadowed as the clouds finally rolled in.

In desperate torment, she closed her eyes, unsure how to get through to him. "Grayson, you love it here in Sun Valley. You belong here."

He said nothing in response, simply stared into the fire with an intensity of deep grief marring his face.

They sat in silence for several seconds—she not knowing what to say and Grayson clearly dreading what he had to say.

"Michael deserves to grow up with his parents—to have a family."

She stood, tossed back the rest of her drink. She gave Grayson a look, daring him to argue with what she was about to say. "Listen to me, Robin left you. She left you! Have you forgotten about all that? You don't share—that's what you said. And she slept with another man."

She knew she was engaging in an unfair fight. She knew it even before Grayson's look of confusion and outright irritation confirmed it.

Keeping his voice steady and even, Grayson stood, clearly now trying to control his temper. "What do you want me to do, Karyn? I have a son—a little boy who needs me. Not part-time, not half-way—he needs a father willing to sacrifice everything to be there for him." He rubbed at the back of his neck. "If that means putting my own needs aside, well that's the way it has to be."

What? He planned to don a red cape and be some kind of superhero? All the rest of this wouldn't matter if he did that part right?

She cast about for what to say next, unsure how to get through to him. He didn't want to listen anyway. His eyes told her his mind was made up. He was leaving.

She could go ahead and argue, of course. What was the point? She wanted something she apparently wasn't supposed to have.

Her heart threatened to pound right out of the walls of her chest.

"Be careful what you give up," she warned.

He met her eyes, tried to encourage her with the slightest of smiles. She looked away.

A bolt of thunder exploded in the sky. It came quickly and unexpected, the rain following, splashing down, a waterfall.

Karyn looked up at the pouring rain, hard, deep pellets hitting her skin.

She shook her head, heartbroken. Heartbroken that he was leaving, but mostly because she didn't think that he was going to find what he was looking for there.

Her eyes took him in—tall and strong in his flannel shirt and jeans. Very much like that first day at the Hemingway Memorial.

Beautiful Robin could have any man in the world, and yet she was entirely fixated on getting Grayson back—and she had the perfect tool to do it—his son.

Did that make his ex-wife entitled to rip Karyn's world apart? So what if they'd had a child. It was selfish to demand what she'd earlier thrown away!

Grayson was *her* soulmate, not Robin's.

He stood, grabbed her face in his hands, tears streaming down his own. "Please try to understand, I never meant to hurt you." He waited until her gaze met his. "Karyn, I will always love you—"

"No." She pulled away, angry. "You don't get to say that anymore."

She looked away from him, her heart plummeting. This was a poorly written soap opera and it was time to turn it off.

She moved for the door. Grayson scrambled, caught her arm. "Wait—"

"No—you've made your decision, while neglecting to consider me in your plans. There's little else now but to let you go and wish you all well." She lifted her chin, pulled a deep breath into her aching soul. "Goodbye, Grayson."

She set her empty glass on the table and walked away.

34

T he next morning dawned bright and crisp, one of those Sun Valley summer mornings that turned warm by ten o'clock.

Leigh Ann, Joie and Karyn all headed to the ranch first thing to check on their dad, only to find he'd already ridden up the draw to take some groceries to the sheepherders. They would all be lying to say their nerves weren't on edge following their recent scare.

"He'll be all right," Joie claimed, as she finished nursing little Hudson on their father's front porch.

Leigh Ann laid her head back against the back of the rocking chair. "Doesn't matter. We could line up a barricade of Bo-Peeps and he'd find a way to get past them and on with his duties here on the ranch. No matter what."

Joie smiled. "That's the truth."

Leigh Ann slowly rocked, watching as a hawk flew overhead. "I can't believe I spent all that time pooh-poohing Nicole and her dreams of becoming a doula." She sighed. "In the end, that training saved the day. Colby's wife spent hours with her nose buried in a book, and I don't know how many hours of training videos she watched." She shrugged. "Guess it doesn't matter. The point is, she was equipped to help you up there on that mountain."

Joie rocked in the chair next to her, tucked the blanket around her son. "She definitely knew how to keep me calm and guided me through a safe delivery." She bent and kissed his downy head. "I will always be grateful."

"And, it was no small miracle that she and Clint showed up when they did. A definite answer to prayer. What would have happened if—"

Joie reached for her sister's hand, squeezed. "It didn't."

Leigh Ann sighed. "Yeah, I guess there's no sense going there when everything turned out all right." She turned to Karyn. "You're being awfully quiet over there."

Karyn closed her eyes, didn't say anything right away.

"Karyn?"

"Yeah, I agree," she finally said. "Happiness is definitely a choice."

Joie and Leigh Ann exchanged glances.

Joie handed off the sleeping infant to Leigh Ann. "So, Nicole tells me Colby received his orders?"

Leigh Ann took a deep breath. "Yes, he reports in three weeks. I don't know if I can take it—I mean, I barely survived his being away at boot camp."

"Colby had been away at college. You survived that," Joie reminded.

"Yes, but this is different. He's—" Her sister shrugged, tried to explain. "It's more than his bulked-up physique. I see how he's matured, how he handles a myriad of responsibilities, how calm and unfazed he seems in stressful situations. The critical thinking and leadership skills developed in those few weeks at basic are on daily display. This isn't the kid who showed up on our doorstep with an unexpected wife." Worry marched across her face. "Despite all that, this time he's going to be in harm's way."

Leigh Ann gave Joie a tired smile, looked down at her little nephew in her arms. "I guess I won't have time to mentally dwell on that." She fingered the soft skin of Hudson's tiny cheek. "My time will be better spend focusing on you—and this little one."

Joie raised her eyebrows. "Does that mean you've forgiven me for representing Candy in the Preston, USA takeover?"

"Not entirely," Leigh Ann told her. There was laughter in her voice, and something more Joie detected. Fear, perhaps?

She felt a spasm of guilt. They'd always fought and made up. Sisterhood was like that, a quilt made up of all the scraps, good and bad. Besides, were her brother-in-law's mistakes any worse than her own?

Her sister needed her support.

"Leigh Ann, I have legal obligations as Candy's attorney. But, you know I'm on your side—right?"

She sighed. "Yes, I do know that. Mark can't rewrite what he's done," Leigh Ann said. "Neither can I. We can only move forward. The next months are going to be grueling in all sorts of ways. There's little I can do to change that." There was a pause. "I'll just have to get employed—at a real job, with real pay."

"You plan on leaving your post as director of the tourism council?" Karyn asked, breaking her silence—this time with no prodding. "That's not fair. This was Mark—not you."

Leigh Ann flinched. "I have no choice."

"Everybody has a choice," Karyn said, anger tinging her voice.

Leigh Ann and Joie glanced at each other a second time.

Concern lined Leigh Ann's face. "I'm sorry?"

Joie adjusted her nursing bra, buttoned her shirt. "Karyn, something's bothering you. Spill."

Their sister's face visibly darkened. "Grayson is leaving and going back to Alaska. He's going to reunite with his ex-wife, a smart blonde who is drop-dead gorgeous, so they can raise their young son together."

Leigh Ann's eyes flew open. "Grayson has a son?"

Karyn nodded. "Appears so."

"Did you know that?" Joie asked.

"No, and neither did he until Robin showed up with a little guy in her arms who looked just like his daddy." She stopped rocking, looked over at her sisters with bitterness. "It's hard to hate someone with dimpled hands. I can't say the same for his mother."

Joie rushed to her side, enfolded her shoulders in a hug. "Oh, Karyn. I'm so sorry."

Leigh Ann came up beside and gave Karyn a fierce squeeze, taking care not to crush little Hudson in the process. "Oh, sweetheart, I don't know what to say."

Clearly shaken, Karyn shrugged. "There's nothing for anyone to say. It's over, and there's little I can do about it."

Leigh Ann pulled away, looked into her sister's eyes. "Still, hate is a very strong word," she cautioned.

Tears were now sliding down Karyn's cheek.

"Or—maybe not," Leigh Ann added. "Just don't park there for long."

Karyn wiped the tears, sighed. "I—I don't *hate* her exactly. It's just—well, this wasn't supposed to end this way."

Her sister's brown eyes were dark with sorrow that came from crumbled hopes.

Joie's heart melted. "Oh, Karyn. I'm so sorry. This wasn't supposed to happen."

Karyn shrugged. "There's plenty of sorrow to go around these days, it seems. None of it is deserved. Mark and Leigh Ann weren't supposed to end up broke—and Colby wasn't supposed to show up with a surprise wife, or enlist and place himself in a dangerous situation."

"I wasn't supposed to be a single mother," Joie remarked. "Not when I only recently got my career back on track. Despite Maddy Crane's unwavering support, it's going to be pretty hard to impress the legal world with no sleep and spit-up in my hair." She took Hudson from Leigh Ann and placed him in the cradle Clint had made, rocked it gently. "I'm the one who barreled through the past few years like a lion in a jungle, always the king. I took stupid risks, hooked up with inappropriate and unavailable men."

Karyn gave her little sister a resigned smile. "We always believed that was not the real you, Joie. Leigh Ann said she suspected you might be hurting, deep down inside."

"Of course, Leigh Ann's always right." Joie quipped, with a slight laugh.

Leigh Ann slapped her hand to her chest in surprise. "Wait— I'm right? That's a first out of your mouth."

Joie rolled her eyes. "Let's all say it together—you're all truth, joy and sunshine every moment."

"That's better," Leigh Ann chided. "But Karyn, has a point— life doesn't always dish what we deserve. Sometimes, life hands us a big bowl of lemons. Take Mom, for example. She died of cancer before she was even thirty-five. She didn't even get to see us grow up. That was not fair. She didn't deserve it—and neither did we."

"Tell me about her, about Mom," Joie prodded. Even now, she kept the letter a secret, a sacred bond between just the two of them—between her and her mother.

Leigh Ann instantly brightened. "She was fun—hard-working —but she never thought twice about setting aside her chores, getting on the floor with us and playing Barbies."

Karyn nodded. "Remember that doll gown she made for my eighth birthday? It was sleeveless and red with silver roses on the fabric. Mom could sew anything."

"And she loved board games, was cutthroat at Monopoly."

Karyn smiled, a little sadly. "She'd actually pout if she landed in jail."

Leigh Ann slowly rocked back and forth. "Remember how she and Daddy danced?"

Joie reached for her glass of lemonade. "They danced?"

"Oh, yes," Karyn answered. "At night, in the living room. She in her apron and bare feet and daddy in his slippers."

"So, she was a good mother?" Joie asked.

"A good mother? Of course!" Leigh Ann said with a smile. "The best."

Karyn reached and placed her hand on Joie's arm. "You don't remember her?"

Her father's sheepdog, Riley, sauntered over and bedded down at her feet. She leaned and scratched his ear. "No—not really. I mean, I remember small snippets of things, but I really don't remember her."

She folded, told them about the letter, how much it had meant to her to read those words written especially for her by the woman she'd longed to know all these years. "There's packages in there for you too, for both of you."

"Yes, Dad gave them to us after you discovered the chest in the attic. It was just like her to save those mementos for us." Leigh Ann paused. "I'm so glad she left you that letter. You were her baby. She really loved you."

Without warning, Joie teared up.

"Oh, honey," Leigh Ann said. "I didn't mean to make you cry."

Joie shook her head. "It's not that—it's just that I'm afraid."

"Afraid?" Karyn asked, concern on her face.

Joie swallowed the emotion choking her throat. "Hudson deserves someone like that—a mom who would remember to keep his baby clothes, who would write him a letter like that. I—I nearly ended it all for both of us up there on that mountain. I mean, I always think the rules don't apply. How can I teach him everything he's going to need to know? How am I going to make sure he eats a balanced meal with food from the four food groups when I eat candy bars for breakfast?" She looked down at her son, miserably. "He deserves better."

There it was, the thing that had crept into her soul like a burglar and robbed her of her peace. All evidence pointed to the fact she would never be enough.

Karyn stood, walked over and placed her palms on either side of Joie's face. "You listen to me—life this side of heaven is hard. Life rarely goes as we expect, or even hope. We face loss, we make mistakes—but in the end, we still have each other. You are a fabulous attorney. You have everything you need to be a good mom." She gave Joie an encouraging smile, then added, "Just do the best you can. If you miss the mark, we'll all be here to fill in the gap."

Leigh Ann nodded in agreement. "Yeah, none of us do this alone—that whole *It Takes a Village* thing, and all."

Perhaps her sisters were right, she could do this—with some help. Besides, there was no turning back now. Her son held her heart in the palm of his tiny hand. She vowed to do her very best. It would have to be enough.

Leigh Ann couldn't help smiling. "And I wonder if Clint Ladner thinks of you as a little more than simply a friend?" She pointed to the cradle. "Maybe you should consider liking him back."

That made Joie laugh. "What, are we—in junior high? Should I pass him a note? *I love you. Do you love me? Check the box: Yes— No—Maybe.*"

Leigh Ann gave Joie a smug look. "I was there when you were in junior high. I think your romantic approach at the time was to tackle the boys and beat the pulp out of them if they failed to do what you wanted."

Joie turned to Karyn. "There's your answer—right there! I'll help you get Grayson on the ground and we'll make him sorry."

Leigh Ann nodded her approval. "I'd even be willing to help!"

Joie bent to sooth Hudson's whimper, picked him up. She grinned up at her sister. "What? And break a nail?"

Leigh Ann looked back in mock horror. "You're right. I can't afford to have them redone."

That made all of them laugh—especially Karyn.

Joie looked out over the familiar vista, the pasture grass bending in the gentle breeze, the way the sun shadowed the cottonwoods lining the creek. "So, Karyn—what are you going to do now? I mean, is it really over with Grayson?"

"Yes, I'm afraid so." Karyn stared at the lane leading to the ranch. "For so long, I was waiting for my life to start, waiting for more. Even before Dean died. It seemed like all I did was smile for the cameras, shop and wait."

She folded her arms around herself. "I had a big hole, and when I met Grayson, I figured he was the perfect person to fill it. Unfortunately, Grayson Chandler wasn't meant to be mine. Not if he was willing to walk away so easily. The fact that he has a son to consider factored into his decision—and rightly so. But, when you really love someone, you can't divert that easily."

The three sisters rocked quietly for several minutes, saying a thousand words with their silence.

Joie breathed in some of the fresh sage-scented air she loved and patted little Hudson's bottom. "Maybe being grateful means recognizing what you have for what it is. Appreciating small victories. Admiring the struggle it takes simply to be human. Maybe we're thankful for the familiar things we know. And maybe we're thankful for the things—and people—we'll never know. At the end of the day, these are the heartbeats of life. The fact we have the courage to face life head-on is reason enough to celebrate."

Karyn gazed over at Hudson sleeping peacefully against Joie's shoulder. "Over these past months, our journeys have certainly wound in directions we never expected," she said softly.

Leigh Ann stood, placed her hands on her sisters' shoulders. "Yes, and there may be more changes ahead."

Karyn clasped Leigh Ann's hand. "But we'll always have each other."

Joie rested her cheek against the top of Hudson's downy head. "Do you hear that, little Hudson? We'll weather whatever lies ahead—together."

AFTERWORD

Hey, everybody—Miss Trudy here. Kellie and I are so glad you joined us for another story in the Sun Valley Series. Don't you just love these three sisters? I hope you'll continue to read on.

I'm not one to spread gossip, but there are a lot of things happening around here lately. Take Leigh Ann, for instance. That poor thing is scrambling after her husband lost everything in a bad business deal. She needs to find a job—and fast!

And, don't we all hope Joie might find true love with Clint? Trouble is, she carries a lot of baggage. (Not all of it is Gucci, if you know what I mean.)

And, Lordy! I'm afraid sweet Karyn had her heart broken yet again—but will a dark-haired stranger be the bandage she needs?

You can bet there are a lot of changes looming in the lives of these three sisters. I, for one, can't wait to see what is on the horizon.

Anyway, sweet things, Kellie is writing as fast as she can. Make sure and sign up for her **newsletter** by clicking HERE so you get notices when future books in the series are available. Don't forget to check out all the information on Sun Valley she has on her **website** at www.kelliecoatesgilbert.com (PS—that's her hometown area!)

You might also enjoy Kellie's new **LOVE ON VACATION** stories. These shorter length romances invite readers to come on vacation with characters who travel to Sun Valley and stay at the iconic Sun Valley Lodge. This groundbreaking series is packed with tales of dating and mating, love and marriage and promises to keep your emotions and your funny bone on high alert. You'll also see a few recognized characters from the SISTERS book show up on occasion. Click HERE to check out the first story, *Otherwise Engaged.*

Well, I've got to scoot. I have an art class to teach. But, we'll see each other again soon!

~Miss Trudy

*Disclaimer – The Sun Valley Series and the Love on Vacation books are not associated with the City of Sun Valley, Sun Valley Resort, Sun Valley Company or Sinclair Oil Co. These books are solely the creative works of Kellie Coates Gilbert and Amnos Media Group.

ABOUT THE AUTHOR

Kellie Coates Gilbert has won readers' hearts with her compelling and highly emotional stories about women and the relationships that define their lives. A former legal investigator, she is especially known for keeping readers turning pages and creating nuanced characters who seem real.

In addition to garnering hundreds of five-star reader reviews, Kellie has been described by RT Book Reviews as a "deft, crisp storyteller." Her books were featured as Barnes & Noble Top Shelf Picks and were included on Library Journal's Best Book List of 2014.

Born and raised near Sun Valley, Idaho, Kellie now lives with her husband of over thirty-five years in Dallas, where she spends most days drinking sweet tea by a pool and writing the stories of her heart.

Please visit her at:

WWW.KELLIECOATESGILBERT.COM

Don't miss out on new releases and special contest information! If you haven't signed up for **Kellie's newsletter** . . . what are you waiting for? **Click here!**

ALSO BY KELLIE COATES GILBERT:

Mother of Pearl

Sisters (Sun Valley Series Book 1)

Otherwise Engaged – a Love on Vacation Story

All Fore Love – A Love on Vacation Story

A Woman of Fortune

Where Rivers Part

A Reason to Stay

What Matters Most

More information and purchase links can be found at:

www.kelliecoatesgilbert.com

A NOTE FROM KELLIE

I love writing about these three sisters and my hometown area of Sun Valley, Idaho. I hope you've enjoyed the *Sun Valley Series* as well!

Thank you for being the most amazing readers in the world! Your emails, tweets, Facebook and Goodreads messages have made me laugh, tear up, and appreciate writing for you all the more. I especially appreciate those of you who take the time to post reviews on all the retailer sites and those who feature me on your book recommend blogs. I treasure you! I'd like to extend a special thank you to my editors, my formatter and to all my dedicated beta readers. You all rock!

~Kellie

Made in the USA
Monee, IL
21 November 2023

47051909R10152